THE MISSING

This Large Print Book carries the
Seal of Approval of N.A.V.H.

THE MISSING

BEVERLY LEWIS

THORNDIKE PRESS
A part of Gale, Cengage Learning

GALE
CENGAGE Learning

Detroit • New York • San Francisco • New Haven, Conn • Waterville, Maine • London

GALE
CENGAGE Learning

Copyright © 2009 by Beverly M. Lewis.
Seasons of Grace Series #2.
Scripture quotations are from the King James Version of the Bible.
Thorndike Press, a part of Gale, Cengage Learning.

ALL RIGHTS RESERVED
Thorndike Press® Large Print Christian Fiction.
The text of this Large Print edition is unabridged.
Other aspects of the book may vary from the original edition.
Set in 16 pt. Plantin.
Printed on permanent paper.

LIBRARY OF CONGRESS CATALOGING-IN-PUBLICATION DATA

Lewis, Beverly, 1949–
   The missing / by Beverly Lewis.
     p. cm. — (Thorndike Press large print Christian fiction)
(Seasons of grace series ; 2)
   ISBN-13: 978-1-4104-1885-2 (alk. paper)
   ISBN-10: 1-4104-1885-5 (alk. paper)
   1. Amish—Fiction. 2. Family secrets—Fiction. 3. Large type
books. I. Title.
PS3562.E9383M57 2009b
813'.54—dc22   2009026560

Published in 2009 by arrangement with Bethany House Publishers.

Printed in the United States of America
1 2 3 4 5 6 7 13 12 11 10 09

To
Virginia Campbell,
whose generosity and dedication
to the Pikes Peak branch
of
The National League of
American Pen Women
are a joyful inspiration to me.

PROLOGUE

I stumbled upon my mother's handkerchief in the cornfield early this morning. Halfway down the row I spotted it — white but soiled, cast in the mire of recent rains. Only one side of the stitched hem was visible, the letter *L* poking out from the furrow as if to get my attention. I stared at it . . . all the emotions of the past three weeks threatening to rise up and choke me right then and there.

Leaning over, I clutched the mud-caked hankie in my hand. Then, tilting my head up, I looked toward the eastern sky, to the freshness of this new day.

Twice now, I've walked the field where Mamma sometimes wandered late at night — weeks before she ever left home. Like our sheep, she'd followed the same trails till ruts developed. I couldn't help wondering where the well-trod path had led her by the light of the lonely moon. Honestly, though, 'tis only in the daylight that I've been compelled to go there, drawn by thoughts of her and the hope of some further word, whenever that might come.

I shook the dirt off the hankie and traced the outline of the embroidered initial — white on white. So simple yet ever so pretty.

My hand lingered there as tears slipped down my cheeks. "Mamma . . . where *are* you?" I whispered to the breeze. "What things don't we know?"

Later, when breakfast preparations were well under way, my younger sister, Mandy, headed upstairs to redd up what had always been our parents' room. The solitary space where *Dat* still slept.

Still shaken at finding Mamma's hankie, I wandered across the kitchen and pushed open the screen door. I leaned on it and stared toward the shining green field, with its rows as straight as the telephone poles up the road, near Route 340. Near where the fancy folk live.

I reached beneath my long work apron and touched the soiled handkerchief in my dress pocket. *Mamma's very own.* Had I unknowingly yearned for such a token? Something tangible to cling to?

With a sigh, I hurried through the center

hallway and up the stairs. Various things pointed to Mamma's long-ago first beau as a possible reason for her leaving. But I had decided that no matter how suspicious things looked, I would continue to believe Mamma was true to Dat.

I stepped into our parents' large bedroom, with its gleaming floorboards and hand-built dresser and blanket chest at the foot of the bed. "I want you to see something, Mandy," I said.

My sister gripped the footboard. *"Jah?"*

I pushed my hand into my pocket, past Mamma's hankie, and found the slip of paper. "Just so ya know, I've already shown this to Dat." I drew a slow breath. "I don't want to upset you, but I have an address in Ohio . . . where Mamma might be stayin'." I showed her what our grandmother had given me.

"What on earth?"

I told her as gently as I could that I'd happened upon a letter *Dawdi* Jakob had written when Mamma was young — when she and our grandmother had gone west to help a sickly relative.

"Why do you and *Mammi* think she might've gone there?" Mandy's brown eyes were as wide as blanket buttons.

"Just a hunch." Really, though, I hadn't

9

the slightest inkling what Mamma was thinking, going anywhere at all. Let alone with some of Samuel Graber's poetry books in tow. "I hope to know for a fact soon enough," I added.

She stared in disbelief. "How?"

"Simple. I'm goin' to call this inn."

Mandy reached for the paper, holding it in her now trembling hand. "Oh, Grace . . . you really think she might be there?"

Suddenly it felt easier to breathe. "Would save me tryin' to get someone to make a trip with me to find out." I bit my lip. "And Dat says I have to . . . or I can't go at all."

"You can't blame him for that." Mandy sighed loudly. Then she began to shake her head repeatedly, frowning to beat the band.

I touched her shoulder. "What is it, sister?"

She shrugged, remaining silent.

"What, Mandy?"

"It's just so awful dangerous . . . out in the modern, fancy world."

"Aw, sister . . ." I reached for her. "Mamma can take care of herself. We must trust that."

She nodded slowly, brown eyes gleaming with tears. Then, just as quickly, she wiped her eyes and face with her apron. She shook her head again. "*Nee* — no, we must trust the *Lord* to watch over her."

With a smile, I agreed.

Mandy leaned her head against my cheek. "I hope you won't up and leave us, too. I couldn't bear it, Gracie." She stepped back and looked at me with pleading eyes. "And if ya do get Mamma on the phone, please say how much I miss her. How much we *all* do." Mandy looked happier at the prospect. "That we want her to come home."

I squeezed her plump elbow, recalling the way Dat's eyes had lit up when I showed him the address early this morning. The way he'd turned toward the kitchen window, a faraway glint in his eyes as he looked at the two-story martin birdhouse — just a-staring. I'd wondered if he was afraid to get his hopes up too high. Or was there more to this than any of us knew?

But this wasn't the time to dwell on such things. I needed to think through what I might say to whoever answered the phone. How to make it clear who I was . . . and why I was calling.

Mandy went around the bed and reached for the upper sheet, pulling it taut. Next, the blanket. She gave me a sad little smile, and after we finished Dat's room, she said no more as she headed downstairs to scramble the breakfast eggs.

I made my way to my own bedroom, down the hall. There, I took Mamma's mud-stained hankie from my pocket. *Will you even come to the phone . . . when you find out who's calling?*

Then, as carefully as if it were a wee babe, I placed the handkerchief in my dresser drawer with a prayer in my heart. *Grant me the courage, Lord.*

For everything you have missed,
you have gained something else. . . .
— Emerson

CHAPTER ONE

Adah Esh slipped from her warm bed, having slept longer than usual. In the quiet, she tiptoed to the end of the hall to the spare room designated as a sewing room. The cozy spot on the second floor had two northeast-facing windows. Adah raised the dark green shade and stood there, looking out at the unobstructed expanse of space and sky. Tendrils of yellow had already sprung forth like a great fan below the horizon.

Since Lettie's leaving nearly a month ago, Adah felt compelled to come here and offer up the day and its blessings to God. She'd first observed this act of surrender in Lettie herself, who as a teenager had begun the day at her bedroom window, her shoulders sometimes heaving with the secret she bore. Other times Adah would find her scooted up close to the glass as she looked out, as if yearning for comfort in the glory of the dawn.

On days when her daughter found the wherewithal to speak, Lettie might point out the sun's light glinting on the neighbors' windmill across the field. *"It's like a gift,"* she'd say, seemingly grasping for even the slightest hint of beauty. Anything to momentarily take her attention away from her grief. Her shame.

Adah's heart ached anew at the old pain of discovering her young Lettie with child, and by the young man she and Jakob had so disliked. Poor Lettie, distraught beyond Adah's or anyone's ability to cheer her. . . . Her heartsick girl had wept at her window like a trapped little sparrow in a cage.

But until recently, those dark and sad days had seemed long past. No more did Adah despise Samuel Graber for wounding her daughter so, nor did she hold resentment against Lettie for her infatuation with him . . . or their dire sin. And never had she forgotten the infant she'd made Lettie give up — her own tiny grandbaby — nor the adoption arrangements made afterward.

Now Adah rested her hand on the sill of the window on this side of son-in-law Judah's big three-story house. She committed the day to almighty God, who'd made it. The One who knew and saw Lettie, too, wherever she might be.

The view from this particular window suited Adah just fine, different though it was from that outside of Jakob's and her first home. In recent years ownership of that house had been transferred to their youngest married son and his wife — Ethan and Hannah. As for herself, Adah was content to live out her sunset years here, under Lettie's husband's watch-care. *If only Lettie might be here, too. O Lord, may it be so!*

She moved closer to the window as she watched the earth come to life. The day sparkled in the sun. Bird-in-Hand was already abuzz with farmers and their mule teams working the green expanse of fields in all directions. Her Jakob would soon stir and she'd leave behind her reverie to go and kiss his wrinkled cheek as he awakened. Then they would dress and head downstairs to breakfast when their granddaughters called them to the table where Lettie had always laid out a big spread. This responsibility now fell to dutiful Grace, just twenty-one and resembling her mother more, here lately, in her diligence to cook and keep house.

"What will this day bring?" Adah whispered before turning from the window. "Can Grace locate Lettie with a single phone call?"

She walked silently to the larger room she shared with Jakob, who she saw from the doorway was still asleep. In that moment, she wondered if they'd made the right decision, giving Grace the address of the Kidron, Ohio, inn where she and Lettie had stayed so long ago. She moved quietly to her husband's side and sat, waiting for his puffy eyes to flutter open.

We protected Lettie's secret this long. Adah trembled as she considered Grace's determination to find her mother, and what she might possibly find instead.

Ach, *have I made a mistake?*

That same Tuesday, after a breakfast of fried potatoes, scrambled eggs, and crackers in warm milk, Grace was surprised to hear Mandy mention Henry Stahl.

Mandy was sweeping the floor when she stopped abruptly and looked up from the pile of crumbs. "I really hate to say anything, but Priscilla Stahl ain't too happy 'bout you breakin' up with her brother."

Grace's stomach knotted up. *Isn't for Prissy to say . . .*

"*She* told you this?"

"Jah." Mandy pushed the dirt into the dustpan.

"Prissy's upset, is all," Grace assured her sister. Breaking up with Henry after the Singing last Sunday night had been downright thorny but not rash. *Had Henry honestly told his sister about it? So unlike him to share much of anything.* She thought of her older brother, Adam — Grace had told *him* already, too.

"Prissy says you *jilted* Henry." Mandy emptied the dustpan into the trash beneath the sink.

"Not sure how she'd know such a thing."

Mandy shrugged. "Well, she's spoutin' off to me — and Adam, no doubt — that you spurned his wonderful-*gut* gift."

Grace couldn't help it; she laughed. "What happened 'tween Henry and me has nothin' to do with that chime clock — my birthday present."

"Your engagement gift, don't ya mean?"

Grace sighed. Surely Adam's meddlesome fiancée would try to understand that Henry had been wrong for Grace — as Henry himself had certainly realized. Goodness, but when Grace had said they should part ways, he hadn't even objected, speaking up for their love.

Maybe love's too strong a word, she thought just then. It had been his silence all around that wore thin over their months as a courting couple. Then Mamma'd left home and it had dawned on Grace that Dat and his aloof manner must surely be the reason. No, it was clear Grace could not marry someone like Henry.

To think Mamma's been gone nearly a month already. It seemed much longer since she had slipped away into the darkness. *How does a daughter get past such a thing?*

Dat never spoke about it anymore — not since he'd fallen so terribly ill there for several days. He kept so busy; perhaps that was how he managed to cope. Adam and Joe, and Mandy, too, also seemed to have pushed their sadness down deep, burying it somewhere in their shattered hearts. *Just as I have . . .*

Mandy left to go to the sitting room and gathered up the throw rugs, carrying them outside to shake.

Meanwhile, Grace went to look beneath the lid of the cookie jar, where her mother kept a phone card for emergencies. But she found nothing at all. *Did Mamma take it with her?*

She wondered if her grandmother might not have a spare one to loan and hurried through the sitting room and the center hall, where wooden shelves and pegs lined either side, to Mammi Adah's own tidy kitchen.

Seeing Mammi cutting Dawdi's graying bangs at the far end of the room, she waited in the doorway, not saying a peep as the scissors snipped away.

Leaning on the doorjamb, Grace was painfully aware that all of her hopes were bound up in the telephone call she felt she must make. The need pulled her chest as taut as a rag rug.

Unconsciously she groaned, startling Mammi, who turned, her scissors slipping as she did so. "Ach, Mammi . . . I'm sorry," Grace said, seeing the bungled bangs.

Dawdi harrumphed, a spew of complaints coming in *Deitsch.*

Mammi stifled a laugh when she saw the damage. "Aw, Jakob, it'll just have to grow back," she said, her hand over her mouth. "Ain't so, Gracie?"

It was a good thing her grandfather couldn't see Mammi's wide smile, not as particular a man as he was.

"Did ya need something, dear?" asked Mammi Adah.

"Our phone card's missin'. Could I borrow one from you, maybe? I'll pay you back when I get my next paycheck." She didn't care to say she was going to call out to Ohio. Mammi Adah would surely gather that.

"I'll have a look-see." Mammi frowned as

she once again appraised Dawdi's botched hair. Then, quickly, she removed the towel she'd fastened around his neck with a wooden clothespin, her usual practice for the monthly haircut. "You might have to wear your hat low on your head for 'bout a month, love," she said before making her way to the back steps. She wiggled her fingers for Grace to follow.

Once they reached the landing, Mammi Adah's face turned solemn. "Have ya heard 'bout Willow's injury?"

Grace had fed their favorite driving horse several carrots just last evening. "What happened between last night and now?"

"Well, since she's older than I am in horse years, Willow's sure to have more problems as she ages." A gray shadow passed across Mammi's face as she stopped beside the worktable in the sewing room. "There's the possibility she is foundered — she injured her leg on the road this morning, according to your Dat." Pausing, Mammi touched a pile of fabric, already cut into squares for a quilt. "She might need to be . . ."

"Might need to be what?" Grace asked.

Mammi sighed, her hand on her throat.

Tears sprang to Grace's eyes. "No, no . . . I can't imagine puttin' her down." She shook her head. "Oh, Mammi . . ."

Her grandmother reached for her hand. "Ach, this is never easy."

Never is right! She choked back her tears. "How was she injured?"

"Your father went over to see one of the ministers bright and early. Willow made a misstep on the road and stumbled on the way back. She's hurt her front right leg."

"Well, what 'bout some liniment? That'll help, ain't so?" The knot of worry increased in her as Mammi glanced out the window, toward the barn.

"You'll have to ask your father 'bout that, dear."

So had Dat already discussed this with Dawdi and Mammi?

"Oh, I'll be talkin' to Dat, for sure."

"I know your father did everything he usually does. He was checking Willow's hurt leg when Dawdi went out there after breakfast," Mammi said softly. "We all know how dear that horse is to you."

"To all of us . . . jah?"

In Mammi's serious gray eyes, Grace saw the pain of the past weeks. Even before Mamma's departure, Mammi Adah had seemed terribly vexed. Things had been tense between Dat and Mamma for much too long, something her grandparents could not take in stride.

Wanting to rush right out to the barn, Grace instead reached for the purple and green squares on the sewing table. *Makes no sense to fret over what can't be changed.* Moving the squares around, she laid out several while Mammi looked for a phone card in one of her sewing drawers. "Putting Willow out of her misery will only add to the sadness round here," Grace said louder than she should have.

"That it would," Mammi acknowledged as she handed her the card.

"*Denki,* Mammi." Time now for Grace to get herself down the road and make a phone call to the faraway inn. Grace had no idea what significance the Ohio inn had for Mamma's present absence, but there seemed to be some link to the past. The mere fact Mammi Adah had given her the address pointed to its importance.

She held the little card and hurried to the steps, where she heard her grandfather still grumbling below. "Dawdi's mighty upset," she called over her shoulder, hoping her grandmother might take the hint and come down to console him. Who could tell what news Grace might soon be bringing back to their ears?

With more than a little apprehension, she headed back down to Mammi's kitchen.

22

Dawdi was facing away from the door, his neck red with frustration. "Adah, bring a hand mirror here to me," he said.

Feeling responsible for his bad haircut, Grace slipped outside. She glanced at the barn, ever so anxious to ask Dat what more could be done for Willow — though, knowing her father, surely the vet would be arriving soon. At this minute, her missing mother required her attention more than the once-sleek bay mare. Grace picked up her skirt and ran past the windbreak of trees to the road.

Best to make the call before another day passes. . . .

CHAPTER TWO

As she strode up Beechdale Road, Grace was aware of the midmorning stillness, broken only by the occasional gust of wind or the lone bleating of a lamb beyond her father's fence. She felt the sharp jabs of gravel and small stones against her bare feet under her long green dress. The stretch of road was the same one where she'd followed her mother, running and calling after her in the early-morning darkness.

A lone white kite floated high behind Preacher Smucker's stone farmhouse in the distance, and a dozen or so red-breasted robins soared silently overhead. Shielding her face from yet another gust of wind, Grace recalled how serene the hour of her mother's departure had been. Uncannily so.

She reached into her dress pocket and located the slip of paper Mammi Adah had given her yesterday . . . and her grandmother's phone card. The mid-May breeze swished at her skirt hem and sent her *Kapp* strings flying over her shoulder as she looked at her grandmother's writing: *The Kidron Inn.*

Is this where you've gone, Mamma? Only one way to know for sure, yet Grace felt dreadfully awkward at the thought of speaking to a stranger. Even with the anticipation of possibly hearing her mother's voice, she was hesitant to place the call. She could not erase the sad truth that her mother had not responded to her pleas that bitter day.

Perhaps she didn't hear me. . . .

Grace liked to give folk the benefit of the doubt. She expected Mamma hadn't wanted her or anyone else to see her go. But did that mean Mamma wouldn't hear her out now? Even though Grace was eager to know something — *anything* — she didn't want to bring further pain to her family. They had already suffered too much.

Am I making excuses?

She sped up as she spotted the wooden shanty ahead. Well hidden behind a clump of trees situated off to the far left, away from the road, it had been placed there by the People. According to Mammi Adah, the bishop himself had chosen the spot a while back, saying it was a bad idea to flaunt the modern connection to the outside world, especially before those English folk who drove past it daily.

A lump crowded her throat at the thought of making the long-distance call in such seclusion, with the fancy world at her fingertips. As it was, she rarely needed to use this phone other than to summon a driver.

I must do this!

She spied the well-trod narrow dirt path and ducked her head under the low-lying branches of an ancient cluster of trees as she reached for the rickety door. Wishing she'd rehearsed what to say, she stopped in her tracks when she heard a dog barking across the way . . . and someone sobbing.

She glanced over her shoulder and saw through the leaves Jessica Spangler, sitting cross-legged in the grass, her face bowed as she wept. The family's golden Labrador came running, hovering near Jessica as if to comfort her.

What the world?

Grace quickly abandoned the phone booth and hastened up the road toward her long-time English neighbor. Forlorn Jessica remained there on the rolling front lawn — her family's handsome redbrick house with its white shutters behind her — as Grace hurried to console her.

I'll call the inn later, Lord willing. . . .

The coffee shop was humming with customers, but Heather Nelson felt unexpectedly relaxed camping out in the corner spot for Wi-Fi hookup again this morning. The same snug location as yesterday. In fact, she'd claimed the table this past Sunday, too — "the Lord's Day," as the Riehl family referred to it. She had waited until Andy and Marian had taken two gray buggies full of children off to something called Preaching service before she'd left to check out this comfortable nook. Here, where she could gaze out at the soothing blue sky.

Today found her too distracted to work on her thesis — terrifying thoughts of what was going wrong with her body lay just below the surface. Instead Heather felt drawn to a particularly interesting health-related chat room. She was intrigued by someone with the screen name Wannalive, who was openly sharing about opting to go the naturopathic route for treatment. Curious to know more, Heather joined in the conversation herself. At first it seemed weird chatting with strangers about something so personal, but after a full hour, she felt as if this newfound connection to other cancer patients was a way of soothing her wounds

27

from her recent breakup. So what if Devon Powers had dumped her for someone new? His calling off their engagement said more about him than her — she would be better off without him. And the truth was, Heather believed she was beginning to get past the initial shock. At least she no longer woke up crying in the night.

And at least I never told him everything. . . . Cynicism had begun to set in, and chatting with someone like Wannalive just might be a productive way to deal with her loneliness. She was smart enough not to offer any pertinent information to this guy. After all, you never really knew whom you were having a discussion with online. But weary as she was of her own thoughts, Heather could definitely see how someone could become addicted to chat rooms. It wasn't that she believed this new friend really cared about her. Not really. But he was *there,* which was a far cry from her former fiancé. Or from the few friends she had back at the College of William and Mary.

When he mentioned his blog — "Food for Thought" — Heather clicked over, wanting to read all about him. She leaned back, devouring the latest entries, then when she was finished, she returned to the chat room to read several more posts before realizing

she had been online far too long already —
more than two hours.

Well, I have the time, don't I?

Looking out the window, she whispered,
"Do I?" Her gaze swept the expanse of the
hilly green landscape, and she was struck
with a desire to talk to her mom. Could
Heather's mother see her from heaven, here,
struggling to deal with her own frightening
diagnosis?

Drumming her fingers on the table, she
hoped her father would keep his intention
to visit earlier than planned, as his recent
voice mail had indicated. Did he actually
want her participation in creating a floor
plan for the house he was so eager to build?
She considered the idea of a modern-style
farmhouse planted in the middle of Amish
country, boasting "electric," as the Riehls
called it . . . and a fully modern kitchen and
bathrooms. Was he concerned at all about
what his Amish neighbors would think,
shunning as they did everything from cars
to televisions? And shunning their own
people, too, if they failed to follow church
ordinances to a tee.

She shivered at the thought of losing one's
family because of such rigid practices. So
much of their lifestyle was mystifying to her,
especially the concept of total yielding, of

giving up one's will for the sake of God and a cloistered society — the opposite of the self-expression she had been groomed to embrace. There was much to be said, however, for the Amish work ethic.

She wondered if the Plain reverence for working the land had somehow gripped her father. *"We'll have more time to enjoy nature — plant a garden together,"* he'd declared in his latest voice mail, as if that was a good enough reason to relocate. But to pull up the roots of their entire life? The state of Virginia *was* congested, sure — at least where they lived, close to Williamsburg. But why sell their beloved family home and move here?

Heather tried to imagine her father gardening — certainly she had never thought of *herself* as an outdoorsy type. Except for afternoons spent at the beach with casual college friends or taking long walks with Mom — before the cancer came and stole away her mother's strength — she had been satisfied to spend much of her time inside. Too, her master's program in American Studies had swallowed up her hours. *Until last month . . .*

Since her diagnosis, she'd read nearly everything online about non-Hodgkin's lymphoma and its supposed cures, both conventional medical and alternative healing methods. It was the latter that had brought her here, to the place where she'd last felt true peace, the kind that propelled her away from the stress of real life. *Ah, Lancaster County . . . a love Mom and I shared for so long.*

Since arriving at the Riehls' tourist home two weeks ago, she had taken frequent walks along Mill Stream. She'd also enjoyed quaint activities like gathering eggs with the Riehls' oldest daughter, Becky, age twenty. And before withdrawing somewhat from Becky and her family, Heather had learned to pinch off old blossoms from the colorful perennials along the walkway, and she'd worked in the family's garden, too.

Yet even in this picture-perfect locale, Heather felt pulled in opposite directions — experiencing both a nagging restlessness and at the same time an inexplicable sense of satisfaction. More so than she'd experienced on the historic Williamsburg campus, surrounded by the trappings of the academia she adored. Nearly more happiness than she'd felt even with Devon Powers. *Before he was sent off to Iraq.*

She sighed, needing to push aside the memory of their breakup . . . the tactless way Devon had handled things. No, she must be free of all that nonsense to focus her energies on the hope of finding a natural cure. Her oncologist, Dr. O'Connor, had referred to her disease as "quite curable." But that cure came with the price tag of chemo, and quite possibly radiation, which she'd adamantly refused. She would not take the route that had killed her mother if another viable means of treatment could be found.

Thankfully, she'd gotten her name on a waiting list with Dr. Marshall — the very naturopath her mom had once hoped to consult. If there was an earlier opening, the clinic would bump up Heather's scheduled appointment, still weeks away.

Heather leaned back in the booth, stretching her neck. As she did, she was quite aware of the large safety pin taking in the waist of her jeans. *Can I beat this disease?* She pondered the question so hard, she thought she had literally verbalized it.

Looking around, she felt somewhat embarrassed, but no one at the nearest tables appeared to have taken any notice of her. She turned her attention back to the page still open on her laptop. Thanks to Wannalive's urging, she was more determined than ever to try the natural approach first.

Will Dr. Marshall be able to help me?

CHAPTER THREE

Jessica was still sitting in a heap on the front lawn when Grace approached. Her shoulder-length auburn hair blew against her pretty face as she wiped away her tears. *What has caused her such sadness?*

Grace sat right down next to her. "I heard ya cryin'."

"My parents are fighting again," Jessica managed to say, tears glistening. "Mom's on the phone with Dad right now."

Grace pushed her bare toes deep into the grass. "I'm ever so sorry."

"They've been arguing a lot . . . and lately Dad's hardly ever home. It makes me scared to death."

"For your parents?"

"Well, them, too . . ."

Grace touched Jessica's arm. "Who else?"

"I'm nearly too freaked to marry." Jessica slid her thick hair behind one ear. "I mean, is this what happens after so many years of

33

marriage . . . people just drift apart?"

Wishing her own mother had stayed put, Grace felt she understood something of Jessica's concern. "Well, don't forget, there are plenty of couples who get along fine, too," she said softly.

"Not *my* parents" came Jessica's bleak reply.

Just then her mother, Carole Spangler, came outside, wearing a long white tunic over her faded blue jeans. Without speaking, she picked up the rubber ball and heaved it over her shoulder, throwing it hard to the beautiful Labrador. The wind carried the ball, but the agile dog leaped high and caught it in his mouth. Then he bounded back across the wide, sweeping lawn and brought the ball to Grace, dropping it in her lap.

"He likes you," Jessica said, a reticent smile on her face.

Grace picked up the ball and threw it, staring now at her father's house in the distance. She wished she might offer some words to encourage her friend. Yet she, too, had struggled with similar concerns about marrying Henry.

The dog gave chase but then stopped, panting, as he surveyed the sheep-filled pasture below, his tail arched and his ears perked straight up. Bemused, Grace wondered how a slow-moving herd of sheep could possibly capture the attention of such an energetic dog.

About the time Grace felt she ought to head home, Carole asked Jessica to go and purchase a dozen eggs from the Riehls. "Looks like you have some time on your hands," she said, to which Jessica groaned softly.

"Oh, let me get the eggs," Grace volunteered, feeling sorry for her friend.

"Gracie . . . no. You really don't have to," Jessica said quickly.

"Well, I want to." Grace rose from her spot on the lawn and brushed off her long dress and apron.

Carole nodded and pulled out a five-dollar bill. "Keep the change for your trouble. I'm much too busy to leave the house even for a few minutes," she said. "I'm running out of time to make several cakes for our church bake sale." The woman was often in a bit of a rush, Grace recalled. Even when Carole had come to check Dat's heart rate and breathing after his recent collapse, she had seemed in a hurry to return home.

Her whole life, Grace had noticed how prone their English neighbors were to living at a hectic pace. Scarcely did they stay at home, Mamma had once pointed out, even fretting on occasion that they were sure to meet themselves coming and going.

"I'll be right back with the eggs," Grace said.

Carole thanked her. "Just so I have them sometime after lunch."

"You sure?"

"I've got enough for the cakes. Afternoon's just fine," Carole said, eyeing Jessica, who was brushing away tears where she still sat in the grass.

"All right, then." Grace shaded her eyes from the merciless sunlight and took the money. Then to Jessica she said, "Come over anytime, jah?"

Jessica looked up briefly, nodding. "Thanks, Gracie."

Heavyhearted, she made her way to the road, turning left toward the house. When she neared the phone booth yet again, it struck her that Dat and Mammi Adah, as well as Mandy, would be eager for word back about Mamma.

"What'll I tell them?" she said right out. *That Jessica's parents are in a pickle, too?*

Truth was, her whole family wanted more than word from Mamma. Better yet for Mamma to simply return home — nothing else would satisfy. With less hope of that each day, Grace filled her hours with work and chores, nearly more than a body could accomplish between dawn and dusk.

Now she rushed past the trees that concealed the phone shanty, its single window facing north, toward the Reihls' farm in the distance. *Tomorrow . . .*

As Grace scurried up the road, past her house, she noticed her father's sheep all clustered in one corner of the meadow and the vet's horse and buggy parked in the driveway. Breathing a prayer for Willow, she headed straight to the Riehls', hoping Mandy or Mammi Adah hadn't spotted her out on the road. She was in no mood to talk of more sad goings-on in the neighborhood.

She turned into the Riehls' lane and saw Becky hitching up one of their driving horses to the gray family carriage. *"Wie geht's?"* she called to her best friend.

"Just fine . . . you?" Becky raised her head, her sad face evident.

Grace hurried to her side. "Oh, you're crying!" *Is everyone in tears today?*

Becky nodded slowly. "Jah, silly me."

"No, no. That's all right."

Becky buried her face in her hands. "Oh, Gracie . . ."

Grace placed a hand on her friend's

shoulder, and she glanced about to see if anyone was watching. "Let's go somewhere and talk privately, all right?"

"Just help me finish hitchin' up the horse." Becky brushed her tears away. "I promised *Mamm.*"

Grace did what she could to speed up the process, but her friend couldn't keep the words back, and she began to pour out her sadness over Yonnie Bontrager, the handsome fellow she'd had her heart set on. "I thought he liked me. Honest, I did."

"I thought so, too." Grace didn't mention having seen Yonnie heading home alone last Sunday night, following Singing.

"Oh . . . I don't know what's the matter between us."

Grace pondered that. "Hard to know with some fellas."

"Ain't that the truth."

She looked kindly at Becky. "Did Yonnie give you anything to go on . . . I mean, did he explain why —"

"He just quit askin' me to go walkin' — out of the blue, really." Becky breathed in slowly, blinking her eyes. "He's been backing away the last couple of youth gatherings."

"Aw, Becky . . . I'm sorry to hear it." Grace had observed Yonnie with Becky often enough to believe they had something special.

Becky rose and patted the horse's mane for the longest time before she spoke again. "To tell the truth, I prob'ly liked him more than he liked me."

"I don't see how that can be."

Becky placed her hand on her heart, a faraway look in her eye. "He's nothin' like he used to be. . . ."

Some fellows lost interest all too quickly. "Well, best to find out before you're engaged or . . ." Grace stopped, thinking of Jessica's parents.

"Or married?"

"All I'm sayin' is, it might be for the best if you part ways . . . since he's actin' like this." She touched Becky's arm. "I'm awful sorry he's made you so sad."

They walked together into the house, and Becky's mother, Marian, greeted Grace with her usual bright smile, wiping her hands on her apron. "I'm glad you dropped by. What can I give yous to snack on?"

Grace suddenly remembered why she'd come. Slipping her hand into her pocket, she pulled out the five-dollar bill from Mrs. Spangler. "Our English neighbors down the road need a dozen eggs." She held out the money.

"You can just put that away. No need to make money off our neighbors. They've done so many favors for us!" Marian promptly went to the gas-run refrigerator and pulled out a carton containing a dozen eggs. "These were gathered yesterday afternoon."

"Des gut." Grace accepted the eggs and opened the back door as she thanked Marian. She thought she heard the mournful neigh of a horse carried on the wind. Anxious to check on Willow and hear what the vet had suggested, she walked as fast as she could without breaking the eggs.

Please, Lord, help Willow recover.

"As you know, Willow's not just a drivin' horse for us," Judah Byler told the vet, Jerry Wilder. "She's become a family pet." *Especially to Grace.*

Jerry did a visual inspection of the mare's knee joints on all four legs, looking for any swelling. He was a stocky man with dark brown hair and glasses, and although he was definitely an *Englischer,* he wore a subdued gray long-sleeved shirt and tan suspenders like an Amishman. Jerry had been looking in on all the Bird-in-Hand farmers' livestock for the past thirty or more years, and Judah appreciated his deliberate way of making decisions — not an impulsive bone in the man's body.

Judah touched Willow's head to calm her some as her ears pricked forward. Her eyes were focused on Jerry as he felt now for any unusual bumps, cuts, or heat, explaining everything as he went. He ran his hands along the mare's shoulders and hips, then lifted each foot to probe its frog and sole. "I'm looking for any bruises or foreign objects . . . checking to see whether the frogs are full of dirt. So far, it all looks good," he said of the first two legs.

He asked Judah to hold Willow still while he stepped back to see if she was distributing her weight equally on all four feet. "Just as you said, her right front leg is the culprit," he noted, indicating that it was cocked slightly. "She's certainly favoring that one."

Jerry straightened and shook his head. "Unless I'm completely off beam, Willow's ailing with the founder, which may have caused her injury. Coupled with her age, it's not good news."

Judah kept his hold on Willow; the mare appeared alert, although he knew she was not frightened. "Can she pull through?"

"Well, quite honestly, it would be a wonder." The vet put his hand on the horse's nose and patted her slowly. "I'd suggest extra attention from family members. If she starts to resist walking, call me and we'll X-ray her hoof. I'll give her medication for pain today." He eyed the stall. "Also, make some soft bedding with sawdust or black walnut shavings . . . that'll be more comfortable for her."

"All right, then," Judah said.

"Hope I'm wrong, but ultimately, I think you'll have to do the humane thing."

Judah shuddered to think of putting Willow out of her misery. What would it do to Grace? She appeared strong, but he was convinced her show of courage was for the benefit of her brothers and Mandy. *And undeniably for me, too.* Losing Willow would be like losing a friend. *One too many losses . . .*

"You know how to reach me, Judah."

He nodded.

Jerry offered a partial wave of the hand. "Good luck now."

We'll need that and more.

"I'll call ya . . . if need be."

The wind came up, scuffling old leaves across the vet's path as Judah stood and watched the man leave. He reached back and squeezed his sore neck. Then, with a great heaviness, he turned back to the stable, to Willow.

"Awful sorry, girl." Bending low, he gently rubbed the injured leg.

"Dat?"

He turned, not having heard Grace come into the stable. "Well, you snuck up on me."

"Didn't mean to." She knelt quickly, leaning her face against one of Willow's good legs. "She's goin' to make it, ain't so?"

He recited what the vet had told him, his heart going out to her. He left out the part about putting Willow down but said, "She's got the founder."

Tears sprang to her eyes. "Ach . . . no."

"It'll be a miracle . . ." he began, then stopped. His daughter knew what was at stake.

"Well, I'm praying, Dat. Is that childish, beseeching the Lord for an animal?"

Empathy welled up in him. "Ain't for me to say." He couldn't help but offer her a tender smile.

"All right, then. I won't quit." She rose to kiss Willow's nose.

The warmth in Judah's heart made him feel alive. But only after Grace had returned to the house did the tears prickle at the back of his eyes and distort his vision, then roll down his face unchecked. *The Lord giveth . . . and taketh away.*

CHAPTER FOUR

After Grace's hot dinner of baked roast and potatoes, steamed carrots and cauliflower, homemade applesauce, and red-beet eggs — even homemade root beer to drink — she confessed to Dat and the others that she hadn't yet made the call to Ohio. She didn't explain what had caused the delay. Mammi Adah had looked surprisingly relieved, Grace recalled as she carried the food scraps to the compost pile behind the barn.

Tomorrow will be soon enough. The less she contemplated calling, the easier it might be in the long run.

Enjoying the feel of the thick grass under her feet, she considered Dat's kindly way when they'd talked in the barn earlier, there with Willow. Despite the sadness of the moment, she was truly heartened at how gently he'd shared the news with her, father to daughter. She'd never heard him speak so

44

freely to a woman.

She was moseying across the backyard, returning to the house, when she heard horse hooves on the driveway. She looked to see who was coming. There, as big as you please — and all smiles, too — was Yonnie Bontrager, perched high in his new courting buggy.

What's he doing here?

Remembering Becky's sadness over him, she did not wave back, not even when Yonnie caught her eye and smiled. *Like last Sunday night.* She recalled his friendly grin as he left the Singing without Becky. What would happen if word got out that Yonnie had come by?

What'll Becky think? Dismayed, Grace hurried around the side of the house and up the steps. Reaching for the kitchen door, she slipped inside before Yonnie could speak to her. She dashed to the utility closet for the mop and bucket and prepared to wash the kitchen floor. There was more than enough work to keep her busy before returning to Carole Spangler with the eggs from the Riehls' hen house.

Hearing Dat and Adam call a cheerful *"Willkumm"* to Yonnie outside, she assumed he'd come to borrow a tool. She shook off the image of handsome Yonnie sitting in his buggy, nonchalantly holding the reins. True, she'd enjoyed his company quite a lot before Henry Stahl had started seeing her regularly. But that was back last year, when Yonnie and his family had first arrived from Indiana, and Yonnie had only asked her to go walking after Singing a few times. He'd explained at length that he'd purposely chosen not to own a courting buggy while he decided whom to court, as if testing to see how she'd react. His was a serious, even careful approach to courtship. To think Grace had been so certain he would decide to court her friend.

Grace stooped to get into the corners with the string mop. Goodness, but Yonnie had ridden right past the Riehls' house to come here! Did he have the slightest idea how fond Becky was of him? *Ain't my place to say.* Besides, Becky was her first concern. *Before any thickheaded fellow!*

When Grace had mopped the dirtiest traffic areas, she poured the gray water outside, rinsed out her sponge, and scrubbed her hands. Another quick look around indicated the buggy was still on the premises.

Then, of all things, she saw Yonnie himself standing near the barn door, carrying a baby lamb like Dat sometimes did. Shocked, she assumed Dat had given him some mighty quick instruction on tending lambs. A full-grown sheep would view him as a stranger and shy away, for sure.

Just why *had* Yonnie come?

Judah removed his straw hat and scratched his head. He had no idea what to make of this young whippersnapper who'd shown up so spontaneously. By all appearances, Yonnie had come to assist with the newborn lambs, but after giving the boy some pointers, something in his gut made him think otherwise.

The lad's father, Ephram Bontrager, had moved here last year with plans to take over his aging uncle's buggy-making business. *"Since there are no farm chores to tie me down just now, I figured I'd stop by here to see if you can use my help,"* Yonnie had said. *"I don't expect any pay."* Yonnie went on to explain that his father wouldn't need him at the buggy-making shop until Ephram was the only one running it. *"Till my uncle retires."*

Now Judah found himself chuckling. He wondered how Grace might feel, especially if the boy was bold enough to stay on for supper. It was still befuddling how this young man had nearly tackled him at the harness shop not long ago, asking for permission to court Grace. He couldn't help but wonder what on earth his daughter thought of Yonnie's peculiar way of doing things.

Taking note of some slipshod work in the bedding areas, Judah called to Adam and Joe. Clumps of straw were strewn about, not having been shaken out hard enough or broken apart from the tight baling.

"*Guck emol datt* — Look at that!" He pointed out the muddled mess and leaned down to pick up a bundle of straw. "No excuse for this."

Adam was first to nod, being the oldest. But it was Joe who fessed up. "Was my fault, Dat. I was in a rush."

"Well, that never pays." Judah wiped the back of his hand across his forehead. *No way . . . no how.* Shaking his head, he sighed, thinking unexpectedly of Lettie. The same old regrets continued to play in his head.

Hindsight was powerful-good; he knew that. But there'd been no chance to make it up to her . . . no time to hear her out.

Glancing over his shoulder, he saw Adam and Joe making right the sloppy arrangement of straw in the nonexpectant ewes' bedding areas. The boys were talking low but fast in Dietsch. He had no desire to listen in — there was enough of that going on in the house. He'd caught Lettie's mother, Adah, lingering near the doorway in the hall last evening, observing his Scripture reading time with his children. Just why, he had no idea. Truth was, Adah and Jakob were both mighty edgy here lately, ever since Lettie's leaving. Downright strange it was — like they were keeping mum about something.

He caught sight of Yonnie again. The lad was coaxing a thin-looking lamb to drink from a baby bottle as doggedly as one of his sons might. *Like he might want to be a sheep farmer, too.*

But no, Judah wouldn't let his mind wander in that direction. He assumed Grace already had herself a beau. Even if she went around with a long face — like Yonnie had pointed out that day in the harness shop — it didn't have to mean she was unhappy with her intended. *Her Mamma's gone, for pity's sake!*

"Judah," called Yonnie. "This here lamb's not takin' to the bottle." He slid the nipple right out of its mouth. "See? No suction." He shook his head, blue eyes exhibiting concern. "No matter what I do, I can't seem to get this one to latch on."

The more Judah worked with sheep, the less he felt he knew. *Just like most any-*

thing . . . a man's always learning till the day he dies.

"Keep rubbing the nipple over its gums," he suggested.

Yonnie nodded and walked away with the lamb's head still snuggled against his shirt. He headed outdoors again, turning to pull the barn door shut.

Not so much lambs but sheep were as wary as any animal the Lord God had made. They were typically terrified of strangers, so Judah had given Yonnie a pair of his old work trousers right quick, to introduce Yonnie to the herd that way. Sheep were also known to wander away. Judah had more than enough fence crawlers — restless sheep — who kept forcing their way through the fence. And the worst of it, they tended to pass on the same habits to their offspring. A bad example to the whole flock.

Ach, like Lettie, he thought and wondered if she would even respond positively to his searching for her. *Like the Good Shepherd and that one little lost sheep . . .*

Heading to the opposite end of the barn, to the mule and horse stalls, Judah looked in on Willow. She was calmer now, after the vet's pain medication.

With yet another glance at the old mare,

he took down his favorite shovel and began to muck out the stalls. The smell scarcely fazed him after all these years. Was that how a person could find himself in boiling hot water? By just sitting, oblivious to the temperature slowly rising over time?

Like a marriage slowly eroding over the years . . .

With each heave of manure, he considered the ministers' stern remarks this morning. *Should* he have gone looking for his wayward wife, as the bishop had suggested? Shouldn't Judah be the one making the call to Ohio, instead of Grace?

Thus far he hadn't lifted a finger to contact Lettie or bring her back. It wasn't that he didn't care to; he wanted her to return on her own, because she loved him. And deep down in the core of him, he was afraid she'd refuse to come home even if he asked.

So much has changed. . . . He'd pursued her at the outset as a young fellow, when Lettie reached courting age. But later, after her return from Ohio with her mother, their getting hitched had been mostly his father-in-law's doing. Jakob had gotten the wheels rolling for Judah to marry Lettie right quick.

He turned to see Yonnie still cradling the feeble lamb in his arms like an infant.

"Ach . . . didn't see ya there."

"Sorry, but this one needs more attention." Yonnie eyed the lamb. "Its ribs are stickin' clear out."

Judah propped up his shovel and wiped his hands on his work trousers. "Give him here."

"Ain't a male," Yonnie said, his blue eyes twinkling.

He took the lamb and the bottle and slowly worked the nipple around the small animal's mouth, then dribbled several milk droplets on the lamb's tongue. Judah held his breath, hoping the gentle approach might do the trick, though he felt ill at ease, being the object of such scrutiny.

"She's awful frail," Yonnie said, moving even closer. Thankfully, the young fellow did not touch the lamb's head. Any movement, and this undernourished newborn could easily become distracted . . . lose the slight suction she had on the bottle now.

Judah heard the steady, even, rhythmic swallowing before the familiar clicking sound of suckling. He was relieved as the lamb began to relax in his arms. This one could most likely be saved.

"I believe you've got a knack," Yonnie said. "A gift from the Father's own hand, my Dat would say."

Yonnie's unexpected admiration made Judah downright nervous. Honestly, he wished the lad would just keep quiet.

Having finally delivered the eggs to the Spanglers, Grace realized she was favoring the far side of the road as she came upon the phone booth. Simply knowing the booth was there made her feel guilty for putting off the call. *What am I so afraid of?*

She forced her thoughts to this last visit, recalling Jessica's eagerness to talk further, which Grace had encouraged her to do. *"Let's go walking sometime,"* she'd said.

Jessica's mother had spotted the unused five-dollar bill on the table. And lo and behold if she hadn't made an awkward comment about Grace's needing it *"for a rainy day."*

Hurrying toward home now, she whispered, "We can take care of ourselves." *With or without Mamma.*

She shook her head as she neared the driveway and noticed Mandy standing at the mailbox on the front porch, holding up the mail and calling to her. "I think there's a letter from Mamma! Oh, Grace, come quick!"

A little burst of air flew from her lips as she picked up her skirt and ran to the front yard. *Can it be?*

Mandy relinquished the letter to Grace, and together they promptly sat on the porch swing. Seeing it was addressed in their mother's handwriting to *The Judah Byler Family,* Grace ripped open the envelope, her fingers shaking . . . and her heart pounding. *Oh joy!*

She couldn't help recalling all the happy times Mamma had sat here on the porch, scribbling off letters to Hallie Troyer, her Indiana cousin, or writing her account of the week in one of several circle letters circulating through the county.

Quickly, Grace read silently.

My dear family,
    I want you to know that I am well . . . and safe. So many times I've wanted to write to you or to call. I long to hear your voices once again.
    I wish I could explain why I am away from home, gone so far from all of you. It is ever so difficult right now. Please trust that I pray for you each day, my dear ones.
                              I miss you terribly.
                                    With love,
                                    Mamma

We miss you, too, thought Grace, fighting

54

back tears. Yet she was puzzled. What could be so difficult?

Glancing at Mandy, who'd snuggled up close enough for her to smell a hint of bath powder, she gave her sister the letter.

Mandy held it tenderly, her eyes glistening. Then she read their mother's note, soundlessly mouthing the words. When she was finished, she folded it again and gently returned it to the envelope. "Here, you keep it," she said, placing it in Grace's hand.

"Have you looked at the postmark?" Grace pointed to the post office stamp: *Kidron, Ohio.* But Mamma had not written a return address. "It's the same city as the inn's address." She reached into her pocket and pulled out Mammi's note. "See?"

Mandy peered at Mammi Adah's writing. "So then, Mammi was right: Mamma's somewhere in Kidron, if not at that very inn." She looked at Grace.

I miss you terribly, Mamma had written.

Seeing her mother's handwriting jolted Grace into action. "I'll go right now and make the phone call . . . surely Mamma's staying there."

"Where else, if not at that inn?" Mandy agreed.

She sighed, not fully understanding why she'd felt so reluctant to call today.

"You want me to walk with you?"

Grace couldn't decide if her sister's presence beside the small phone booth would give her the moral support she needed or make her more nervous. But Mandy got up and followed her down the sidewalk and through the front yard. With each step, Grace felt an impending mixture of anxiety and anticipation. Just how close was she to finding a mother who might not wish to be found?

CHAPTER FIVE

The ring tone on her iPhone gave off a jingle, alerting Heather that someone other than a relative or a college friend was calling. She answered and was surprised to hear a congenial receptionist informing her there was an unexpected opening tomorrow morning at Dr. Marshall's office.

"Great. I'll take it, thanks." For a fleeting moment, Heather was absolutely elated. But as the receptionist gave the driving directions and the office suite number, she experienced a sinking feeling. After thanking the woman again, she hung up. She hadn't expected this cloud of sadness. It was as if a door had creaked open, and she was being propelled through it to an unknown land.

She breathed slowly, turning to look over her shoulder at the many enticing sweets in the display window across from her. Something told her this might be her last chance to indulge in the "Standard American Diet," or SAD, as some online sources called it. In fact, one article had asserted the typical American diet could eventually kill you.

Nice, she'd thought.

Returning her attention to her laptop screen, Heather hit Save and closed her thesis. Then, opening another Word file, she began to add another section to her daily journal. She typed a new heading: *Life As I'll Soon Know It.*

Grace was glad Mandy wasn't disappointed at her suggestion to wait outside the phone booth. Even so, she felt like a *Laus* — louse — excluding her sister this way. Still, it was better that Mandy not overhear the conversation. Who knew what might transpire? Besides, as Grace closed the door behind her, there didn't seem to be enough air inside the shanty as it was. Or maybe she was simply breathing it all up too quickly.

Trembling, she lifted the receiver and held it against her ear, listening for the automated prompts. Next, she punched in the phone card number.

At last, a phone rang on the other end. Then . . . a woman's voice.

"Kidron Inn — Tracie Gordon speaking."

Grace's thoughts froze.

"Hello? Anyone there?"

"I . . . I'm sorry." She swallowed hard. "I'm lookin' for someone."

"Yes?"

"Well, it's my mother. Is she there, by any chance?" Suddenly Grace felt ever so silly, like a tongue-tied youngster. "Ach, her name's Lettie Byler."

"No, not presently. But . . . she was."

Grace's heart leaped up. "Oh, that's wonderful-*gut,* really 'tis." She hardly knew what to say next.

"Lettie was here for several weeks, in fact."

Several weeks?

"I wish you'd called earlier, dear."

"Me too. And I should've told you my name. I'm Grace Byler, calling from Bird-in-Hand, Pennsylvania, where my mother lives." *Where she used to . . .* Grace tightened her grip on the phone. "Did she happen to say where she was going?"

"I really can't say, no." A short pause.

Ach, please try to remember. . . .

"Oh, wait." The innkeeper's wife spoke up suddenly. "She did say something about looking for a midwife."

Grace's breath caught in her throat. *A midwife?* "My mother's still in the area, then?"

"She may very well be."

Grace felt her throat closing. *So very close and yet . . .* "Is there anything else you remember? Was she goin' to see cousins in another state, maybe?" She just had to know more.

"You know, now that you mention it, your mother *did* talk some about a cousin in Indiana — I do recall that."

"All right, then. Denki — thank you — ever so much."

"You are most welcome, Grace. And if there's anything else I can help you with, please don't think twice about calling."

"That's kind of you. Good-bye."

The word *midwife* spun around in Grace's head. And even though it was nearly suffocating in the phone booth, she stayed there for a moment after hanging up the receiver. "What can it mean?" she muttered, staring at the sky through the little window. And how could she begin to explain this to Mandy, who was waiting but a few feet away?

And Dat . . . wouldn't he know if Mamma was expecting a late-in-life baby?

Leaning her head back so hard that her Kapp pushed forward, Grace decided she best not share that part of the conversation. *What other reason might there be for Mamma to search out a midwife? Oh, goodness . . .*

what next?

She struggled not to show her frustration. Taking a long, slow breath, she opened the shanty door and stepped outside.

Mandy came rushing over. "What did you find out?"

"Mamma's not there — but she was. It's possible she's gone to visit her cousin Hallie Troyer."

Mandy stared at her as if Grace looked ill. Did her confusion show on her face? "Sounds like Mamma's movin' from place to place. Why on earth?"

Grace could do nothing but agree with her sister's suggestion. Yet why would Mamma write them a letter saying she missed them, if she wasn't heading home?

"You goin' to write to Cousin Hallie?" asked Mandy.

"Well, I doubt Troyers have a phone, so maybe I'll have to." But what she really wanted to do was just go there and see for herself.

"Mammi Adah surely has the Troyers' address," Mandy pressed. "Ain't so?"

"I haven't decided what to do." They moved out from under the shadow of the dense thicket of low branches.

Mandy shook her head and gave Grace a sharp look as they headed home. "I don't see why everything's up to you, Grace."

"It's not." She wouldn't let her ire up. After all, Mandy had every right to wonder. "What's clear is Dat's not able to go lookin' for Mamma — not now, anyway."

"But even if he were free to go, I doubt he would," Mandy blurted.

"What a miserable thing to say," Grace chided her . . . but she had thought the same thing earlier.

"Jah, I have some time on my hands," Yonnie said as Judah walked with him from the barn. "I'm caught up on my work over at the deacon's place . . . for now."

"Well, there's plenty to do here," Judah replied.

"And the injured mare needs tending to, jah?"

Grace will be out there with Willow. Judah bowed his head. "Just can't see how Willow's goin' to make it."

"My family once had to make a difficult decision about a horse," Yonnie said. "Dat says he's known some farmers to give up too quick. His motto is to just hold steady."

"Doesn't seem right . . . with Willow still sufferin'."

Yonnie looked him square in the face. "Can ya give her more time?"

Judah thought again of poor Grace. "All right, then. We'll see what tomorrow brings." Yonnie sure seemed to be one persistent fellow. But he'd grown up around horses, having helped his father and uncle raise them in Indiana, before moving here.

Yonnie tapped his straw hat and hurried off to hitch up his horse and buggy. "I'll be back bright and early tomorrow!"

Judah was puzzled at his optimism. Yet he couldn't fault Yonnie for his helpful spirit. Then, looking out toward the road, he saw Grace and Mandy talking as they headed this way. A smile formed on his lips, and he found himself curious at what might transpire if Yonnie bumped into his eldest daughter before he left for home.

Knowing it was best he keep his distance on that, Judah muttered, "Ach, old man . . . just let things be."

What with so many interruptions this afternoon, Grace was glad she'd planned a supper of fried chicken and noodles with brown butter. "We best be showin' Dat what Mamma wrote in her letter," she told Mandy as they set the table for the evening meal.

"*You* show him," Mandy urged as she folded the paper napkins. "He'll be eager for some word 'bout your phone call, too, won't he?"

Grace stewed. Really, what was there to tell? That Mamma had stayed exactly where Mammi Adah suspected she'd gone . . . but was now heading somewhere else? "Instead of comin' home," she murmured.

"What?" Mandy turned.

"Just thinkin' out loud."

Mandy offered a reassuring smile and finished placing the utensils on the table. "You seem awful jittery. Is it the phone call? Something you ain't tellin'?"

"I'm more confused than upset. Can't understand why Mamma's staying away . . . and why she doesn't just tell us what's botherin' her."

"Jah." Mandy's eyes turned serious. "Makes not a speck of sense."

Grace sighed, wanting to change the subject.

Mandy asked quickly, "Is it too soon to call Dawdi Jakob and Mammi Adah over for the meal?"

"No, go ahead. I'll let Adam and Joe know we're ready." Going to the side door, Grace called to their brothers. She was aware of Dat's footsteps overhead in his room, directly above the kitchen.

She was just stepping back inside when

Yonnie Bontrager waved to her from near the stable, where he had finished hitching up his horse. He straightened to his full height as he caught her eye. "Have a *gut* evening, Grace," he said with a big grin.

Uncertain why she was blushing, Grace returned to the kitchen to get the food on the table, all the while wondering why Yonnie had stayed this long. She doubted Dat would volunteer as much, and she wasn't about to ask. Certainly not during the supper hour, when Dat's mind would more than likely be on Mamma's letter.

With yet another prayer for her mother's safe return, Grace slipped the envelope with its telltale postmark next to Dat's white dinner plate.

CHAPTER SIX

Alone now, Judah picked up Lettie's note, his eyes hungry for word from his wife. *The Judah Byler Family,* she'd written on the envelope — the only mention of him. He read the short letter, noting that she'd simply signed off, *Mamma.*

Not *with love, Lettie.*

He placed the letter on the Bible and rose from the chair near the window where he'd sometimes sat with Lettie through the years. He leaned down to remove his socks. Tomorrow promised another long day of work, with new lambs still coming fast, according to the birthing schedule he'd meticulously planned. Soon, though, the numerous births would taper off and they would fatten the lambs for market.

In the past couple days, Grace hadn't again brought up going to Ohio to look for Lettie. He could only hope she might push aside that nonsense. How would it look to have two women from his household running about? Judah rose and reached for the dark green blind on the first window and pulled it flush with the sill. He did the same at the second.

Removing his suspenders, his mind wandered to Willow, and he hoped for Grace's sake — and the horse's — that the vet's treatment today might turn things around some. *And Yonnie's efforts, too, for whatever they were worth.*

He walked to his side of the bed, glancing once more at Lettie's note. Why *had* she written? Did she think they'd forget her if she remained silent?

Going to their shared dresser, he opened the middle drawer and removed a clean pair of pajama bottoms. *Do you ever wonder what we're thinking, Lettie?*

One thing was sure: He was tired of waking up alone. It was time his wife came home and fessed up about her disappearance. "Time for a long talk, too."

When he'd slipped off his work trousers and put on his pajamas, he pulled back the quilt and got into bed. "Why am I muttering to myself?" *'Tis laughable.* He reached for the Good Book and his wife's letter. Judah was mighty tired, but he read two psalms, one after the other, before going over Lettie's note once more. Why hadn't she written one just to him?

Weary of the day, he pushed the letter beneath his pillow and fell promptly asleep.

Heather woke up Wednesday thinking about a discarded necklace box she'd found last month when she was sorting through her bedroom closet. The small box where her mother had kept all of her baby teeth and her first snippets of soft baby hair.

Stretching, she smiled at the memory of those childhood "treasures." She slipped out of bed in her rented room, knowing it was wise to claim early the only bathroom on the second floor. She gathered up her brush, shampoo, and robe and darted across the hall.

She showered in record time, and later, after she'd dressed and towel-dried her hair, she realized she had no interest in eating. *Zero appetite.* She was too nervous about her doctor appointment to share in Marian's "big spread," as the gregarious Amish-woman liked to describe breakfast. The Riehls' house was packed to the rafters — each of the guest rooms filled. *"Springtime in Lancaster County is a real draw for tourists,"* Becky had explained yesterday while she and Heather had fed the chickens. All the quaintness had begun to wear off, but she hadn't wanted to offend Becky, who had undoubtedly noticed Heather's backing away since they'd first connected.

She's figured me out . . . like everyone eventually does, Heather mused, heading downstairs.

Marian stood at the kitchen counter, wearing a plum-colored dress and matching apron, her blondish hair pulled into a smooth bun at her neck. The strings from her Kapp draped over her slender shoulders as if she'd pushed them back, and her clear blue eyes sparkled as she turned from stirring the pancake batter. "Well, you're up mighty early, Heather," she said, her smile contagious. "Can I pour some fresh-brewed coffee for ya?"

"Coffee's good, thanks." She wasn't in the mood for small talk, but she supposed she'd have to endure it if she was to have her needed shot of caffeine.

"I'm serving blueberry pancakes this mornin'," said Marian cheerfully. For as much as the woman apparently enjoyed eating, Marian was quite thin. "Becky went over to Cousin Emma's yesterday afternoon, where we rent a freezer, and brought back some of the blueberries we put up last August."

"Sounds delicious, but I need to leave for an appointment this morning."

"We picked more than a little mess of berries last summer . . . most of 'em with dew still sittin' on them when we brought them in for breakfast." Marian's smile seemed to grow. "For some reason, more blueberries than even raspberries last year."

Heather turned to look out the window as she waited for the coffee. She missed her mom on mornings like this. The smell of pancake batter — one of the breakfast foods her mother often enjoyed making — brought so many happy thoughts flying back. At first, immediately after her mother's death, Heather had resisted the memories. She'd existed merely in survival mode, as though moving through dense, deep waters. She'd gone so far as to remove all the pictures of her mom from her bedroom — it tore at her to see her mother looking so healthy and vibrant . . . so alive.

But in recent months, she'd begun to welcome the past and was conscious that Mom was never far from her remembrance. With the realization of great loss had come a yearning for the memories.

"Here's your coffee, dear . . . just the way you like it."

"Thanks." Heather turned, smiling her

gratitude.

"Wouldn't you like something more? Something to take with you, just maybe?" Marian sounded somewhat concerned.

"Not this morning, but thanks anyway." She did not go to sit at the table as usual but rather carried the mug back to her room and set it on the coaster on the dresser. Scrutinizing her well-scrubbed face, she began to apply eyeliner and mascara, then brushed her still-damp hair again.

By the time she arrived at the doctor's office, Heather was pleased to see only two cars in the designated parking area. The many times she'd accompanied her mom to the doctor, to the oncologist especially, had led her to realize doctors were primarily aware of their *own* schedules, or so it seemed. But if you were the first patient of the day, now that was a plus. And as Heather stepped up to the receptionist's window, she could see by the sign-in list that she was indeed the first.

Off to a good start . . .

Grace found Mamma's note tucked under Dat's pillow when she made his bed that morning. She didn't bother reading it again but set it on the small round table next to the bed, wondering if Dat — or Mammi

Adah — might have an idea about Mamma's need to locate a particular midwife. And why one so far from home? *Might such a woman be able to help Mamma with midlife issues?* Grace had never been so befuddled.

Smoothing the top quilt, she looked about the room. Was there something of Mamma's here, in the bedroom she'd shared so long with Dat, that might point to her need to go away? Was there anything at all that offered a clue, besides the missing poetry books?

Hesitantly she opened the dresser drawers that had belonged to Mamma. Finding each one empty, she went to the foot of the bed and lifted the lid on the blanket chest. Surely there was something she'd missed before, hidden in the crevices or beneath the coverlets.

But she found nothing. At least nothing that hinted at an answer.

When she'd closed the lid, she again ran her hand over the bed quilt, sighing. *Oh, Dat,* she thought, *I'm so sorry for you. What might I have done differently?*

Downstairs, Mandy was stirring up the waffle mix, having offered to make breakfast the night before. *"It'll give you time to check on Willow,"* she'd said. Grace gave her a peck on the cheek and hurried outdoors, under the tall trees Dat had planted years ago. *Shady as umbershoots,* she thought, breathing in the freshness of morning. She noticed the first few blossoms on the trumpet creepers, their bright orange trumpet-shaped flowers climbing the newly painted white trellis Adam had nailed to the back of the house years ago. Mamma had always called them hummingbird vines, because they attracted the lively little birds the whole family enjoyed watching.

In the spring and summer, Mamma had liked to sit in this shaded yard, delighting in the many types of birds that called and flitted from branch to branch in the cool of the morning. Come evenings, if Mamma wasn't already settled in the front porch swing, Dat sometimes carried lawn chairs out to the backyard for Dawdi and Mammi, as well. The four of them liked sitting there, all lined up, drinking root beer or meadow tea, tired from the day yet with contentment on their faces. Always it was Mamma and her parents who carried the conversation, with only an occasional nod of the head from Dat — if that.

Her musing over Mamma quickly turned to dismay when she walked into the barn and saw Willow sprawled out on the bed of sawdust, her injured leg drawn up close to her barrel. Whatever the vet had attempted must not be working.

Touching Willow's mane, Grace blinked back tears. "Such a dear pet." Gently she massaged the injured leg, mindful of even the slightest reaction. She and Dat had taken time last night to ice the limb, alternating cold and hot applications. Her father had assured her stable rest was the best way to heal Willow's leg.

Adam had also come out to check on Willow, although he'd seemed particularly keen on talking about Yonnie. He'd wondered aloud how Grace felt about his helping Dat.

Grace hadn't owned up to Adam how she felt. She suspected her brother was still licking his wounds, so to speak, from her decision to release Henry from their engagement. It was clear, though, that Adam assumed Yonnie was quite interested in her. *"Taken with ya, really,"* her brother had said almost accusingly.

Grace wondered how he had gotten that idea. *For Becky's sake, he'd better keep such thoughts to himself.* Now she finished massaging Willow and gave the horse a pat, fairly sure Mandy was ready to serve the waffles. Making her way back to the house, she pulled on the rope a single time, to ring the dinner bell. Once was enough, as the menfolk would be mighty hungry.

She moved back indoors to pour coffee, thinking again of Mamma's absence. More than a dozen times a day, she caught herself turning to ask her mother a question, momentarily forgetting. Or she'd think of something just before retiring for the night and want to share it with her mother. *Why's she wandering around Ohio? And why can't she talk to one of the midwives here?*

Grace was ever so glad to hear her father and brothers coming in the main door. The familiar *clunkity-clunk* as they removed their work boots in the hallway brought her comfort. Soon they'd come stocking-footed into the kitchen for Mandy's nice hot breakfast. She stood back, eyeing the table. Everything was set as it should be. And when Dat, Adam, and Joe were washed up for the meal, she was surprised to see the corners of Dat's smile spread clear across his tanned face.

"You and your sister outdid yourselves," he said quietly, going to sit at the head of the table.

She wanted to show her gratitude for her father's unexpectedly kind remark but said nothing as she took her seat. The spot where

Mamma had always sat since Grace could remember remained achingly unoccupied.

After the silent blessing and their unison, "Amen," Grace said she'd seen how feeble and ailing Willow was this morning. "Can't something more be done?"

"No change overnight," Dat said in a low voice.

"Well, Yonnie's certainly giving his know-how a try," Joe piped up, across the table. "Yesterday he talked to her and just a-stroked her a *gut* while."

"What does he know about horses that we don't?" Adam eyed his brother. "I say, best not to get your hopes up" — and here he looked directly at Grace. "Willow's had many *gut* years. Isn't that what counts?"

Grace's heart sank at this, but she nodded.

Dat said not a word, and they began to silently enjoy breakfast — Dat and the boys all smacking their lips in appreciation. She was terribly conscious of the occasional sound of neighing, sad and pitiful, coming from the barn. It wasn't right to let the animal suffer so. *Poor, dear Willow . . .*

She rose to pour another cup of coffee for Dat, struggling not to cry. Just as she was returning to the table, Adam suggested, "Maybe you could scoot over and sit in

76

Mamma's place . . . fill in the gap a bit." Across the table, Mandy and Joe were focused on refilling their plates with scrambled eggs, bacon, toast, and hot oatmeal — they hadn't seemed to hear Adam's startling remark.

But Grace was even more stunned when Dat gave his subtle consent with a quick nod of his head. His instant agreement served to heighten her fears. For some unknown reason, he must not believe Mamma was returning home soon.

Grace said nary a word, glancing instead at her mother's place on the wooden bench between her and Dat. Why was her brother suggesting this now, on the heels of Mamma's letter? After all, she'd written that she missed them. Didn't that count for something?

Adam urged her again, "Why not, Grace?" The question annoyed her. Adam, too, seemed to disbelieve their mother would ever return. *Makes not a whit of sense . . .*

Truth was, she felt reluctant to slide over, even though her father had given his approval. Yet being a single young woman, she was expected to obey her father and older brother.

"It's a hard reminder that she's gone, is all," Adam explained softly.

"Dat?" She looked his way.

He drew a long breath, then gestured with his head. "You and Mandy can both move over . . . for the time bein'."

Without hesitating further, Grace did as she was told. She moved her plate and utensils, and Mandy followed right behind her, sitting in Grace's usual spot. Looking across at Adam, and then glancing at her father, Grace felt slightly disoriented, but she continued with her meal. She felt ever so strange sitting there.

Dawdi Jakob and Mammi Adah walked in just then, joining them late for breakfast — Mammi made the excuse that Dawdi hadn't been feeling well. Then, sitting down on the opposite side of the table, they gave Grace a stern look.

"Why's Gracie sittin' there?" Dawdi asked with a disapproving frown.

"Can't hurt nothin', Jakob," her father spoke up. "There's a vacancy at this table."

"Ain't that the truth," Dawdi grumbled.

Later, after breakfast was done and Grace walked back with her grandparents to their side of the house, nothing more was said. For that, Grace was greatly relieved. It wouldn't do to question Dat further. After all, they were in a state of transition — "flux," Dawdi Jakob had said recently. And no one, not even her father, knew how to get things back to normal.

CHAPTER SEVEN

Grace and Mandy were finishing up the breakfast dishes when Yonnie flew into the driveway in his courting buggy. "Show-off," Grace said under her breath. Mandy must've heard because she shrugged before reaching for the next dish.

It was apparent Dat wasn't surprised by Yonnie's return. In fact, by the way they came out of the barn to greet him, Joe and Dat actually seemed to be expecting Yonnie.

Grace turned away, not caring to discuss her surprise with Mandy, who was staring at her now with curious brown eyes. Wanting to complete the chore of redding up the kitchen, Grace hastened to scrub the sink, then rinsed it thoroughly. That done, she moved to the stove and wiped it down.

"You all right?" Mandy said.

"Of course."

Mandy forced air through her pursed lips. "You sure don't look it."

Her sister most likely assumed Yonnie's showing up again annoyed her. But Mandy couldn't possibly know why that would be, unless she, too, had observed Yonnie's interest in Becky, then his leaving alone after the last two Singings. "I'm just fine, really," Grace insisted.

"Ain't foolin' me, Gracie."

"Will ya bring up some potatoes for me?" Grace asked, hoping her sister might take the hint and leave her be. Besides, it was past time to start preparing the noon meal — thick and hearty beef stew — so it could simmer while she did her other chores.

Without another word, Mandy headed for the steps to the cold cellar. Relieved, Grace went to the window, still wishing she had concealed her emotions better. It was then she noticed the Spanglers' big dog — the golden Lab she'd played fetch with yesterday — tearing through the sheep pasture. "For pity's sake, no!" She rushed to the kitchen door and was thunderstruck to see Yonnie heading across the barnyard. He slipped beneath the fence and pushed his straw hat back on his head, strolling briskly toward the middle of the field.

The terrified sheep were all huddled together in the far corner. Some of the pregnant ewes would be so frightened they might birth too early, and that would never do. Dat needed every single one of the new lambs this season, just as he did any other springtime. The lambs were their main source of livelihood.

Yonnie crouched low in the middle of the pasture, holding out his hand to the excited dog. Although Grace couldn't be sure from where she stood observing, she thought he might be talking to the Labrador.

She continued to peer out, her nose almost touching the screen door. "Well, I'll be . . ." The dog ceased its barking and moved slowly toward Yonnie until he was licking his hand, and then Yonnie's face, nearly knocking his hat off. "Unbelievable," Grace whispered.

"What is?" Mandy asked, startling her as she came up from behind.

"Over there." She pointed to Yonnie, now leading the neighbors' dog by his collar, up the hill toward the Spanglers' house.

"Ach, that dog's been watchin' the sheep for several days now," Mandy replied. "I wondered if this might not happen."

Grace, too, had noticed the dog's interest in the sheep — just yesterday, in fact. "It's a *gut* thing someone was there to calm that Lab," she said, thinking of the ewes.

"You mean the lion tamer?" Mandy teased.

Grace gave a small smile. "He sure has a way with them."

"Well, with dogs, anyway."

They laughed at that. Then Mandy said she'd seen Yonnie carrying one of their sickly lambs yesterday. "Dat says Yonnie's keen on savin' the weakest of them. You know which one?"

Grace knew. Adam and Joe had continued bottle-feeding the pitiful creature after Yonnie left. "Mandy . . . did Dat say anything 'bout needing extra help?"

"Not a word. Why?"

It was Grace's turn to shrug. "Just curious."

"Ain't troublesome, havin' Yonnie Bontrager here . . . is it?"

"Why would ya think that?" But it *was* a strange predicament, and Grace knew full well that Mandy was smarter than she was letting on. Still, Grace was weary of talking about the boy who'd hurt Becky so badly. She wondered what Becky must be thinking. *Surely she saw him coming this way.* She simply could not let her dearest friend wonder if Yonnie was sweet on *her.* Not for the world!

Once Mandy emptied her apron full of potatoes onto the counter, she left to assist Mammi Adah with a pile of mending. Grace breathed a sigh of relief, letting out her pent-up frustration as she chopped potatoes for the stew. *That Yonnie — he's a charmer, for sure.* Goodness, but sweet Becky was the perfect choice for him. How could he not know this? Quite unexpectedly, Grace realized he might've broken *her* heart, too, if she'd let him a year ago.

What would happen if the object of Becky's affection kept coming to help Dat in Mamma's absence? For now, Grace could only hope Yonnie wouldn't be so presumptuous as to stay over for the noon meal. *Like he's hired help — or worse yet — family!* Mandy's teasing she could take; it was her brother Adam's seeming disapproval that truly bothered her.

The young receptionist and subsequent nursing staff were so friendly, Heather was caught off guard. As a result, her apprehension slowly began to subside as she followed the brunette nurse down the hall to the examination room. Instead of the typical stark décor of a doctor's office, the room was enhanced by earth tones and a skylight, which lent a bright and tranquil feeling. Sinking into the comfortable chair, Heather willed herself to relax.

She was equally impressed with Dr. Marshall, a pretty, vivacious blonde with an infectious smile and twinkling blue eyes. "First of all, I want you to call me LaVyrle," she began. "I hope we'll become good friends."

Encouraged, Heather nodded. "I'm counting on you to help me," she said. "I've been diagnosed with non-Hodgkin's lymphoma, stage IIIA. That's why I'm here."

"A confusing disease, to be sure," Dr. Marshall said. "Rituxan is the conventional medical treatment for B-cell lymphoma — it's a monoclonal antibody that targets the CD22 antigen on the surface of the lymphoma cell."

"A complicated name for chemo, right?" Heather talked about the horrors her mother had endured. Then she said, "Believe me, I'm not interested in that."

LaVyrle leaned back in her chair and offered an understanding smile. "You may know that our bodies have the amazing ability to fight off cancerous cells, given the right kinds of foods." She went on to describe the effects of a poor diet.

"Obviously, I've been the product of my parents' lousy eating habits," Heather admitted.

"That's true of most of us. But remember, it's never too late to start anew."

"That's what I was hoping to hear." Suddenly Heather felt less alone.

LaVyrle gave her a brochure about a health lodge. "Perhaps you might want to consider my wellness program. It's the most effective way I know to help undo the harm done by eating poor-quality food or from exposure to environmental toxins. Think of it as jump-starting your own personal program to health."

A ten-day commitment? She scanned the information, surprised to learn that the lodge was located in the vicinity of the Riehls' tourist home. "Thanks. I'll read every word."

LaVyrle smiled. "Before you decide on that, I'll need to order a battery of blood tests to help me move ahead with a plan tailor-made for you. I want to know exactly what we're facing."

Heather attempted to disguise her surprise at being subjected to yet another test. *Needles are anything but natural.*

Following the appointment, Heather sat waiting to be called into the lab for blood work. Dr. Marshall's nurse had asked her to refrain from wearing perfume or hair products at her next clinic visit. Besides several patients, some of the staff members were allergic.

She thumbed through a nutrition magazine, intrigued by an article about enhancing the immune system.

"Heather," the nurse called.

She rose and carried the magazine into the lab with her, reopening it again to the article. Reluctantly she pushed up her sleeve for the blood draw, wishing she'd requested her medical records from home. Except that this clinic was searching for things her regular clinic hadn't even considered, like thyroid deficiencies, potential liver enzyme irregularities, or a possible toxic overload of heavy metals. Even mercury from eroding dental fillings could compromise the immune system, she'd learned.

She winced as she anticipated the initial poke, followed by the steady stream of dark blood into the vial; she dreaded needles. But she *had* been surprised at the forty-something doctor's vibrant demeanor. Heather could sense how much the optimistic woman loved her work. Best of all, LaVyrle believed she could help her beat her illness. The road to good health seemed to stretch ahead.

"You may actually feel worse before you feel better," the naturopath had warned during the appointment. *"Nausea, headaches,*

cramping, skin eruptions — all of these symptoms can occur as diseased cells and toxins leave the body . . . but they are early signs of recovery."

Heather realized this was going to require a steely commitment on her part. A lodge stay would mean not eating any solids, enabling her body's energy to go toward healing rather than digestion. Plant-based juices and broths would free her body of toxic buildup. And in addition to daily liver and colon cleansing, steam baths and saunas, she would learn to do a dry-brushing technique to detoxify her largest organ — her skin. But the juice fasting was central to it all. "Consuming freshly extracted organic greens and veggies will detox your body at the cellular level," LaVyrle had explained, giving her an approximately one-hour crash course on health and wholeness.

Heather had jokingly said, "Garbage in, garbage out?" when LaVyrle spoke of feeding the body the right kinds of foods to prevent disease and to maintain optimum well-being.

Surprisingly, after all of this, Heather had maintained her determination to give the natural way her best shot, starting today, by purchasing the list of necessary herbal teas and food supplements, including zinc and B and C vitamins.

So, with LaVyrle's encouraging remarks lingering in her mind and a Band-Aid in the crook of her elbow, Heather left the lab and headed for her car. She wanted to get to Eli's Natural Foods, on the east side of Bird-in-Hand, right after lunch at a local natural foods restaurant . . . before she lost heart or began to second-guess LaVyrle's holistic plan for eating and living. Aside from the snippets of information her mother had shared before she passed away — most of which had come from books on strategies for fighting debilitating disease — Heather had never received so much information on naturopathic medicine from a reliable source.

She slowed as she spotted the Wellness Lodge, operated year-round by LaVyrle and her staff. She already knew its exterior rather well, having driven by it several times, intrigued by its stately presence. The place was something of a contrast to the Riehls' quaint homestead, although both boasted similar white signs on the front lawn near the road. The brick red farmhouse-turned-lodge was actually within walking distance of her father's newly purchased land. Broad white shutters trimmed the front and side of the house, and a large bay window gleamed to the left of the black entry door. All around were purple lilacs dense with blossoms. The yellow-green hue of draping willows beyond highlighted Mill Creek, which ran through the large piece of property.

While creeping past the lodge, Heather was amazed again at her luck in getting into LaVyrle's office weeks ahead of the initially scheduled visit. *Or was it luck?* She could not dismiss the significance of that as she considered she was now steering toward a new path, a major fork in the road of her life. *And to think I have Mom to thank for setting all of this in motion. . . .*

"Time to kick those CD22 B cells in the teeth," she said, glancing in the rearview mirror. "And time to level with Dad about my diagnosis."

Heather drew a long breath and remembered the phrase Marian and Becky Riehl often said as they went about their daily chores — "Lord willing."

"That too," she whispered.

Lettie Byler locked the motel-room door behind her and removed her lightweight shawl and blue cape and apron, dropping the garments onto the nearby chair. She glanced around the small yet clean room.

The off-white walls were brighter than even hers back home, but the gray carpet and matching drapes made the place gloomy, nearly depressing — such a contrast to her pleasant room at the Kidron Inn. Tracie Gordon had been quite apologetic when she had informed Lettie that the entire bed-and-breakfast had already been reserved for the past week. Thankfully Lettie had managed to acquire another room in the Kidron area for much of that time, at least until she felt she'd made every attempt to locate Minnie Keim, the midwife who'd assisted with her first baby's birth.

Twice, prior to leaving Kidron, Lettie had slipped into the weekly livestock auction, where farm folk bid on dairy cows, hogs, sheep, and goats. Though the place was packed with mostly men, she'd encountered a few women — wives and daughters of the bidders — hoping to talk to someone who might know Minnie or her husband, Perry.

As Providence would have it, on her walk back from the auction one Saturday after-noon, Lettie had stopped to toss a stray ball back to a towheaded schoolboy. He was standing around the U-Wash It, of all things, with his two younger brothers, all three of them wearing wide-brimmed straw hats. The adorable trio had been waiting for their mother to finish scrubbing down their black buggy for Preaching services the next day. When she heard Minnie's name, the pretty blond woman had brightened, certain the midwife had relocated to near Baltic. *"Minnie's staying with an uncle and aunt, is what I heard."*

"Why's that?" Lettie asked.

"Her husband got laid off recently," the woman said, sympathy pinching up her face. *"Lots of folk have fallen on hard times lately."*

So Lettie had come here to quaint little Baltic, a few short miles southeast of Charm. It *had* been something of a godsend to find this affordable place, one offering a discount for longer stays. Even so, she'd decided she might not need to be here much longer. Already she had nearly exhausted her few leads in *this* rural town, as well as the outlying areas north and east of here. All but one slim lead, which had come from an Amishwoman she'd met in Kidron, a talkative clerk at Lehman's Hardware who had known Minnie's only daughter, Dora. She had been told that Dora's fiancé worked at Green Acres Furniture, just north of Mt. Eaton. So Lettie had traipsed all over that area, including Apple Creek and the surrounding villages, surprised at the sight of many red barns, something she'd rarely seen in Lancaster County. She'd also hired a Mennonite girl to drive her around Goose. Bottom Valley, in Walnut Creek, but had come up empty-handed. No sign of Minnie, Dora, or Dora's fiancé.

Lettie was beyond perturbed that the folk she'd encountered hadn't the slightest inkling of Minnie's present whereabouts. Some said she was possibly visiting extended family in Wisconsin, while others said she sometimes did missions work in South America. Even the post office no longer had a residential address listing for her. Lettie was beginning to think Minnie Keim had gone missing.

In her heart, she refused to give up her search, but her physical body was weary of the continual roadblocks. She could only wonder if the midwife had become reclusive out of necessity. Was it possible the benevolent Amishwoman who'd arranged the adoption of Lettie's baby was doing something other than midwifery now? Minnie had been the one responsible for acquiring the trusted doctor, a man highly regarded by her and the local Plain community. Both Lettie's mother and the sympathetic midwife had assured her that all was taken care of properly. In short, Minnie had been anything but flighty or elusive back then, but the years had a way of diminishing one's memory.

What she *did* recall was being told by her mother not to fret, that the doctor had already set up the baby's legal adoption with a local attorney. *But with which law office?* she wondered now. *Was I ever told his name . . . or the doctor's?*

Trudging to the mirror, she lifted off her Kapp and began to pull the hairpins from her bun, letting down her waist-length hair. *My mother made me remove my prayer veiling and hair bun for the birthing. . . .*

The frightful day rushed back, and Lettie felt as helpless in that moment as she had in the hours before and after delivering her first baby. The precious child she'd never seen and never held had been born so far from home, in an inn full of strangers. So unlike her children with Judah, who were born upstairs in Judah's and her own bedroom, with their father sitting near the window, eagerly waiting to hear each newborn's cry. Such blessed births those had been, yet even they had been overshadowed by the first.

" *'Tis best this way,*" Mamm had repeated the midwife's words to Lettie hours after her firstborn was bundled away. *"For the baby and for you, dear one."*

"Dear one," she whispered now. Shaking off the injustice, she let her thoughts drift homeward. She pictured Grace or Mandy finding her letter in the mailbox, the girls vying to read it, their heads nearly touching.

"How can I bear this?" Lettie whispered. In her mind's eye, she saw Judah coming in from the barn to wash up. "Mamma wrote us," one of the children might say, handing him the envelope. Would he be curious enough to look for the postmark, see Ohio, and wonder why she had chosen to travel there?

He never knew what happened to me in Kidron, she thought with a mix of regret and sorrow.

There were times when she wished her mother had not demanded their secret be kept from Judah. The unsuspecting young man had married a girl he had scarcely courted. She was not the innocent bride Judah Byler had assumed he was getting. And for that, Lettie was still sad. Sad . . . and terribly sorry.

Yet she had never dared question her parents. Why had she been so willing to let Dat and Mamm make all the decisions for her, whisking her away? Oh, but she knew. As their daughter, Lettie had been expected to obey, to go along with whatever they had deemed right and good for her. Her idolatry of Samuel had created a wound in her family, and giving up her baby was her punishment. Certainly she had let her parents down, and there was no forgiving that. No forgetting, either.

She had been so terrified those weeks and months. Afraid Samuel would no longer love her, cast her away if he discovered she was with child. At night she stared up at the sky from her bed, terrified that her future was doomed . . . that if Samuel left her and the secret got out, not a single boy in the church district would ever want her. She would end up living her life as a *Maidel,* trapped with her unyielding parents.

And now here I am alone, and by my own doing. . . . The past continually plagued her, as did a new and growing fear that the longer she stayed away from home, the angrier Judah might become. Had she waited too long already?

Lettie pulled her hair over to one side and lowered herself onto the bedspread. *Will I be put off church soon?* she thought, becoming anxious about the *Bann* and shunning.

She gripped the edge of the pillowslip as tears rolled down her cheeks and across the bridge of her nose. *Oh, dear Lord, help me,* she groaned, feeling lost. She must find Minnie Keim. Somehow she must. And the doctor, too, who would surely know something about her baby. Anything.

A train rumbled through the downtown crossing, and its whistle startled her. She curled up on the bed, tucking her chubby bare feet beneath her long skirt. Ever so spent, Lettie gave in to sweet and irresistible sleep.

Grace watched her fifteen-year-old brother dart across the yard, lean and nimble as a katydid. "Hope you cooked enough," Joe said, glancing back over his shoulder at the barn as he came into the kitchen.

"Enough what?"

"Food, silly." Joe's light brown hair was matted under his ratty straw hat, which he had just removed to fan himself. "Yonnie's goin' to be putting his feet under your table today." His brown eyes sparkled as if delighted.

"Today?" She drew in her breath.

"And every day, prob'ly . . . 'cept for Saturday and the Lord's Day." He scratched his oily head. "Dat wants him workin' here, seems. At least till birthin' season is past."

"Dat does?" She puffed the words out of her mouth.

Joe nodded. "Yonnie's mighty *gut* with the frail lambs. That's his job, makin' sure the new ones that're rejected by their mothers are bottle-fed frequently." He went on, lauding Yonnie as if he was his long-lost brother.

"You best be washin' up," she told him and headed back to the table. Grace did not like this unforeseen turn of events, not one bit. Her hands shook as she filled each glass with water. *Cooked enough food, indeed!*

CHAPTER EIGHT

At dinnertime, Yonnie sauntered indoors with Adam and Joe to wash up. Grace felt awkward and disconcerted with Yonnie staying for the noon meal. And he was looking her way, of all things.

"Where would ya have me sit?" he asked quietly, drying his hands.

In your own kitchen, she thought. His steady gaze unnerved her as he waited for her response. Did her expression give her away? Could he tell she was displeased?

"Right there's fine." She pointed to an empty spot on the bench down near where Dawdi Jakob always sat.

Not only did he slide in next to her grandfather, but he chattered like a magpie before the silent blessing. Dat's frequent blinks seemed to suggest Yonnie's yammering surprised him, as well.

After Dat's prayer, Yonnie lost no time in dishing up a generous portion of beef stew.

Grace had made hot biscuits, too, serving those alongside dishes of pickled beets, chowchow, and Mamma's delicious dill pickles.

But she could hardly wait for the meal to end. Goodness, but other than Adam and Joe, she'd never fed another young fellow in this kitchen, including her former fiancé.

She sat stiffly next to Dat, in her mother's usual place, her hands fidgeting beneath the oilcloth. She picked at her apron and tried to avoid Yonnie's eyes. This fellow seemed downright indifferent to their traditional ways — either that or he was just plain stubborn.

Like her father and brothers, Yonnie cleaned his bowl several times. Grace lost count how many. If there was anything to be relieved about, it was that Yonnie brought an air of surprising ease with him, an arresting confidence she'd not seen in other men his age.

As he talked with Joe and Dawdi Jakob, who seemed quite friendly toward him, she considered that Becky must be right now pining for Yonnie, next farm over. Clenching her teeth, Grace reached for her water glass. *I must talk to her soon.*

Then, because Mandy had insisted earlier that her sweet tooth needed some attention,

Grace brought out two snitz pies made with dried apples. Her sister could not conceal her delight; food always seemed to do the trick with her. And the pies weren't lost on Yonnie, either, she noticed.

When the pies were gone but for a few slices, Yonnie thanked her across the table. "Denki, Grace . . . a wonderful-*gut* meal."

She could hardly believe her ears. What a peculiar thing to do! Although there was no denying how nice such a compliment was to hear, rather than the slurping and burping men traditionally used to show appreciation at the table.

Later, when the kitchen was empty, except for Mandy at the sink, Joe pulled Grace aside. He steepled his fingers. "You're scheduled to work at Eli's today, ain't?"

"Jah, and I need to leave right quick." Grace noticed the mischievous twinkle in his brown eyes and drew a long sigh. "Joe . . . why are you askin'?"

"Just thinkin' something might be a *gut* idea," he said.

"Listen, I'll be walkin' to work if it's not *you* who's drivin' me. Ya hear?"

Joe's expression changed from comical to more serious as he glanced in the direction of the barn — and probably Yonnie. He ran his hand through his light brown hair, making his bangs stand straight up. "All right, then." With that he headed for the hallway to get his straw hat. "Let me know when you're ready to leave," he called back.

Mandy started giggling. "What was *that* about?"

"Pure nonsense," Grace told her. But to herself, she wondered why her younger brother wanted to push her off on Yonnie for the drive to Eli's. *Why, when Joe surely knows what Adam thinks about me ending things with Henry Stahl?*

While removing expired items from the shelves, Grace pondered her next step in finding her mother. *Should* she write to her mother's cousin Hallie — ask if Mamma was visiting there? Considering how mysterious Mamma had been, she realized that contacting Hallie might present a problem, especially if Mamma hadn't gone to Indiana . . . or if her cousin wasn't aware of Mamma's leaving home.

No sense in embarrassing Mamma further, Grace thought, *no matter how badly I want to locate her.* She was deep in thought, wishing she might somehow call a community phone in Hallie's area and find out something, when she sensed someone standing nearby.

She turned to see a tall but slight young

woman. "Ach, sorry. I must've been day-dreaming." Grace stood up quickly.

"No problem."

Grace balanced her clipboard on top of several cans on the second shelf. "Can I help you? I hope you haven't been waiting long."

"Not at all." The young woman looked to be close to Grace's own age. "Do you carry herbal teas? Especially Japanese green tea. I understand it's a detoxifier and an antioxidant."

Grace nodded. "Sure, follow me."

The customer nodded and looked around. "It's a little dark in here."

"Jah. Our fancy English shoppers sometimes find it hard to get accustomed to the gas lamps."

The girl tilted her head, a peculiar expression on her pretty face. "There's no electricity?"

"No."

"Wow." The customer's eyes lit up. "How do you refrigerate your foods?"

"We use gas-run refrigerators in the store."

The young woman seemed befuddled; then she said, "Well, I see you carry organic carrot juice. And bulk foods, as well as organic meats and cheese. Eggs too. Hey, I think I've hit the jackpot."

Grace shook her head. "Beg your pardon?"

"Sorry, just an expression. You know, the pot of gold at the end of the rainbow?" The girl laughed. Her brown hair fell forward and she reached back, pulling it high into a ponytail and securing it with a hair tie from her pocket.

"I don't know much 'bout jackpots and rainbows." Grace smiled, going along with her little joke. "Here we are." She pointed out an array of herbal teas.

Leaning over, the girl asked if she knew how to choose the best ones for anti-inflammatory benefits.

"Oh, I'd be cautious 'bout sayin', really. You best look through that book." Grace pointed to the reference material they kept on hand to answer customers' questions. "We can't recommend any particular product."

"That's okay, thanks." The girl went to the table and picked up the book, leafing through its pages.

After helping other customers, Grace noticed the young woman was still standing there, perusing the reference book. She walked over to her and asked if there was anything more she could do to help.

The girl pressed the book against her chest. "Have you ever heard of a dietary approach to curing serious diseases? I'm talking colonic cleansing, juice fasting . . . organic teas?"

Grace stepped back in surprise. Other than being almost too thin, this young woman didn't look sick. The girl's face had good color — although maybe that was due to makeup. "Do you mean just any type of illness or . . . ?"

"I mean . . . have you heard of this kind of thing?"

The young woman seemed desperate for reassurance. But most of what Grace knew about home health remedies had come from Mammi Adah, who'd taught her as a young child all about the herbs in their garden.

Without waiting for an answer, the Englischer continued. "I was told today that there's a cure found in nature for nearly every disease known to man . . . or woman." She sighed and glanced quickly at the ceiling. "The medical community views these guidelines as radical, even ridiculous. And yet, in spite of that, there are some very lucky people who are cured of . . . well, serious diseases."

Sounds like she wants a magic pill to take to make her well. Grace didn't dare ask if she was referring to herself. "Feel free to jot down any of the information in the book,"

Grace told her.

The girl reached for a box of green tea with mango, peach, and pineapple. " 'Individually wrapped for freshness,' " she read, turning the box over to look at the back. And just that quick, tears welled up. "I'm so sorry. . . ."

Grace suddenly realized this was the young woman she'd seen out on the road, walking and crying, not many days ago. "There is someone you could talk to 'bout this," she said, wishing she had a tissue to offer. "Our preacher's wife cured herself of cancer. I know you'd like her quite a lot. Her name's Sally Smucker."

"Really?" The girl raised her eyebrows. "Well, I'd hate to intrude on her."

"Believe me, Sally would never feel that way."

"She wouldn't mind fielding a gazillion questions from . . . an outsider, I guess you'd call me?" She stopped a moment. "A fancy Englisher, right?"

Grace laughed softly. "Ach, sorry . . . earlier I didn't mean —"

"No . . . perfectly understandable."

"But Sally would truly enjoy sharing her journey with you," she added. "She's helped lots of folks. Back some years ago, she tried to get my aunt Naomi to make a drastic

106

change in her eating habits . . . to no avail."

"Like what?"

"Oh, it was a peculiar diet, I daresay."

"It couldn't be much more peculiar than what I learned today."

"This was mostly fresh and raw fruits and vegetables each day. Very little cooked food — and no meat or dairy at all."

"That *is* extreme. And radical diets are hard to stay committed to, or so I'm told." She looked sad again, working her mouth. "I really don't know . . ."

"I'd be happy to take you to meet Sally. Honestly."

"And you say she's presently in remission?" The girl's pale blue eyes shown with the slightest measure of hope.

Just then Grace knew for certain that all the questions were about her. *She must be terminally ill. . . .* Hardly anyone Grace had ever known made drastic changes in their eating habits unless they were dying. "Jah, Sally's blood tests keep comin' back just fine every three months or so."

A slow smile spread across the girl's face. "Thanks, uh, miss. I didn't mean to keep you from your work." She reached out her slender hand. "I'm Heather Nelson, by the way, and I really appreciate your time."

"Grace Byler . . . ever so happy to help."

Heather remarked on the warm weather as they walked to the cash register together. Then she mentioned that she was staying in a private tourist home. "And with the kindest hostess — Marian Riehl, on Beechdale Road." Removing her wallet from her purse, Heather looked up with a smile. "She's Amish, too."

At this, Grace was truly delighted. "Well, for goodness' sake . . . I wondered if perhaps I hadn't seen you before. Marian's our neighbor! And her daughter Becky is my dearest friend." To think this was the young woman from Virginia both Becky and Mammi Adah had spoken of. *Jah, the very one!*

When Heather had paid her bill and was heading for the door, she asked Grace again about visiting Sally Smucker. "If you're sure she wouldn't mind."

"Absolutely not." She followed her outside before she realized what she'd done. "Let's get you on the road to health right quick."

Heather's eyes pierced her own.

Touching her arm, Grace said, "I'll do whatever I can."

"And . . . I'd really appreciate it if you kept what I told you to yourself."

"Goes without sayin'," Grace assured her.

"Since you and Becky are good friends, I

mean. And the community here is . . . well, pretty close-knit." Heather's voice faded away.

"For sure and for certain."

"My father doesn't even know yet," Heather added, frowning.

Grace wondered at this revelation, but it wasn't her place to question her new acquaintance. "Well, you have my word." She paused. "And let's decide soon on a *gut* time to visit Sally."

Heather's face lit up. She waved and made her way to the dark blue car Grace had seen at the Riehls', with its sleek silver stripe across the side.

"I'll be seein' ya." Unable to move away just yet, she watched Heather back out. All the while Grace hoped she might remember all the wonderful-good things Mammi Adah had taught her about healing herbs. And that Sally might be able to help Heather as much as she'd helped so many others.

There were no accidents where the dear Lord was concerned — Preacher Smucker called it Providence. *Help Heather find whatever she needs most, Lord.*

CHAPTER NINE

Later on Wednesday afternoon, Adah sat at the worktable with her friend Marian Riehl, glad for help on her piecework for a niece's hope chest. Between household duties and meals, she liked to slip away to the cozy sewing room. There, she found a bit of tranquility, especially when Jakob went outside to work with Judah and the boys for a while. Truth be known, her husband had become ever so fretful since Lettie's leaving.

Fond as she was of him, Adah chafed under his unrelenting worry over Lettie nowadays. His concern weighed her down, made her sorry she'd ever given Grace the address for the Kidron Inn. And while Grace had shared that her mother had indeed stayed at the inn, Adah suspected her granddaughter had learned even more from the phone call than she was telling. Ever since making the call, Grace's eyes had carried her apprehension. She'd also kept the phone card, so Adah assumed she planned to track her mother down further.

"You're off somewhere in a daydream," Marian said, leaning forward on the table.

"Oh, s'pose I am. I was thinking of Lettie," she admitted. "We received a letter from her yesterday."

Marian arched her eyebrows. "Did you, now?"

Adah nodded.

"So . . . is she comin' home?"

"Only the Good Lord knows."

"Lettie didn't say in her letter?" Marian stopped her sewing altogether. "Why'd she bother to write, then?"

Adah had wondered the same. "To let us know she's all right." She shook her head slowly, not wanting to say more. Besides, she knew Jakob would caution her not to reveal their family secret to even a dear friend like Marian. The burden weighed heavily after these many years.

"Well, Lettie's surely missed around here. I see it in Grace whenever she comes by to visit Becky. She yearns for her Mamma." Marian pushed her thimble down onto her finger and picked up her needle again. She ran it through the fabric, pulling it taut.

"Jah, we all miss Lettie," replied Adah,

her lower lip quivering. "Something awful."

Marian reached across the table, her thimble resting on the back of Adah's hand. "You mustn't bear this alone, dear friend."

Adah swallowed, close to tears. Nodding her head, she managed to say, "You're ever so kind."

They resumed their sewing for a time. Then Marian spoke up again. "What I don't understand, I guess, is how Lettie can ramble all over the countryside, expectin' she can come home whenever she pleases." Her words jelled right there in the air.

Adah's breath caught in her throat and she began to cough. So hard, in fact, she had to get up and go downstairs for a drink of water.

In the kitchen, Jakob looked up from his sunny afternoon spot near the window. "For pity's sake, love, sounds like you're chokin'." From his comfortable chair, he could look out and watch the birds. Sometimes he simply got up and wandered outside to sit on the small back porch for some fresh springtime air, if he wasn't needed in the barn for an easy chore. These days, Judah was relying on him less often. Though Adah didn't like to admit it, her husband was in decline.

She took several sips, patting her chest as

the water soothed her throat. "It pains me . . . Lettie didn't think to write specifically to Judah." *Among other things.*

Inhaling slowly, Jakob agreed. "Seems she's avoiding her husband."

"Which makes me think she might be out there visiting someone. . . ." Here she lowered her voice to a whisper. "Maybe that so-and-so fella, Samuel."

"Now, why on earth?"

"I ask myself the selfsame thing every day." She looked toward the stairway, and Jakob seemed to understand, giving her a nod.

"Marian's upstairs askin' questions," she said, carrying her glass with her across the kitchen to the steps.

"Seems everyone is."

She turned around. "Ach, Jakob?"

He smoothed his uneven bangs. "The bishop, most recently. Judah was on his way back from a meeting with the brethren when Willow injured her leg."

A shiver ran through her. "I hope there's no talk yet of the Bann."

"Well, it's sure to come" — his face was solemn — "if Lettie doesn't get herself home."

Adah turned sadly to head back upstairs to Marian, Jakob's words echoing in her mind. She couldn't help but worry the plans they'd set in motion long ago had miserably backfired. And even worse damage might be done if they lost Grace to the world in her search for her mother.

Grace was relieved when Mandy offered to redd up the supper dishes. In fact, she fairly flew out of the kitchen door, leaving much of the cleanup undone. The past several evenings had been remarkably warm; it was nearly impossible to stay inside. She walked along the road toward the Riehls', fingering the phone card in her pocket as early evening breezes ruffled the meadow grasses.

She enjoyed the shimmering twilight — the way it cast its long shadows over the cornfield to the east and beyond. She wondered how Heather was faring this evening. She had sensed the girl was different than most fancy folk who came into Eli's. Heather had been guarded, even discreet in her curiosity about the Plain-run store, not asking any prying questions. *Refreshing, for a change.*

Grace truly hoped a new approach to eating might provide Heather with the help she needed — she certainly seemed up for it. And, as frank and open as the girl had been, Grace wished to talk with her again soon. But first things first. She wanted to visit Becky tonight — tell her Yonnie was going to be working for Dat for a while. *Certainly not my idea!*

She hadn't gone more than halfway down the road when she heard a carriage coming up behind her. Turning, she was surprised to see Henry Stahl and his mother, Susannah, nearing her in their gray enclosed buggy. They were close enough for her to see Henry's hand go up in a stiff sort of wave. Goodness, but when she and Henry were engaged, he had scarcely greeted her on the road. Momentarily she relived the awkwardness of their last date — the night she broke things off. She felt sorry for him . . . but not at all for herself.

She continued walking, somewhat hesitantly now, as she watched the horse and carriage turn into the Riehls' lane. Henry's mother glanced her way with a cheerful smile. *She must not know . . . yet.*

It felt awkward going to see Becky with Henry probably waiting in the buggy for his mother to run in and visit with Marian. Grace had seen Marian earlier, waving a fond good-bye to Mammi Adah as she left the big house. She and Mammi often spent several hours together each week, sewing and whatnot all.

Grace purposely focused her attention away from the back of the buggy, looking across the road at the old woodshed, overtaken by kudzu vines. Talk amongst some of the young people was that the harmful vine was getting inside the shed and spreading all over the place. Becky's brothers had actually hacked the giant green leaves and their tendrils down to nothing last year, even though Adam had urged them to report it so the fast-growing vine wouldn't spread and kill off every plant in sight. *"We don't want it to devour houses,"* he'd told her with a smile, but she knew the kudzu was no laughing matter.

She tugged on her apron as she made the turn into the Riehls' lane. *Slow down,* she told herself, trying to pace things so she wouldn't encounter Henry face-to-face. She could see the horse and carriage parked near the side door. "Can ya believe this?" she whispered to herself.

But as she continued walking, it turned out that Susannah was the one who stayed in the buggy while Henry carried a box of canning jars to the back door. Ach, but Grace did not want to run into him there on the back stoop!

Just as she was eyeing the pasture, planning to make an escape if necessary, Henry handed the box to Marian and headed back toward the buggy. "Hullo, Gracie," he called to her.

She felt her heart pound, worried what else he might say. "Hullo, Henry." It was ever so awkward, trying to be polite when she wished he'd just return to the carriage and ride away.

"Well, have a nice evening." He tipped his hat.

"You too." She hoped she hadn't seemed too quick to speak. Truth was, she'd endured two uncomfortable moments in the space of a few hours. First Yonnie's imposition at noon, and now this. She stood there, counting the seconds as Henry and his mother drove around the curve in the lane to head out toward the road.

It was then she spied Becky across the side yard in the dirt, pulling weeds from soil that had been dampened with a garden hose. It was still light enough to see her expression tighten for a second as Becky looked up. But she didn't look glum for long, not once Grace waved and smiled. Grace dashed across the lane to her friend and knelt down in the dirt to begin helping her weed the garden patch.

"Aw, you mustn't," Becky protested.

Grace heard the catch in her voice. "I

came over to talk about Yonnie." She paused, aware of Becky's long face. "He's helpin' my Dat . . . for a time."

Becky's lips formed a nearly straight line as she pressed them together. She didn't respond, choosing instead to keep her attention on weeding.

The silence unnerved Grace. "Please, don't be put out with me. I couldn't bear it."

"I heard he was over there . . . from my brothers." Becky rubbed her hands together to brush the moist dirt off her fingers.

"He's helpin' with the lambs."

"And coaxing Willow back to health, too, I s'pose," Becky said.

"Well, he'll have a time of that." The beautiful old horse was surely suffering. She took a deep breath. "I'm sorry if Yonnie's hurting you by doing this . . . truly I am."

"Well . . ." Becky's light brown eyes were sad. "Remember, he liked you from the very start?"

"Oh, Becky . . ."

"No, he talked 'bout *you,* Grace. Quite a lot, in fact."

She straightened. "This is silly. I came over to tell you I have no interest in Yonnie . . . which is the truth."

Becky looked toward the pastureland and

her father's cows. "Seems strange that you'd break up with Henry Stahl . . . then right quick, Yonnie comes a-callin'."

"Well, he's not comin' to see me. I can tell ya that."

"Ach, Gracie . . . the timing's suspicious, ain't so?"

She hadn't even thought of that. "Guess it might look that-away."

Becky shook her head. "Jah, to me and anyone else who saw Henry head home alone after Singing last Sunday night."

A stab of gloom hit her between the ribs once again.

"No, I don't mean that — not many of the youth saw him by himself."

They just stared at each other, not speaking. *I despise this,* thought Grace.

Suddenly, Becky squeezed her arm. "Oh, Gracie, I'm bein' too hard on ya, ain't? If you say you're not interested in my beau — I mean, my *former* beau, then . . ."

Grace was surprised at the way she described him. "So Yonnie broke things off?"

Becky's head dipped, and her chin nearly touched her chest. "Frankly, we never courted. Not really."

Grace frowned, unbelieving. "But the two of you looked so happy together."

"I did hope it might lead to courtship,"

Becky continued. "That's what hurts so bad."

"I wish I could do something to take away your sadness." She sighed. "And I'm not interested in Yonnie Bontrager. Anyway, with Mamma gone, it doesn't seem right to be thinkin' of a beau."

Becky brushed away her tears. "Aw . . . Gracie, I'm sorry. I know you're missin' your Mamma."

Grace's shoulders tensed, and she swallowed hard, lest she give in to crying, too. She told Becky, "I called an inn, out in Ohio . . . and I must've just missed her."

"Honestly?" Becky frowned. "Did they say where she was headed?"

Grace shook her head. " 'Tween you and me, I'm not sure I'll ever get over this. . . ." She couldn't go on.

Becky touched her hand. "I cannot imagine what yous are goin' through. I just can't."

Instinctively, they both set to work again, weeding. The ensuing hush was somehow freeing, and Becky's sadness faded from her pretty eyes. Grace refused the temptation to say what her girl cousins often whispered to each other: There was no use worrying over a relationship gone sour when there were lots of good fish in the deep blue sea. For now, Becky needed only Grace's loyalty . . . and a listening heart.

And *she* needed Becky, too.

For that reason, she would not encourage Yonnie one iota.

When Grace and Becky had finished in the garden, Grace asked if Heather Nelson was around. "I met her at Eli's today." That was all she said, wanting to keep the promised confidence.

"Well, let's just go and see if she's back." Becky led the way into the house, where a box of empty canning jars sat on the floor in the kitchen. "Who's this from, Mamm?" she asked.

Marian brightened. "Susannah Stahl had extra, so she and Henry stopped by a little while ago. Guess they're sorting through their cold cellar before all the berries start comin' on in June."

"We should have oodles, too, Lord willin'," Becky said, nodding her head at Grace. The two girls had spent many happy hours together in the berry patches growing up.

Marian added, "Grace, your grandmother and I hope to sell all kinds of jam this summer."

Grace wondered if Mammi Adah was hoping to make up for Mamma's lost income at their roadside stand, with a bit of help from Marian, but she didn't ask.

Becky's younger sisters — Rachel, ten, and Sarah, nine — crept into the kitchen and sat on the wooden bench like two pudgy birds, their thick blond hair twisted into a bun. Seeing the close-in-age sisters made Grace think of Mandy, and because she didn't want to be gone much longer from the house, she asked Marian if she knew where Heather might be.

"She's been out all day," Marian said as she sat down next to Sarah, who leaned her head against Marian's arm. "Anymore, she's gone a lot."

Grace guessed Heather must have important things on her mind. "Will ya tell her I stopped by when you see her next?"

"We sure will," Marian said, pinching Sarah's cheeks. "Won't we, honey-girl?"

Sarah nodded, eyes sparkling. It was clear she and Rachel were fond of Heather.

"Well, I should be headin' home," Grace said, moving toward the back door. "I'll be seein' ya."

Becky followed her to the door, past the Stahls' canning jars, and together they headed outside. "Mamm didn't tell ya that most days now, Heather rushes out of the house to charge up her laptop batteries and her fancy phone that does near everything 'cept cook." She laughed a little.

"Where's she go for that?"

"A nearby coffee shop, I guess," Becky said. She lowered her voice. " 'Tween you and me, I think she's more comfortable round my mother than me."

"Wonder why?"

"Just a feelin' I have." Becky scrunched up her face. "For all the communicating she says she craves, she doesn't seem to know the first thing about friendship. *Erschtaunlich* — astonishing."

This surprised Grace. "Well, she seemed outgoing enough today at Eli's."

They had reached the end of the drive, and Becky sat up on the fence, her bare feet dangling. "Heather, bless her heart, started out ever so friendly — real curious about the farm and even wanting to help out some. But mighty quick she disappeared into a shell, almost like a turtle. Now I think she uses that college paper she's writing as an excuse to be alone." Becky sighed, shaking her head. "I don't understand a'tall."

"That's odd."

"She just pulled back." Becky smoothed her apron, shaking her head. "Can't tell ya what happened." She looked toward the road. "Maybe she got scared . . . hard to say 'bout outsiders, really."

They saw the Spanglers' car coming down the road, zooming past a horse and buggy less than a quarter mile away. Grace cringed, holding her breath. "Right there's one of the big differences 'tween the English and us." She breathed a prayer for Jessica and Brittany and the things Jessica had shared with her.

Becky nodded and jumped down off the fence. "I best be goin' inside for evening prayers. Dat likes to fire up the gas lamps 'bout now and get started with Bible reading."

Grace glanced toward her own house, then at the sky. "My father does the same. Starts out with a song, though — 'They say I have nothin', but they are wrong. . . .' "

Becky smiled, reaching for her hand. "Glad you came over, Gracie." Then she added quickly, "Don't be surprised if Heather does the same with you in due time that she did with me."

Grace pondered Heather Nelson's present absence from the Riehls' as she walked up the road. According to Becky, the pretty English girl was just plain *ferhoodled.* She sighed. *And no wonder, if she's searching and hoping so hard for a cure for her illness.*

Whatever it is.

Hurrying toward home, she decided then and there she'd try to be a good and consistent friend, no matter how turtle-like Heather might just end up to be.

CHAPTER TEN

"Mighty *babblich* you are," Judah said as he and Yonnie worked together, filling the sheep's feeding troughs that Thursday afternoon.

"Sorry . . . don't mean to talk your ear off," Yonnie replied with a smile. "My next youngest brother's a bit chatty, too."

"Runs in the family?"

Yonnie paused a moment. "I guess you could say we talk so much because we're fond of each other."

"Oh?"

"My parents discuss everything, it seems. 'Course, it's only natural to want to talk a lot with someone you love, ain't?"

Judah had never considered this; he hardly knew what to say. But then, he rarely did. He turned his attention to refilling his feed bucket, the sheep pressing in hard against his legs, *baa*-ing all the while.

"It's *gut* to voice your opinions, my father

126

says," Yonnie added. "Anytime he's unde-cided on one thing or another, he talks it over with Mamm."

Judah was thunderstruck. "She helps your father make decisions?"

"Why, sure." Yonnie gave a chuckle. "Lots of couples check with each other, far as I know."

"Well, ain't so much that way round here." *And a gut thing, too.*

Yonnie frowned. "That's too bad. Mamm says no woman wants to live under the thumb of a man. If she's to feel truly loved, her opinion has to matter to her husband."

"Ain't very Amish."

"Well, livin' here, I'm finding out there are nearly as many different church ordi-nances and ways of doin' things as there are kernels on a corncob."

He's a thinker, this one.

"But bein' best friends seems to work for my parents — it's given 'em a relationship that's prepared for the long haul." Yonnie went to get more feed for his bucket, then carried it to the trough. "I hope to have the same sort of marriage one day."

With Grace? Judah coughed, stifling his sudden amusement. Yet in spite of his urge to chortle, he could not dismiss what the lad had just shared.

■ ■ ■ ■

Lettie knew she would be hungry well before breakfast if she didn't get up from her nap. She couldn't just skip supper that evening. Still groggy, she was disgusted with herself. *Ach, sleeping in the middle of the day!*

Yawning, she slowly rose from the bed and shuffled to the bathroom sink. She turned on the warm water and reached for a scented bar soap on the ledge. She paused, aware of the water dripping off her face and hands into the sink. It had been weeks since she'd shared a meal with family. *Will they forgive me someday?*

Reaching for the small white hand towel nearby, she patted her face dry. She touched her cheeks, her fingertips lingering over the crinkled lines around her eyes. When had they appeared? And my, but she was pale. Yet she must not stare for long, as giving too much attention to her appearance was sinful.

Reaching for her brush, Lettie prepared to wind her thick hair back into a bun. She yearned to return to the comfort of the bed, but soon she set her Kapp on her head and went to find the cape and apron she'd removed prior to her nap. She found them slung over the chair where she'd left them hours before. They looked a bit rumpled now. "Won't matter."

She sat on the edge of the bed and leaned down to pull on her dark hose and black leather shoes for the walk over to East Main Street, downtown. She'd spotted the sign for Miller's Dutch Kitch'n after riding over winding roads from Sugarcreek, past Dunkard Road and Bob White Quality Feeds. Even her Mennonite driver, who'd hailed from nearby Berlin, recommended its delicious home cooking. *"And don't forget their three-dollar-off coupons!"* he'd advised. The thought of a hot meal perked her up some, and Lettie checked her purse for the room key before pulling the door securely closed.

The evening was still plenty light as she made her way through the small parking lot to the narrow sidewalk, hoping the brisk walk might invigorate her. Walking certainly had helped back home. Here lately, though, she felt almost too tired to even eat at the end of the day. Exhausted in spirit, too.

As she went, she prayed for help in finding Minnie Keim, concerned at being gone from home this long. She'd kept track of the days on the little paper calendar she'd tucked away in her purse. No doubt her family was in turmoil over her leaving. Yet she couldn't help wondering if they were also mighty put out with her, too. *What if they don't* want *me back?* She sometimes caught herself considering this, falling prey to pity. But how could she expect sympathy when she'd brought all of this on herself?

As she walked, she noticed the area's black V-shaped buggies, which still seemed peculiar to her. And small as this town was — even smaller than Bird-in-Hand — she felt awkward being the only soul out walking at this evening hour, when most folk were heading home for supper or already gathered round the table.

The restaurant had a hitching post in back and a rustic Alpine-looking exterior in front, complete with black shutters. As she entered, she noticed immediately how busy it was, even for a weeknight. With many people gathered around family-style tables that seated eight, and others sitting in booths along the windows, she hoped it might be easy to blend in. But hers was the only heart-shaped Kapp, a sure signal of her out-of-town status.

Once she was seated, a waitress about her age came over to take her drink order. The woman wore a blue short-sleeved dress with a white frilly-sleeved apron on top, a style

Lettie had never seen before. The waitress smiled warmly, almost as if she knew her. "Welcome to Miller's." She glanced at Lettie's prayer cap. "You ain't from around here."

Lettie shook her head. "No." Secretly, she preferred the more graceful style of the Lancaster County Kapps, if she dared to think that way. Something about the seam sewn down the top made it prettier.

"Well, I hope your stay here is real nice," the waitress said. Lettie noted the name *Susan* pinned to her apron. "What would you care to drink?"

"Lemonade's fine."

"Right away, then." The cheerful woman left, leaving Lettie surrounded by numerous Plain folk in a sea of colorful shirts and dresses. She was intrigued by the aqua blue and even bright orange men's shirts, having seen some of the same colors up in Kidron. But here, with so many Amish gathered in the dining room, most of them talking in their primary language, she suddenly felt like a fish flapping on a shoreline.

When Susan brought the lemonade and set it down, she asked if Lancaster County might be Lettie's home. "I can tell by the style and color of your dress. And your Kapp."

Still unsure of herself yet glad for the woman's friendliness, Lettie smiled. "Jah, 'tis."

The waitress nodded. "Here, we have many pleats in our prayer caps."

Lettie could easily have said she was all too familiar with the ironed-in pleats and the heavily starched Kapp. She'd observed one such covering closer than she'd ever cared from a birthing bed while in intense labor. "If you don't mind, I'm ready to order my dinner," she said, realizing she'd been terribly abrupt.

Susan nodded and removed a tablet from her apron pocket. She clicked the pen several times, smiling. "What looks *gut* on the menu? Our specialty is broasted chicken — the best in three counties."

"Everything looks delicious, really." And because she had been rude to someone who might well be her own distant cousin, Lettie offered an apology. "I'm awful sorry."

"Don't fret. It's all right."

She still felt sheepish. "I'll have the smoked sausage and a side order of corn nuggets."

"Homemade rolls with that?"

Lettie nodded. "Some strawberry jam, too, please."

"Sure." Another welcoming smile and the

waitress left Lettie's table.

Beginning to feel hungry, she looked at the dessert section of the menu printed on the paper placemat. The angel food cake caught her eye. She just might have to indulge — she'd given up watching her weight years ago.

While she waited for her meal, she glanced around the large room, not daring to make eye contact with anyone. She recalled that the innkeeper's wife in Kidron had told her of a woman who made a thousand Kapps each year, and in twenty or more different sizes. Such meticulous work had to be similar to piecing together a quilt. *Takes perseverance,* she thought, knowing it might take just that to find her son or daughter. Minnie Keim was surely the key to unlocking the past . . . leading her to her first child.

Lettie traced the tan latticework design on the burgundy tablecloth. She stared at the wall clock with its small pendulum across the room, then glanced at the wallpaper border of colorful fruit high on the wall. Feeling terribly conspicuous, she looked out the window at the flour mill across the street before reading every single word again on the menu. She was quite relieved when the waitress returned with the meal.

But she was startled, though somewhat

pleased, when Susan later pulled out a chair and sat down with her. "I thought I'd take my break now . . . keep you company. That is, if ya don't mind."

"Well, it's awfully nice, but you don't have to . . . if there's something else pressing."

"I don't have to do near half what I do round here," the woman said softly. And leaning forward, she said, "I've lived here for a long time . . . worked here for quite a few years, too." She bowed her head for a moment. "I daresay I'm as lonely as you look."

"Ach, I . . ." In the Plain community, a woman stood out if she was by herself. And Lettie was fairly sure that's what had prompted the waitress to feel sorry for her. Why else?

"Are you visitin' someone in Baltic?"

"I hope to, jah." She was hesitant to say the midwife's name in the midst of all these people, unsure if the vivacious waitress just might announce it.

"I'm Susan Kempf," the brown-eyed waitress said.

"Glad to meet ya, Susan. I'm Lettie . . . Lettie Byler."

Susan glanced around the restaurant. "I know how it feels bein' single in a world of couples and families."

She thinks I'm a Maidel. . . .

"The sadness of loss . . . I see it in your eyes." Susan sighed, frowning tenderly. "I'm a widow, too."

"Oh, but you're mistaken," Lettie blurted out. "I'm quite married."

Susan apologized, nearly falling over her words, her face red with embarrassment. "I'm so sorry. I thought . . ."

"No hurt feelin's at all," Lettie was quick to say. "That's understandable." She admitted she was traveling without her husband.

"Well, I hardly ever see that." Susan explained that most Amishwomen in these parts were accompanied by their husbands or another woman when they came to the restaurant. "You're one courageous soul, I 'spect."

She shook her head. "I'm anything but that." She half expected her companion to ask why she'd come alone. Instead Susan asked where she was staying, and before Lettie realized where the conversation was leading, the thoughtful woman had invited her to stay at her big, empty house.

"For the time being," Susan said.

"That's awfully kind of you, but I've already paid the motel through this Sunday, so . . ."

Susan looked disappointed. "I just thought

it might be more comfortable for you . . . and we could get better acquainted."

"Maybe we'll meet again, here, at the restaurant. Maybe for supper tomorrow?"

"Well, I've got some vacation days coming. . . ."

At that moment, several customers entered. Lettie was astonished to see Sylvia Fisher, an employee friend of Grace's. *What's she doing here?* Sylvia worked at Eli's Natural Foods with her sister Nancy, who was also standing right there next to her near the cashier, talking and smiling.

Oh, goodness! Lettie's heart sank; the girls would know her in an instant. She ducked her head. The Fisher girls would surely contact Grace if they spotted Lettie here.

"On second thought," she said quickly, "maybe I'll take you up on that, Susan. If the motel will refund the next three days, that is."

"Well, let's just see what they say." Susan's eyes twinkled. "Since you've already paid your supper bill, we'll go through the kitchen to get my purse. My horse and buggy's out back."

Relieved at the prospect of leaving the dining room, Lettie rose and headed straight for the bustling kitchen. *Whew! Too close for comfort!*

■ ■ ■ ■

As Heather packed up her laptop at the coffee shop, her father called to say he was only a few miles away. "Will you meet me for supper? I have a few stops to make first."

"What are you hungry for?" she asked.

"Oh, you pick. I'll bet you've discovered some great places to eat by now."

She suggested the Bird-in-Hand Family Restaurant & Smorgasbord, and they met there some time later.

Her dad gave her a big hug in the parking lot. "I've missed you," he said as they headed inside.

"Me too," she said, eyeing him. Right now she didn't care to make small talk. What she really wanted was to blurt out that she was seriously ill — get it all out in the open at last. But Dad was busy talking about his work and how famished he was.

At her father's urging, Heather joined him in ordering the full buffet, and her resolve to eat only fresh raw vegetables and fruit quickly disappeared.

"It's much too quiet at the house," Dad said as they settled in at a table for two. "Besides that, Moe and Igor miss you."

"Aw, they're such sweet little kitties," she

said. "Did you bring them along?"

He shook his head. "No, and your mother wouldn't be happy if she knew her beloved felines are winging it." He poured more sugar into his coffee and stirred it. "I asked the neighbor to look in on them — feed and water them — while I'm away."

"That's great, Dad. The cats like her."

He set down his spoon and picked up his knife and fork. "Well, eat up, kiddo. I'd say you could use it." Her father took a bite of pork and sauerkraut, smiling at her as he chewed. It was obvious he had something on his mind. "I've been thinking a lot about this house. I don't know when I've been more excited about anything."

"It's all over your face, Dad."

"At first I thought it would take a few months to get the ball rolling, but I asked around, and it turns out there's an Amish carpenter who can start right away." He chuckled. "Guess even the downturn in the housing market has its silver lining." He suggested they drive together to the home of the Amish carpenter he'd hired to construct the new place. "I want you to meet Josiah and his family. He's touted as the best Amish builder in Lancaster County. . . . I saw several of his houses earlier today."

In spite of his drive from Virginia, her dad

looked better rested than Heather remembered. "Everything's falling into place so quickly," he said.

"Sounds like it." She could hardly believe this was her dad talking — it wasn't like him to be so impulsive.

He reached inside his tan sports coat and pulled out a sketch of a floor plan. "It's rough, but what do you think?" He passed it across the table to her. "Three bedrooms are enough, right?"

She nodded, assuming he would use one as a home office, as he did at their present house. "Dad . . . you know I'll be going back home to Virginia in the fall." *If all goes well.*

He frowned. "You're working on your thesis, right?"

"Well . . . not so much."

"I thought you came here for that — to get away from distractions."

"I've just lost some steam, that's all."

Suddenly he looked worried. "Honey, what are you saying? You had such passion before."

She sighed, knowing this was lousy timing. She couldn't possibly reveal her terrible news when he was so exuberant about the new property . . . and the house plans.

"I'm just saying I won't need my own space there, except when I come to visit."

She had to play down whatever he'd picked up on in her voice. Sometime soon — perhaps tomorrow — she would tell him about her enlightening appointment with the naturopath.

She stared at her plate of chipped beef, potato salad, baked beans with brown sugar, and her tall glass of Coke. She'd certainly blown it at this meal. *I'll eat better after my cleansing program,* she told herself.

Her dad referred again to the Amish master carpenter. "Josiah Smucker has an amazing reputation here. And not only is he a carpenter, but he's a preacher, too . . . though he makes his living building."

Smucker? Could this be Sally's husband, or were there lots of Smuckers in the area?

"Amish ministers aren't paid a salary," Dad explained — strangest thing she'd ever heard. Yet she was intrigued by her father's seemingly avid interest in all things Amish.

"What exactly does being a master carpenter entail?" she asked.

"Josiah's in charge of planning barn raisings and other local building projects. He's had tons of experience, and he's really great. I think you'll agree soon enough that we're lucky to have caught him and his crew at the perfect time."

"We're lucky . . ." Heather was worried her

dad was including her too much in all of this. And she found it hard to believe when he said the house could be built and ready to move into within about five weeks. Maybe less. "Sounds like *Extreme Makeover: Home Edition,*" she quipped.

Her dad laughed and raised his coffee cup to her in a sort of toast. "It does sound incredible, but with the kind of teamwork Josiah has, he can raise a two-story barn in a day."

Their young Amish waitress returned to the table. "Will there be anything else this evening?" she asked before tallying up their order.

"I think we're fine." Dad looked across the table, grinning. "Unless the young lady would care for more."

"Oh, I've had plenty." She smiled up at the rosy-cheeked girl, who couldn't be a day older than eighteen. "Thanks anyway."

Her dad also thanked the waitress and accepted the bill. They got up from the table — *the scene of my latest dietary crime,* thought Heather, recalling her discussion with LaVyrle.

Weaving through the maze of tables and diners, she followed her father to the cashier's table, noting the many Amish and Mennonite customers, as well as Plain waitresses, some with white netting prayer caps. As many trips as her family had made here throughout the years, she still was not completely accustomed to this somewhat foreign place nestled within the bounds of the contemporary *real* world. And now here was her dad, ready to put his job on hold to build a new house and start up a gentleman's farm on former Amish land. It was hard to wrap her brain around that, but the past eighteen months had taught her the death of a spouse could alter a person's thinking.

Like the loss of a mother?

Observing him pay for their meal, she felt as if she was seeing her father for the first time in a very long time. The prospect of building a house had definitely put a spring in his step. A man his age needed purpose in life, something to get him out of bed every morning. Supposing he kept it up, his successful career couldn't be his only reason for living.

As long as Dad doesn't use the new house as a place to retreat from the world . . . like I am. . . .

Together they walked through the parking lot, to their individual cars. Dad suggested they caravan over to Josiah's. "I'll lead the way," he told her. "I'd like to get some of

your ideas down on paper as soon as possible. I can only stay around for a few days."

*Long enough for a serious father-daughter
talk,* she hoped.

"Sounds like you know where you're going." She clicked the remote to unlock her
car.

He chuckled. "That I do. I've already
visited Preacher Josiah at his farmhouse,"
he admitted, opening her door.

"Wow, Dad . . . aren't you full of surprises."

Smiling, he touched her elbow. When she
was inside, he closed the door and patted
the window. "See you there, kiddo."

Kiddo . . .

Thinking what her news might do to him
made her depressed. And no amount of
wishing could change the fact Heather was
still somewhat skeptical about Dr. Marshall's natural approach to healing. *Is it too
good to be true?*

CHAPTER ELEVEN

"There's going to be a hen party next Wednesday morning," Susan Kempf said as she took the reins in her all-black buggy.

"We call our baking get-togethers back home Sisters Days or baking bees," Lettie said. She was quite taken by the openness of Susan's carriage. *Not at all like our buggies back home.*

"I think you'd enjoy meeting my neighbors, 'specially May Jaberg. She helped me pick up the pieces . . . after Vernon died." Susan went on to talk more about her "dear neighbor," who was hosting next week's work frolic. "May's Amish-Mennonite, and the most nurturing woman you'll ever meet. She has three adopted children, and a whole bunch of biological kids, too."

Adopted? The word tugged at Lettie's heart.

"We'll be baking cookies and pies for her church's bake-sale benefit."

Lettie was still deep in thought about May's family. "How old are May's adopted children?"

"Oh, let's see: The two older girls are in their twenties. I'm not sure about their son," Susan said. "Believe me, Lettie — May would be ever so pleased to have you join us."

"Well, it would be nice, but I doubt I'll be here that long," Lettie said, though she did wonder whether she might catch a glimpse of May's children there. The idea she could be very close to finding Samuel's and her missing child gave her pause.

Oh, dear Lord, could it be?

Susan continued to sing the praises of her neighbor, and Lettie found the woman's winning way quite infectious. *Is meeting her the answer to my prayers?*

Except for some occasional prattle with Tracie Gordon in Kidron or the heartbreaking visit to Samuel Graber, Lettie had been cut off from any real fellowship since departing Bird-in-Hand. Being with jovial Susan was ever so encouraging.

"Would you happen to know how May and her husband went about adopting their children?" she asked somewhat apprehensively. "Was it through an agency . . . or a private adoption?"

"You know, I never heard." Susan glanced at her. "But as forthcoming as May is, she'd pro'bly be glad to talk about it."

"Ach no, I don't need to be that nosy." *Though I'd love to know . . .*

"We can drop by right now, if you'd like." Susan smiled. "Are you thinkin' of adopting?"

"No, no," Lettie protested. "It's just so interesting how families come together." She felt bad, fudging on the truth to this good-natured woman.

Susan mentioned several other families in their farm community who'd actually gone overseas to places like Romania and China to adopt children.

"Amish couples?" Lettie asked, surprised.

"Some, jah. Lots of Mennonite families especially have gone the route of foreign adoption."

As they rode, Lettie was aware of the sound of the carriage wheels *click-clack*ing on the road, the occasional snort of the horse's nostrils. Wonderful-*gut* sounds. Susan lovingly referred to the bay mare as "Molly." Watching the horse's head rise and fall with her rythmic movements, Lettie couldn't help but enjoy herself in the front seat of the old carriage.

They talked of the pleasant springtime

weather, and Susan brought up May's hobby of beekeeping. "Ach, Lettie, I've never seen anyone so pleased as May was last month when she received nearly four pounds of honeybees in the mail. They come in a wooden crate, ya know."

Lettie nodded. "Our neighbors back home are beekeepers, too. They sometimes share their raw honey with us."

"There's nothing like it, is there?" Susan commented as they rode down the main street, toward the little motel where Lettie was lodging.

Lettie quickly thought ahead to what she might say to the owner. She could not afford to lose the money she'd paid in advance for her room. No telling how much longer she'd have to be away — how much cash she would need to stay afloat.

Feeling impolite for letting her mind drift, Lettie focused again on Susan, who continued to describe the many aspects of beekeeping: the queen cage, the worker bees, the new hive, and the building of honeycomb for a bee nursery. "May's just so excited to watch the bees come back to the hive, all laden with pollen." She sighed happily. "Seems to me, spring creeps right up on a person, ain't so?"

Lettie agreed. She'd experienced that

while staying in Kidron last month, seeing the newly planted fields turn from brown to dazzling green, a sight she'd always enjoyed during this season. And the gold of daffodils and pink dogwood trees . . . and dozens of beautiful hummingbirds.

"There's nothin' like a new honeycomb in a new hive to bring that home, seems to me," Susan continued.

Never having kept bees, Lettie could only listen. But the way Susan talked so warmly of her "bee-lovin' neighbor" — and Lettie's own curiosity about May's adopted children — made her hope all the more she might be able to get her money refunded. She was so drawn to the idea of staying with Susan.

"Is this here the place?" Susan asked as they approached the motel with window boxes filled with red and white petunias.

"Jah, just park in the back." Lettie was torn between pulling up stakes here to go to Susan's house, and longing for her own house on Beechdale Road. But she'd already committed herself this far. *Sure hope I'm makin' the right choice.*

"You'll be very comfortable at my home," Susan said.

True, but I can't stay long, thought Lettie. She opened the buggy door and made her way to the motel entrance.

■ ■ ■ ■

"*Nee* — no, I wouldn't think of startin' on another house till the work's done on yours." Josiah Smucker was leaning over his wife's kitchen table. Younger than Heather had expected — perhaps in his mid-thirties — Josiah was drawing a rough map of Heather's father's plot of land, taking into consideration the location of Mill Stream. He pointed out the creek to Heather but continued directing his conversation to her dad. "I can tell ya this, Mr. Nelson, I have no slackers on my crew. That's how we get things done quickly. That, and I've got me a *gut* many workers, all doin' their jobs at once."

"Please, call me Roan."

Josiah grinned, ran his hand through his thick brown hair, and accepted a tall glass of homemade lemonade from his darling pink-faced daughter. "Would ya like some, too?" the girl asked Heather next.

"Sure, thanks," Heather said.

Her dad marked the area where three massive trees stood on the property. "You should know my daughter and I are tree huggers," he told Josiah, winking at Heather. "Is it possible to preserve them?"

149

Josiah nodded his head vigorously. "The way my men and I look at it, whatever the Lord sees fit to put on the land stays there."

Her dad nodded. "Wonderful." He glanced at Heather, smiling. "My daughter and I will meet with the draftsman and go over the blueprints tomorrow. She's staying at an Amish bed-and-breakfast close by . . . and I'll try to get a room on Route 340 somewhere."

Josiah peered over his shoulder at his pretty wife, who stood at the sink, washing dishes. "Well, if that doesn't work out, let us know. We have two spare rooms. So anytime you're in town, Roan, just let us know."

Heather was again struck by the uncommon hospitality of these people. And because there had been no talk this evening of cost, she assumed her father had already discussed price and payment with this man who could raise a two-story barn in a single day, as well as preach a sermon to a houseful of Amish folk. It boggled her mind.

Mom would never believe this!

The thought of her mother and the courageous battle she'd fought and lost with cancer brought Heather's thoughts back to the radical approach to eating LaVyrle had advocated. But first the hardest part — the ten-day lodge program down the road.

Surely LaVyrle's way would be easier than chemo and radiation. *Anything else would have to be!* She'd witnessed the conventional medical route firsthand and had no desire to go there. Marian Riehl, on the other hand, had been completely accommodating of Heather's request this morning to steep some green tea for her in lieu of the usual coffee. And Heather had taken her food supplements in the bathroom upstairs before coming down for breakfast. Other than her slipup this evening, things had gone pretty well since yesterday's appointment.

So this is how best-laid plans go awry, she thought, once more realizing that the diet she was considering was going to take some remarkable willpower. Not to mention a fair amount of reprogramming. *I'll have to send out a memo. . . .*

Sighing, she was conscious again of her gaping waistband, surprised her dad hadn't made more of her weight loss. *He's being polite . . . or he's too caught up in his new adventure.*

She cringed at the thought of laying her bad news on him — she felt distressed even trying to imagine such a conversation. But how long could she afford to wait on the recommendation LaVyrle had so whole-

heartedly urged?
Am I playing Russian roulette?

Without any pleading whatsoever, Lettie was pleasantly surprised to receive a refund for the balance of her intended stay at the motel. "God bless you," the kindly woman said after counting out the bills.

Lettie thanked her and pushed the money into her purse, then headed for the parking lot. "It won't take me but a few minutes to pack my things," she told Susan as she hurried off to the room.

When she'd double-checked the vanity and bathroom area for her personal items, she folded her clothes into the suitcase and zipped it shut. Before leaving, she placed several dollar bills on the desk as a tip for housekeeping, along with the room key.

A small miracle, this, she thought, returning to the buggy.

Susan agreed when Lettie mentioned it. "God has a way of directing our ev'ry step, I'll say."

Even when we run away from home? She pondered her own decision again, what it meant to be absent in the midst of the busiest time of the year. Lambing season had always been so hard on Judah, and she breathed a prayer for strength for her hardworking husband even as the sound of Molly's *clip-clopp*ing began to ease her nerves. She relaxed in the seat, traveling for at least a mile without speaking. It was odd, because Susan had been so talkative earlier.

"You must be weary from the day," Lettie said.

"Not so much tired as nervous." Susan pointed ahead to the tall house on the corner. "See a ways up there? For the past few weeks, every time I've made this turn, I've been pelted by either small stones or acorns. They just come flyin' right into the carriage."

"What on earth?"

Susan looked surprised. "You mean you don't have this problem in Lancaster?"

"Occasionally, but it's not something we hear much about. There are more incidents of cars speeding round buggies and whatnot."

"Well, it happens too often here. In the summer and fall, the boys even throw rotten fruit, most often apples. And there are many thoughtless pranks, 'specially during the harvest. Plenty of troublesome things go on in October all over Ohio Amish country, I'm afraid."

"Because of Halloween, maybe?" Lettie couldn't imagine another reason.

"Maybe so. I don't know so much about the English. It's even become something of a tradition amongst the *Amish* here to pull tricks on each other — at least at harvest."

"Like what?"

Susan laughed a little now. "Well, for instance, putting two buggies on top of a house. That happened not long ago."

"On the roof?" She could scarcely even picture such a thing! "How'd they get up there?"

Susan gave a wave of her hand. "Oh, there's ways, if you've got a bunch of young bucks with too much to drink."

There was some trouble with alcohol back home, too. Lettie shuddered to think of their young people choosing to go down that dead-end road. It seemed the newspapers made a heyday of that from time to time . . . playing up the rebellion of only a few of their youth to boost subscriptions.

Now they were approaching the corner house. Lettie leaned forward cautiously to study its white clapboard and dark green shutters, watching for the culprits to come running across the lawn.

She held her breath as the horse slowed up to make the turn at the corner and then hurried to a trot. With arms stiff, Susan held the reins. "Be sure and cover your eyes if something comes flyin'," she advised.

Lettie clenched her jaw, suddenly thinking of Judah. Did he ever worry about her, away from the safety of his covering and care? Poor man, he did not even know if she was living in the modern world or with their kinfolk.

Wishing she'd written more details in her recent letter, she recalled his loving concern during her pregnancies . . . the tender way he had helped her in and out of the family carriage. *Not so long ago.* Would they ever have such tenderness between them again?

The fond memory slipped away as the horse and buggy passed the white house and moved along the length of the backyard. "We're almost in the clear," Lettie said, hoping it was true.

"For this trip, maybe." Susan glanced at her, eyebrows raised. "Are you all right?"

Lettie said she was. "Frankly, I wish you hadn't told me. I'll be ever so jittery now . . . there, at that corner."

"Well, if you come to town on your own, you'll know what to watch for."

Lettie appreciated Susan's concern.

"My husband had a kindly way of unnerving those kids, back when he was still alive." Susan's voice cracked. "Vernon would turn and wave and grin at them while the rotten fruit just came a-flyin'. The nicest man I've ever known . . ."

They were quiet for a time. Then Susan said softly, "Seems like just yesterday he was sittin' here, driving me to town. Ach, I miss him so." She dabbed at her eyes with a hankie. "Still, I wouldn't wish him back, not since he's gone to Glory."

Lettie's heart went out to Susan. "How long ago?"

"Nearly three years now."

Lettie shared that her dearest sister had also passed away. "Naomi was my closest friend . . . as well as my sister. I don't think I've ever gotten over her passing."

"I know that feeling all too well." Susan nodded knowingly. "And what a blessing when two sisters are that close."

"Oh . . . don't misunderstand me: The Lord gave me some wonderful-*gut* siblings. But Naomi was mighty special. She not only loved me . . . she liked me, too."

"There *is* a difference." Susan seemed more relaxed now. The lines lay loose on her lap. "Do any of your siblings live in Ohio?"

Undoubtedly Susan was itching to know why she'd come to Baltic. "Most all my relatives are back in Lancaster County," Lettie told her. It struck her once again that her grown firstborn son — or daughter — could very well be living nearby, unknown to her. The thought nearly took her breath away.

"At the restaurant, you mentioned hopin' to visit someone."

She drew in a shallow breath. "Jah, I've been looking but can't seem to find this person."

"I wouldn't mind helping . . . that is, if I'm not pushin' my nose in."

Lettie hoped Susan wouldn't be confused or even misled if she revealed her eagerness to locate a particular midwife. She considered what she ought to say, recalling that her mother often urged her to at least say *something.* To get the words out rather than to think it through till she knew precisely how to express herself. *Sometimes that's the hardest part of all.*

Feeling suddenly tired, she asked quietly, "Do you know of a woman in the area named Minnie Keim?"

Susan frowned. "You mean Perry's Minnie?"

"Jah." Lettie gave her a searching look.

"Sure, I know her. She's a well-known midwife . . . and a counselor for young girls. Unwed mothers, mostly."

"Oh?" Lettie's hands went limp. "That's just who I came to see."

"Well, I know right where she and her husband are stayin'." Susan explained that they'd recently moved in with Minnie's uncle and aunt, after Perry had been laid off and was unable to afford their rent.

"How far from your place?" asked Lettie.

"Three miles, if that."

Only fifteen minutes away by horse and buggy, she thought, her heart aching with anticipation. *Soon, ever so soon, I'll know something about my child. . . .*

CHAPTER TWELVE

The musky sweetness of lilacs hung in the air the next morning as Grace made haste to the stable. She'd gotten up extra early to be with Willow, anxious for even the smallest sign of improvement. *"Such miracles are few and far between,"* Adam had cautioned her yesterday after evening prayers.

It had also been last evening that she'd bumped into Mammi Adah in the hallway, half hidden amongst its assortment of sweaters, black shawls, work jackets, and boots. There her grandmother had stood, face beet red in utter embarrassment, as if she'd been eavesdropping on the family's time of Bible reading and prayer. *Awful strange . . .*

For some time now, since before Mamma had left, Dat had been reading Scripture from the English Bible. Plenty of Amish folk did this, and it wasn't against their bishop's wishes . . . not like some Grace knew. Even so, it troubled her to think Mammi was spying on them. Or was she merely looking in on them with pity?

Who's to know, tight-lipped as Mammi Adah can be when it comes to Mamma.

Grace knelt in the soft sawdust and pressed her face against Willow's. "Hullo, sweet girl. Did ya sleep at all?"

Grace was heartened to see the horse was more relaxed today, her injured leg not so tightly pushed up against her belly as before. How many feeble old horses had been nursed back to health with various home remedies passed from one neighbor to another? Adam and Joe had given her little hope last night at supper. Dawdi Jakob had sided with her and Mandy, arguing with the boys to give it more time — *"and more homemade liniment, just maybe."* Mammi Adah had remained silent on the matter, which surprised Grace, now as she thought about it. Mammi wasn't one to hold back her opinion, no matter what the supper table discussion.

Grace touched Willow's head, tenderly petting her. "You'll be up soon and walkin' round the barnyard, *gut* as new." The words sounded deceptive even to her own ears as she looked at the beautiful horse lying there. God had made horses to sleep standing up.

She wondered what Mamma would say if she knew of Willow's condition. Surely she would be distraught, too. "Did Mamma tell you where she was going?" she whispered to Willow. "Did she come here and talk to you before her night-time walks?"

Grace had slipped out of the house several times to see if her mother was indeed pouring out her heart to Willow. *Like I sometimes do.* But she'd never seen her mother do any such thing.

Willow turned her head slightly and gave a muffled whinny.

"You know I'd make ya well if I could, hmm . . . ?" She leaned forward, rubbing the upper part of the mare's injured leg as she softly hummed a hymn from the *Ausbund.*

Then, sitting ever so still, she absorbed the sounds around her. From across the road, she thought she heard the soft babbling of Mill Creek. And then . . . the crunching of gravel underfoot.

"Dat must be up already," she said, still stroking Willow's neck. "We're all so worried 'bout you."

Grace heard a shuffling sound and the barn door creaking open.

She turned toward the door, straining to see. If only there was a smidgen of light from the moon. But she'd crept here *"on the deepest side of the night,"* as Mamma sometimes referred to the span of time after midnight, before sunrise.

Returning her attention to Willow, she said softly, "A lantern would help, jah?"

When the footsteps were nearly upon her, she jerked around and saw the dim silhouette of a young man. She wouldn't have known who it was, except that he spoke her name in such a gentle, hushed manner, she recognized him immediately. "Yonnie?" she asked. "What're ya doin' here?"

"Same as you . . . looks like." He squatted down close to Willow and opened a bottle of liquid that smelled like turpentine mixed with vinegar. Methodically, he began to apply it to the injured leg. "I mixed in some egg to make it creamy. My Dat always used this on our horses out in Indiana," he said.

Her eyes were accustomed enough to the darkness to see his hands making light, flowing circular movements.

"You don't mind, do ya? My comin' here to help Willow."

"No." She surprised herself by not thinking before speaking. Yet how could she say otherwise?

"*Gut,* then."

She shook her head. "Maybe you misunderstood."

"Oh?"

"Willow's our pet."

"Why, sure she is, Gracie." He clucked his tongue as he leaned closer to Willow. "And I can see why you're fond of her. She's one special mare. Mighty good-lookin', too."

Grace was wary of his tender talk. What right did he have to sit out here in the dark like this with *her* wounded horse? *Or with me, for that matter?* "I best be goin' inside." She rose quickly.

"Well, I'll be right here."

She considered that. "Ain't at all necessary, really."

"Jah . . ." He paused, and she waited to hear what he'd say. "Grace, I'm doin' this for your father. Just so you're clear on that."

She blushed in the darkness — she'd sounded awfully presumptuous. The air felt ever so still, as it often did just before dawn. In but a few minutes, Dat and Adam would come to look after the sheep and the new lambs, flinging their arms into jackets, their boot tongues flapping as they trudged into the barn. What would they think if they saw her here with Yonnie?

"All right, then," Grace said gently. "Make Willow *gut* and well . . . for Dat."

163

■ ■ ■ ■

Martin Puckett's van was filled with Amish-men. He was glad to be receiving frequent calls for transportation again, particularly since he'd lost some days of business following Lettie Byler's disappearance last month.

His wife was right — the strange rumors about his running off with Lettie had blown over, and he'd come out smelling like a rose, just as Janet had predicted. Her kiss as he left the house this morning had lingered on his cheek.

Presently he was driving a whole smattering of farmers, carpenters, and one draftsman named John Stoltzfus to different locations. John, the youngest of the group, wanted to go to the Bird-in-Hand Family Inn, where he was to meet an out-of-towner.

"His name's Roan Nelson," John told his cousin and the others in Pennsylvania Dutch. "To think a fella from Virginia with a good-payin' job would want to pull up stakes and build smack-dab in the midst of us."

"Jah . . . what's wrong with him?" said one, to which the passengers in the van burst into laughter.

"Doesn't this Roan fellow know he'll be surrounded by slow-movin' traffic?" said another. "And smelly road apples, too?"

Martin smiled, enjoying all the fast-talking Deitsch. Eavesdropping was one of the perks of his job. Daily he heard tittle-tattle, putting the pieces to an enormous mosaic together in his head at the end of each week — the struggles of living "in the world but not of the world." To think these good folk adhered to the lifestyle of another era altogether while living in the twenty-first century. *Searching for happiness is like trying to catch a feather in the wind no matter who you are.*

"Hey, is Mr. Nelson the one who bought the undersized piece of land over on Gibbons Road?" asked John's cousin.

"That's right," said the oldest-looking man in the bunch. "I guess Roan Nelson told Preacher Josiah he's always wanted to run a small farm of sorts."

"What'll he grow on such a small acreage?" a farmer piped up from the backseat.

"Guess he'll have to get his house built first," John replied. "Which is why I'm meetin' him today . . . and his daughter, who's staying over at Riehls' for the summer. Preacher says Roan wants some Amish influence in the look of his house, but he also hired an English guy to rough out the blueprints."

Martin wanted to interject a niggling thought: *Don't you find it peculiar when outsiders want to live among you?* The Amish he knew best wanted to keep their neighborhoods cloistered and free of worldly ways. Folks like Roan Nelson had a tendency to break down the long-held barriers within the Anabaptist community — bring in too much of a modern mentality. Martin assumed no amount of the contemporary world, even in small doses, was any good for the young people of this tight-knit community.

"Why was that parcel of land sold off to an Englischer?" John's cousin asked. "Who slipped a cog on that?"

Several of the men chuckled, and one mentioned that a Mennonite named Bender was the original landowner. A man in the second seat spoke. "The way I heard it, the owner's attention was caught mighty quick by the first person who came along with the right amount of cash in hand."

That was precisely what Martin had suspected, too. *Some folk will sell most anything, if they're desperate enough.*

But this Virginia businessman they were joking about . . . Martin was very interested in meeting him. Likely he would have the opportunity when he was hauling Josiah Smucker and his crew of workers over there every day.

What's Roan Nelson's motive for worming his way into an Amish neighborhood, anyway?

Heather badly needed a morning caffeine fix, but the naturopath had strongly advised giving up coffee — all day, every day. Anything with caffeine, including chocolate, she recalled. Even the green tea she was allowed to drink had to be decaf. As a result, she was dragging around like the old-fashioned string mop Marian Riehl used to wash her big kitchen floor. Once again, Heather had taken her supplements upstairs before breakfast, then downed two full cups of the Japanese green tea.

She sat respectfully studying the rough blueprints in the pavilion near the Bird-in-Hand Family Inn, where her father had acquired a room last night. Her dad and the draftsman — an Amishman named John Stoltzfus, whom her father had met last month at an animal auction — sat across from her, drinking their coffee and tossing ideas around. The smell of the rich brew taunted her nose with its aroma.

John finally posed a question directly to

her. "Do ya see any changes you want to make, Miss Nelson?" A flat pencil was pushed through his cropped brown hair and perched just above his ear.

"Well, let's see." She looked over the blueprints, wishing she felt more interest. She scrutinized the placement of the bedrooms but her thoughts wandered. It was still so disorienting to think her father was building a new house.

What would Mom suggest they do about the number of proposed bedrooms? Wouldn't she be heartbroken at all this talk of moving away from their longtime family home?

As if to center her thoughts, Dad pointed to the sheet that depicted the upper level. "What about the layout of the upstairs bathrooms, kiddo?"

His enthusiasm for the plan was evident in his cheerful tone. *What sort of daughter discourages her widower father?* "How about a private bath for the second bedroom?" she ventured.

"Separate bath it is." He leaned back and clapped his hands.

Oh boy, Heather thought.

Focusing on the floor plan was difficult, almost impossible, when she should be prying open her heart and telling Dad about her illness. And she wouldn't mind his input on the Wellness Lodge program she was still deliberating. Insurance wouldn't cover the cost, and it would be tough for her to devise a way to pay the considerable expense on her own. And, too, if she enrolled in the program ASAP, she'd be disappearing from life in general even more than she already had here in Amish country.

Her father's chin jutted forward as he moved his attention to the area of his future home office. *What use will he have for an office here?* she had to wonder.

As she studied the blueprints more carefully, it seemed apparent a woman had been involved on some level. Maybe Josiah Smucker's wife, Sally? The dining room was only a few steps away from the compact yet serviceable kitchen . . . where a smallish breakfast nook was situated near a fireplace at one end of the room. *Perfect for morning coffee and sweet rolls,* she thought, but caught herself. *No . . . perfect for raw-milk yogurt smoothies and fresh fruit.*

"You look tired," Dad said unexpectedly.

She glanced up. "Guess I am."

"Late-night party?"

"Right, Dad . . . with *you* at the buffet, pigging out, remember?" She smiled, feeling slightly embarrassed, thanks to the

Amishman sitting across from them. "Besides, most people go to bed with the chickens around here. Isn't that right?" She looked at John.

The man chuckled, his beard touching his chest as he nodded.

"I'd like to sign off on this today, but perhaps a short break would do us all some good." Dad motioned for her to walk with him. "Excuse us, please," he told John, who politely said he could use a moment to review the revisions up to this point. "My daughter needs to stretch her legs."

I do? Startled, Heather rose and followed him around the inn and out front.

"Everything all right, honey?" he asked.

She inhaled quickly.

"Are you disappointed in the house? Am I moving too fast?"

The worried note in his voice stirred her heart. Why *did* he want to leave Virginia? Their lovely house held sentimental value for them both, especially with Mom gone. How could Dad possibly walk away from all the cherished reminders of their years together? Like hers, Dad's life had become unraveled after Mom's death. Maybe it *was* time for him to make a massive change, just as she had needed this time away for herself. *But a permanent move?*

"I'm fine with whatever you want to build, Dad — however you want to build it."

"You're sure?"

She nodded. "It's your house . . . it's what you want."

His features relaxed into a smile. "I want you to visit often."

"Sure, Dad . . . and I will. If I can." They headed through the parking lot toward the quaint farmers market, housed in a barnlike structure. She wrapped her arms tightly around herself, gathering strength . . . or perhaps courage. She'd put this off for too long. "Dad, I'm sorry . . . it's really hard to think about building a house right now. I'm happy for you, I really am. But I need to talk to you about something completely different. Something I should've discussed with you before."

He stopped walking abruptly. "Honey, what is it?"

She paused, catching his eye. "I'm sick, Dad." There was no turning back. "I wanted to spare you the bad news. . . ."

He winced. "What do you mean, sick?" His eyes were dark with concern.

She looked down at the ground beneath her feet. "This is so hard."

"Heather, you're scaring me — how sick?"

"It hurts to think of adding more worry to

your life." She began to tell him the results of the initial blood tests and the other medical findings. Everything she could possibly remember that had led to her cancer diagnosis.

"How long have you known?" he asked.

"Too long, and for that I'm sorry."

Dad's eyes were blinking fast. "I wish you'd told me right away." He was frowning, struggling to absorb the news, to contain his emotions.

"Oh, Dad," she whispered as he pulled her into his arms. "I couldn't bear to tell you at all. And . . . I almost didn't."

"You're my daughter." There was a catch in his voice. "You're all I have now."

When he released her, she explained that the oncologist had said she needed to have chemo immediately. "But that's a dead-end, in my opinion," she said, quickly moving forward to the very different approach the local naturopath had suggested. "I really want to give this a try instead."

"Heather . . ." He shook his head. "I think you should return home and start the chemo immediately."

"Dad . . . please, no."

"Why not?"

"Remember what Mom went through? It was a nightmare . . . and worse."

"Well, her cancer was different."

That's what the oncologist said.

"Why not give it your best shot with medically sound treatment?" He was practically arguing now. "Then, if chemo doesn't work, I'd be open to your little experiment."

She'd figured he might respond this way. "You're saying I should take the normal route, and if that doesn't work, then I can get inventive?"

He nodded. "Precisely. Why not?"

"I want to do what Mom thought might have worked better for her." She gave his hand a squeeze. "Let me do this my way . . . please?"

"This lodge program you're so keen on — it must have a hefty price tag."

She'd wondered when to reveal this. "Not surprisingly, yes."

He was quiet for a time, as though processing the reality of her words. But before they reached the farmers market, he raised her hand to his lips. "I have strong reservations about rejecting conventional medicine, Heather. It seems ridiculous. I want to hear what this so-called naturopathic 'doctor' thinks about your type of cancer before you decide anything."

"LaVyrle's pretty amazing. I think you'll like her."

"Well, liking your doctor and thinking you're doing the right thing are worlds apart. But I do want to meet Dr. Marshall as soon as possible. Will you set it up?"

"Sure, Dad. Thanks." She linked her arm through his and they turned back toward the inn again, this time in silence.

She felt the strength in his arm as they walked. The pastureland toward the north made her miss the Riehls' farm setting, and she thought of Grace Byler, the friendly Amish girl over at Eli's. *Will she even remember my desire to meet with Sally Smucker?*

They reached the entrance to the inn, and Dad stopped suddenly, his eyes searching hers. "In all fairness, I don't want to get your hopes up. The lodge program sounds like potentially dangerous hocus-pocus to me. At best, a money-sucking gimmick." He guided her through the lobby again, back to the quaint patio area and the blueprints. "I won't let you do something foolish, kiddo."

And I won't let you stand in my way. . . .

"How about we sign off on that beautiful new house of yours first?" she suggested. When they returned to the pavilion, they found the Amishman sitting contentedly with his coffee, making pencil notations on the plan.

Please, please . . . be on my side, Dad. Heather sighed, hoping LaVyrle might somehow change his mind.

CHAPTER THIRTEEN

Lettie hitched up Susan Kempf's horse and carriage at mid-morning and headed off to see Minnie Keim. Susan had graciously offered her best driving horse and buggy.

She clucked her tongue to the bay mare and held the reins. She'd long imagined this meeting with the woman who'd helped deliver her first wee babe. Lettie felt almost the same level of anticipation as before visiting the baby's father, Samuel. When she passed the house Susan had pointed out as May Jaberg's, she couldn't help gawking. A curious thought crossed her mind: *What if I could observe May's older children from afar?*

Watching the road now, she felt restless about meeting Minnie again. She was also quite relieved that Susan had offered to let her make the trip alone while she attended to household chores. *Will Minnie remember my child . . . or the name of the doctor who placed my baby?* Lettie wondered as she drove along the winding road. *She's delivered so many babies over the years.*

Even at this hour, a dense mist hung close to the ground — a common occurrence in Holmes County, she'd learned. The sun would take some time to penetrate the damp fog. That and the long tunnel of a road, overshadowed by trees, gave her the unsettling sense of going backward through the years. . . .

In the mist Lettie saw that long-ago day. The day she had tearfully stood in the hayloft as young Samuel vowed his love. *"We'll be together, I promise you,"* he'd said, gently pulling her down into the soft hay. *"We love each other, don't we?"*

"We do, but . . ."

"With all my heart, I love you, Lettie Esh."

She'd resisted only slightly that first time, enjoying his touch on her face, her hair. "Daed *might check on the horses,"* she'd whispered amidst his repeated kisses. *"He always does, right after supper."*

But all too quickly she was lost in Samuel's ardent embrace.

"We'll build us a house, not far from here." He had pressed her warm cheek against his own. *"Trust me . . . won't you? Oh, my darling girl."*

And she had trusted him. More than once. Sometimes in the haymow and sometimes deep in the woods under the light of the moon.

"If only I'd waited," Lettie whispered, wishing away the shameful memory. She glanced at the little map Susan had drawn for her, aware of the narrow road ahead — and the pounding of her heart.

Lettie still could not dismiss her anger toward her mother, who'd had it in for Samuel from the start. True, she and Samuel had been very young. Nearly too young to court, let alone to marry and raise their baby. Samuel had also been opposed to certain aspects of the Old Order church — he hadn't wanted Lettie to go through with the expected church baptism. *Wasn't that the real reason I had to give away my baby?*

Aside from the tidbits her mother had revealed to Dat, her father had known precious little about Samuel's romantic interest. It had been Mamm who'd several times caught Lettie with Samuel as they'd read poetry to each other high in the barn. *We were nearly able to touch the cobwebs in the rafters.*

Guilt overtook her each time Lettie allowed herself to return to the past in her mind, as if the vivid memory of her first love sustained the transgression.

And here to think she held Minnie Keim's address in her hands. She must thank the midwife for helping her understand, as a teen girl, what was happening to her that frightening day. The early contractions, the exhausting labor, and ultimately, the final excruciating pushes. After the birth, Minnie had stood with her back to Lettie, cradling the baby in her arms, whispering to Mamm for several minutes before leaving the room.

Both Minnie and Mamma know whether I birthed a son or a daughter. They know to this day. . . .

When Lettie pulled into the dirt lane, several kittens scurried in front of the horse. Clusters of cats and their kittens were typical at a dairy farm, and especially at such a large farm operation as this one looked to be. Lettie was surprised not to feel a speck of hesitancy now, so anxious was she to know the truth.

By the time she tied up the horse and straightened herself a bit, the scent of rain permeated the air. A few drops drizzled down from the thick haze as she headed across the sidewalk to the front door. It struck her as odd that the swing on the porch was positioned exactly as Judah had placed theirs at home. For a moment, she had to compose herself.

When she knocked, an older woman with graying hair and a sagging chin answered. "Why, sure, Minnie's home. Let me get her for ya." Lettie was heartened, then suddenly fearful. Her nagging thoughts threatened to overwhelm her. *I've come too far . . . waited too long.*

Minnie came to the screen door. She'd become a rather stout matron in the twenty plus years, but her face was as round and pink as Lettie remembered. Her hair was a mix of white and golden blond in the natural light of day, and she wore a gray dress and black cape apron over it, both similar to the style Lettie sewed for herself.

"Hullo?" Minnie opened the door a few inches. "My aunt said you're askin' for me."

"Oh, am I ever glad to find you . . . at last!" Lettie said. "You delivered my first baby, years ago. You knew me as Lettie Esh."

Minnie's eyes swept her face. "Lettie, you say?"

"My mother, Adah, contacted you . . . then we came from Lancaster County and met you in Kidron."

"The two of you?" Minnie's brow pinched into a frown. "I've assisted hundreds of

180

women, you must know. Most of the younger girls come with their mothers."

Lettie nodded. "I wouldn't expect you to remember. Not right away."

Minnie moved out from behind the screen door, smiling for the first time. She suggested they walk down to the gazebo. "Can you stay for a while?"

"I surely can." *As long as need be . . .*

"Tell me more. What were the circumstances of the birth?" asked Minnie.

"Well, I was unmarried . . . just sixteen." She held her breath, aware of her disgrace once again. "My parents were opposed to me bringin' up a baby without a husband, lest I never marry otherwise." She sighed. How painful it was to rehash her family's rejection of her . . . of her child. "I loved the father of my baby. Very much, in fact."

"I s'pose he loved you, too," Minnie surprised her by saying.

"That's what fellas tend to say, jah."

Minnie nodded slowly, a twinkle in her eye. " 'Specially the ones who can't wait for marriage . . . or won't."

They sat next to each other in the protection of the enclosed white gazebo, far enough from the house so as not to be heard. The humidity hugged the earth, a gentle rain falling around them. The sounds

181

of spring were alive in the song of the chickadees pecking on seeds at a nearby feeder . . . small children calling back and forth behind the house. The question on Lettie's mind demanded a voice.

"I don't mean to put you out, but I was hoping you might remember me . . . and my mother. And, for my own peace of mind, whether I had a boy or a girl." Lettie added suddenly, "And, too, if you might recall the name of the doctor who arranged the adoption."

"Goodness, such a tall order." Minnie's expression was somber. She thought for a moment, frowning and studying Lettie.

"Mamm and I came to you in the spring — twenty-four years ago in April."

Minnie silently took this all in.

"We'd come to help my father's ailing aunt, as well," Lettie said, hoping to trigger some recollection.

"Ah, sure . . . jah." Minnie's memory was flowering; her eyes held a glint of recognition. "If I'm not mistaken, wasn't your Mamm interested in herbs — 'specially those for teas?"

Lettie felt she might burst. "Jah . . . that's Mamm."

Minnie began to whisper to herself, as if solidifying the past. "Her name was Adah, spelled with an *h.*"

Tears spilled down Lettie's face.

"And you . . . you were ever so young." Minnie straightened her long dress, turning to face her. "If I recall correctly, my dear, you gave birth to a daughter." A gracious smile appeared. "A healthy, pink-faced baby girl."

Lettie's heart leaped up. "A daughter, then?" She brushed back her tears. "All this time, deep in my heart, where I couldn't get to it, so to speak, I believed I'd given life to a son."

"Hopin' for a miniature of his father?" Minnie seemed to understand so much of what she was feeling. Uncanny, unless Lettie's emotions were typical of most women in her shoes.

"I was so lost then," she confessed. "How I wanted to keep my baby . . ."

Minnie's eyes were moist. "Oh, dear girl, you're still lost, ain't so?" She placed her hand over Lettie's. "Lost, till you find your child."

There was no holding back the tears. Lettie yielded to Minnie's welcoming arms, sobbing just as she had on the day of the birth. But this time, someone truly cared how very fragile and heartbroken she was.

Before starting to cook the noon meal, Grace pinned Mammi Adah's dress pattern to the fabric. She'd laid out the material on her grandmother's kitchen table. That way, if she didn't finish before time to set the table on Dat's side of the house, she wouldn't have to put everything away before dinner. *Before I see Yonnie again.*

"You were all smiles just a bit ago," Mammi Adah said, moving away from the sink, where she had been washing some store-bought tomatoes. She went to the table and sat down, watching Grace work while she did some tatting. "What's a-matter, dear?"

She didn't want to mention the fellow who was showing up every single day. *And with Dat's blessing, too . . . of all things.*

"Ain't about your Mamma, I hope."

Grace drew a long breath. Her mother was never far from her thoughts, but Mammi Adah surely knew that. After all, hadn't they also been close at one time? "I mourn her leaving most when I'm alone in my room at night."

Mammi stopped her tatting. "You know, if I didn't have your Dawdi to look after, I

184

might go lookin' for her."

"I've wondered 'bout that."

" 'Tis only natural."

"I don't know what it is 'bout twilight and after . . . when the darkness falls. Or maybe it's just bein' alone that helps me feel comfortable talkin' to the Lord 'bout Mamma . . . and whatever made her leave us. That way I don't cause others more sadness. I just take it to the Lord. Don't you?"

"Oh, honey-girl, I certainly do."

Grace placed the left sleeve on one side of the table, away from the bodice, which she presently began to cut. "Mamma's out in Ohio, or she was. For what reason? You must know something." She held the pinking shears in her right hand, letting their point rest on the table.

Mammi Adah rubbed her forehead for the longest time. Then she looked at Grace. "I can't possibly know what's in your Mamma's heart. Only the Lord sees that."

"Sometimes I ask the Lord if He wouldn't consider putting a *gut* word in for us with Mamma. Well, for *me* anyhow." Grace's voice quavered unexpectedly.

"Aw, honey-girl, it's so awful difficult. For you, 'specially."

"Instead of getting easier with time, it's

harder. The reality sets in more with each day."

"Like it did when your aunt Naomi passed so suddenly . . . In some ways, your mother's absence is nearly like a death."

She hadn't thought of it that way, not since Mamma's short letter.

" 'Course, Naomi never had a chance to say good-bye." Mammi Adah shook her gray head.

Grace turned back to her cutting and pondered her grandmother's words, struggling with her memory of Mamma on the road that night. "Jah, life's too short not to stop and at least say good-bye."

Mammi Adah reached across the table for Grace's hand. "Let's not fret, dear."

Grace looked down at their intertwined hands. "Mothers don't leave their families on a whim. I'm convinced Mamma is missing because of something important . . . at least in her own mind."

"I believe you're right." Mammi released her hand.

Grace began to pile up the pattern pieces and cleared off the snibbles and extra fabric. Ought she bring up the innkeeper's remark about a midwife? *Too hard to comprehend,* she decided.

"It's not like your Mamma to up and disappear without a powerful-*gut* reason," Mammi Adah said thoughtfully.

"Well, I mean to find out what . . . the minute lambing's done." Grace hoped Adam might be able to spare a few days to accompany her to Indiana in early June or even sooner, though she hadn't discussed the impulsive notion with him or with Dat just yet. And, things being what they were, there was no sense in bringing it up to Mammi Adah.

CHAPTER FOURTEEN

It was a rare morning when Adah could sit and tat for an hour. Today she listened carefully as Grace poured out her concerns, her fingers working the tatting shuttle. Adah glanced up for a moment, beginning to feel wrung out. Yet what could she do? *It's too late to change the past.*

She sped up, wanting to complete the handkerchief trim to give to her next younger sister for an upcoming birthday. Several other siblings and a good many girl cousins had their birthdays in August and September, too — amongst the People, many birthdays fell in the late summer months and early autumn. *Biggest months for birthdays, what with winter calling for warmth . . . and tenderness.*

She was silent as she watched Grace gather up the fabric pieces for the dress. "Awful nice of you to help me like this," she said. "My eyesight being what it is . . .

well, I'm just so grateful."

"No need to thank me, Mammi, with all you do for us."

Adah worried about Judah and his four with each passing week. "Still, I daresay your family needs you more than ever."

"Seems so."

For the life of her, Adah could not understand why Judah had asked Grace to move into her mother's place at the table. Made no sense to her or to Jakob. It seemed to them that Grace had too much on her shoulders now. Even as a youngster, she'd often been too willing to accept responsibility. Grace was, after all, supposed to have time for courting, but Adah doubted she was seeing anyone anymore. In fact, Grace often headed upstairs for bed even before Mandy.

Each day Adah recognized anew her growing frustration with Lettie, who hadn't bothered to consult her before embarking on her unreasonable journey. *Was* she visiting Samuel — telling him about their baby? Adah realized she must never underestimate either Lettie's grit or her determination.

Grace left the sewing room to go and start the noon meal, and Adah stretched a little before examining her stitching. As she continued her tatting, she wondered why

Judah rarely spoke of Lettie — not even to Jakob. Was he just too pained over her leaving? Or was he put out with her?

She'd heard tell from the bishop's mother-in-law that there'd been a gathering of sorts early Tuesday morning, confirmation of what Jakob had brought to her attention. She'd made a point of finding out more — Lettie *was* her daughter, after all. As it turned out, the bishop's wife had kindly taken her into confidence, saying that if the brethren were fixing to slap a probationary shun on Lettie — long-distance, of all things — then Adah certainly had a right to know.

And, according to what Grace had learned from talking to the innkeeper's wife, Lettie just might be heading to Cousin Hallie's in Indiana. If so, Adah figured she could easily write a letter of warning to her daughter. On the other hand, if Lettie hadn't gone there at all, Adah would be setting herself up for a dozen or more questions from too-curious Hallie. *I surely don't want that!*

Adah put down her tatting and went to her bedroom to sit on the cane chair near the window. Jakob and Judah had made the lovely chair together the year Lettie and Judah were newlyweds. She was torn, truly, between wishing Judah might be more interested in wanting to search for Lettie . . .

and worried that if he did, he might discover his wife's terrible secret.

So Adah sat there and stewed and pondered and fretted till she had no better idea what to do than when Lettie had first left the family. Still, Adah knew one thing for certain: She felt responsible for the whole jumbled-up mess.

"Two doctors come to mind," Minnie told Lettie as the rain slowed to a mist. "One's in Haiti with Christian Aid Ministries. But since he and the other fellow worked together for years in Kidron and Apple Creek, I daresay what one might know about the placement of your baby, the other would, too."

"Who's the second doctor?" Lettie was breathless.

"Joshua Hackman. Everyone calls him Dr. Josh."

"Here, in Ohio?"

Minnie shook her head. "Not anymore. Last I knew, he took over a practice near Nappanee, Indiana."

Immediately Lettie thought of Cousin Hallie. Then, because Minnie seemed so willing to give answers, Lettie asked the question she'd never breathed to a soul. "Do you know if the couple who adopted my baby was Amish?"

"That would make *gut* sense, I 'spect. But I wasn't privy to their identity, although I wouldn't be surprised if they were local."

An adoptive mother like May Jaberg, perhaps?

Minnie paused, eyes searching Lettie's. "I can see this troubles you greatly."

Lettie willed her pounding heart to slow. "If only I'd specified Amish parents . . . how much easier it would now be to find my child. My *daughter.*" Her words caught in her throat.

"Have you ever considered that she might not want to be found?" Minnie's words fell like stones to the ground. "What if she's not aware of her adoption?" Minnie patted Lettie's arm. "You might bring heartache, instead of joy, if you go knockin' on her door."

Samuel had brought this to her attention, as well, two weeks ago.

Lettie groaned softly. "I must seem awful selfish."

"Well, you surely feel cheated . . . having missed out on raising your child." Minnie offered a considerate smile. "But have you seriously considered your daughter in all of this?"

"Searching for her isn't only for *my* benefit." Lettie began to describe how Samuel's wife had died, leaving him alone and without offspring. "I wanted to somehow make up for keepin' the truth from him all this time. Wanted to help ease his sorrow . . . with the news of our child."

"I guess I don't understand."

"It's ever so complicated." The awkward turn in the conversation embarrassed Lettie further. Minnie seemed to indicate she'd done something wrong in wanting to find her daughter . . . for Samuel's sake. "I don't intend to be selfish." Lettie rose.

Minnie continued to frown, and Lettie felt increasingly chagrined as the seconds ticked by. Then at last, and with a slow breath, Minnie replied, "Turning this situation over to the Lord is the best suggestion I can make."

"Well, I've done that repeatedly . . . all these years."

Minnie's expression turned to disbelief. "If I may be so bold, I believe you're holdin' on to the past, embracing it longer than necessary," she said quietly. "Coming before God with hands filled and leaving with them empty . . . *that's* relinquishing control."

Lettie's lips parted, but she could not speak.

" '. . . Behold the handmaid of the Lord;

be it unto me according to thy word,' " Minnie quoted Scripture. "The mother of our Lord Jesus was truly a model of submission."

And I certainly am not, Lettie thought sadly.

"Ach, since I'm meddling already, I can't help but wonder if your mother has been a help to you in your struggle with these hidden things."

Lettie began to cry.

Minnie leaned near. "You've never forgiven her, have you?"

"She made me give my baby away," Lettie sobbed into her hands. "You must surely know she forced me to."

"You're not alone. Many girls have been coerced by their parents into doing the same."

"But you don't understand. I would've brought up my dear baby alone, Minnie. You must believe me."

Minnie slipped her arm around Lettie. "Let's stop and pray right now."

Before she could respond, Minnie had begun to lead out in a plea for divine guidance. "Please direct this precious, brokenhearted child of yours, dear Lord." She also asked for the will of God to be done, and while she prayed, Lettie thought of how confident she sounded — much more so than Lettie herself had ever been in prayer.

When Minnie finished, her eyes fluttered open, bright with tears.

Lettie said, "I can see why so many young women are drawn to you."

"I feel called to tend to the poor little lambs, wounded as they've been by wrong choices."

"Denki for takin' time for me, Minnie. Truly."

The midwife smiled. "Trust the Lord to lead you, Lettie. And I believe when you understand why your mother demanded what she did — for both you and for your child — you'll be ready to forgive her fully."

Lettie tensed at her words, unready to wipe away the painful memory even if she could muster up the forgiveness. She *had* offered it up to God, only to keep taking it back and harboring it — stuck now with the weight of the burden.

"I can't be more grateful to you." Lettie rose and walked with Minnie back toward the house.

Minnie looked her way. "You know where I am if you need anything more. Anything at all."

Lettie made her way to the horse and gave Molly a sugar cube before she untied her. Then from the lane, she waved again to

Minnie, who was still standing on the porch steps. Lettie gave the kindly woman a wistful smile. *I will long remember this day.*

"You can't mean it, Gracie." Adam held his frown for several seconds as he poured himself a glass of water before the noon meal. Then his solemn expression turned to a half smile. "I really hope you're pullin' my leg."

"No, seriously, we can use some of my money from Eli's to catch a train or a bus . . . or even hire Martin Puckett to drive us," Grace replied.

"I s'pose you think we'll bring Mamma right back?"

She brightened. "Why not?"

"Well, you aren't thinkin' straight. Ya can't just go out there hopin' to run into Mamma. Besides, what if you *do* find her and she doesn't want to come home? What then? It'd break your heart all over again."

She didn't know how to respond to that.

"The lambs are comin' on fast, in twos some days. It's a terrible idea to leave now." Adam pressed his straw hat down on his head. "Besides, I promised Priscilla I'd take her to the next work frolic with a bunch of other couples from our district."

Grace smirked. "Well, I s'pose Prissy

wouldn't like it much if you went off lookin' for Mamma, jah?"

"Well, say what ya want, but she's awful concerned 'bout Mamma goin' missing," Adam replied.

"Maybe *too* concerned?"

Adam's eyebrows shot up. "What's that supposed to mean?"

"Mamma's absence didn't seem to bother Henry much at all," she ventured.

Adam frowned. "Maybe if you'd stayed put with him, you would've found out what he *really* thinks."

"Ach, you know as well as I do that Henry has trouble opening his mouth."

"But you hardly gave him a chance." He grimaced. "According to Prissy, he talks a-plenty."

Just not to me . . .

Adam went on. "Henry's not the only one hurt over it. Prissy had high hopes for the four of us being extra-close family."

She knew that, all right. "But I'll still be her sister-in-law, even *not* marryin' Henry, if you go ahead with your wedding plans to her," she said. "Besides, are you sayin' it didn't matter that Henry and I weren't right for each other? That Prissy just wanted me to go ahead with a bad match?"

"Maybe you —"

"No, really. Is your sweetheart that thick-headed?" Immediately, she regretted saying it.

"Well, this is goin' nowhere, and mighty fast. And it ain't becomin' of you, Grace."

She felt bad — she hadn't meant to insult her closest brother's fiancée, but she found Prissy's meddling unbearable. "Aw, Adam . . ."

He raised his glass to his lips, emptying it all in a rush. Wiping his mouth on the back of his shirtsleeve, he said, "And another thing, too: It's obvious Joe's pushin' Yonnie off on you."

She'd hoped this wouldn't come up, especially now.

"Dat too." Adam frowned, catching her eye. "Mind you, Grace, I've nothin' against Yonnie, but if you accept him as a beau so soon after Henry, you're as fickle as Prissy says."

"You best be gettin' back to work," she suggested to keep the discussion from escalating further. Then, to try to smooth things over, she asked, "Would ya want a thermos of cold water to take along?"

His face was devoid of expression. "Sure, sister."

She hurried to open the cupboard beneath the sink and reached for the thermos, then ran the faucet, waiting for the cold water. "So . . . will Yonnie be stayin' for dinner again today?"

Adam peered out the screen door, his back to her. "What's a-matter? Does Yonnie talk *too* much for ya?" He chuckled and reached for the thermos before heading outside.

Relieved, Grace watched him go.

When Lettie passed the white house with the dark green shutters, she hurried the horse to a town trot. It wasn't until she'd made the turn past the dreaded corner that she began to feel calmer again. But the strain she'd experienced was far less than the turmoil inside her. Truth was, she carried around the burden of not only guilt but of self-centeredness, just as Minnie had so sympathetically pointed out. What if Lettie's first daughter *was* content with her adoptive family?

Do I want to upset her security for my own happiness? Or for Samuel's?

The idea her child might not have been adopted into an Amish home upset her as she rode back to Susan's. The springtime breeze blew right into the front of the carriage, against her bare feet.

Thinking of chillier weather, she recalled

a dreary and cold November Sisters Day a few years ago. She and her friend Sally Smucker had each taken their mothers to bake dozens of loaves of bread and pies at the bishop's wife's house. It was the start of wedding season, and the day was so cold Lettie had placed several hot bricks on the floor of Judah's carriage before piling heavy woolen lap robes on top of them. *"Enough to weigh us down to nothing,"* Mamm had said with a hearty laugh.

But the thing that stuck out in Lettie's memory was all the chatter among the women about an Amish couple waiting to adopt an infant. Her ears were antennas, and Mamm had glanced her way several times, till Lettie refused to look back. Oh, but the sting of loss had flown right back into her tender heart.

She refocused her attention on the road leading to Susan Kempf. By the time she arrived and unhitched Molly, then led her back to the barn, Susan was standing on the back stoop, waving.

Lettie looked at the sun's position, wishing she could simply snap her fingers and renew the past. If only wishful thinking could undo her failings. *My unwise choices . . . my sin.*

Hurrying across the yard, she could not

forget Minnie's disquieting remarks. *When I understand why Mamm did what she did,* Lettie thought, *then I'll forgive her.*

She brushed away the morning's visit while Susan carried the food to the table. Making her way to the sink, Lettie reached for the bar of homemade soap, wishing with all of her heart she could not only immerse her hands but bathe her soul, as well.

CHAPTER FIFTEEN

Grace stuck her pointer finger beneath her Kapp to scratch her head. She momentarily turned her back to Mandy to watch Yonnie return to the barn with Adam and Joe after dinner. He'd had a toothpick in his mouth when he'd caught her eye and smiled broadly before leaving through the kitchen door with her brothers. Now he fiddled with it as he walked, talking especially to Adam. Together, they heaved open the barn door and disappeared inside, Joe following behind.

Mandy interrupted her thoughts. "Do you want to wash or dry?"

"I'll dry." Quickly Grace went to gather up all the dirty utensils left scattered around the table. Despite what he'd said, it was hard to understand why Yonnie was hanging around all day. Was Dat paying him to help, or was he volunteering?

Just then Mamma's place at the table

caught her eye, the seat Grace had so timidly claimed. She'd wondered while serving and eating her dinner of fried salmon patties, mashed potatoes, and coconut squash what Yonnie thought of it. Had he even recognized what she'd done? As unconventional as his family was, perhaps he didn't realize there was a seating arrangement at their table.

And why should I care what he thinks?

"You comin' to my room again tonight to pray for Mamma?" asked Mandy as she dipped two plates in the hot rinse water.

"Sure."

Mandy was silent for a moment as she went on washing one plate after another. Then she said more quietly, "Do you think prayer changes the Lord's mind 'bout things?"

Grace straightened a bit. "I only know what the Scripture says: We're called to pray for God's will to be done on earth as it is in heaven. You remember the Lord's Prayer?"

"But isn't God's will goin' to be done no matter what?"

Grace pondered that. "I 'spect if we knew such hard answers, we might consider ourselves equal with our heavenly Father. And you know what happened to one so-

and-so who got all puffed up with pride like that."

"Jah, pride goeth before a fall."

Grace gathered up a handful of clean utensils and laid them out to air-dry on the table as Mandy hummed a church hymn behind her, seemingly content with her sister's answer.

Glancing out the window now, Grace saw a young woman and a middle-aged man walking along the road toward the Spanglers'. She moved closer to the window and realized it was Heather Nelson walking with an Englischer about Dat's age. "Wait just a minute, Mandy." Grace tossed the tea towel on the table and ran out the door.

It was a warm, bright day, the kind she liked to go wading in Mill Creek, across the road. But now she stood barefoot in the driveway, waving. "Heather . . . is that you?" she called, hoping it was indeed her new friend. The slender girl tugged gently at the man's wrist, and they began to walk up the driveway toward Grace.

Despite her initial exuberance, Grace felt suddenly shy in the presence of this clean-shaven man in dark blue jeans and a pale blue shirt, sleeves rolled up. Up close, he looked older than Dat — early to mid-fifties, she guessed — with hair and eyes nearly the same color as Heather's. He radiated poise and well-being.

"Grace, I'd like you to meet my father, Roan Nelson."

Grace returned his cordial smile as he reached to shake her hand. "Hullo, I'm Grace Byler. I can certainly see you're father and daughter, you look so much alike."

Heather grinned at her father.

"Very nice to meet you, Grace," Mr. Nelson said. "Heather's been telling me about meeting you at the local natural food store."

"Oh . . . jah. I enjoyed our chat very much."

"Grace 'lives neighbors' to the Riehls', as Becky likes to say," Heather replied, the highlights in her light brown hair shining gold in the sunlight.

"I see," Mr. Nelson said, eyes twinkling.

"I ran out hopin' to catch you . . . so we can plan our visit to Sally Smucker."

Heather pushed her thick hair behind one ear. "Great. I was hoping."

"Does the day after tomorrow suit ya?"

"Okay with you, Dad?" Heather asked. "Do you have anything planned for Sunday?"

"Don't worry about me, kiddo. I can manage alone for a few hours," Mr. Nelson said,

205

offering a smile to Grace. "You girls go and have your fun."

"Sounds good," Heather said. "How about that morning?" Then, quickly, she frowned and shook her head. "Wait. I wasn't thinking — don't you attend church on Sundays, Grace?"

"Ev'ry other Lord's Day we go to Preaching service — same as the Riehls."

"Are you members of the same group?" Mr. Nelson asked.

"Jah, my parents joined this church years ago — long before I was born."

"Then your preacher must be Josiah Smucker?" Heather asked.

"That's right . . . Sally's husband."

Excitedly, Heather told her father, "Your building contractor is Grace's minister." Then to Grace she said just as animatedly, "Josiah's building my father's new house, up the road."

Simultaneously they turned to look toward the north as Heather pointed in the direction of the newly purchased land. "We'll soon be neighbors," Mr. Nelson said. "Well, at least *I* will be." He reached an arm around his daughter's shoulders.

"Then let me be the first to say it: Will-kumm to the neighborhood." Grace almost said "our neighborhood," but it was one thing for a modern family like the Spanglers to have lived amongst them for many years. *But for Englischers to move in from out of state?*

"I'll come over after dinner Sunday, then, if that's all right," Grace said.

"Dinner? Let's see — at noon, right?"

Grace nodded. "Some folk call suppertime dinner and dinnertime lunch." She laughed, feeling much more relaxed with the two of them than at first. "Mandy and I'll put on a light spread for my father and brothers. Mandy's my sister — maybe you'd like to meet her sometime."

"Terrific."

"Oh, and I'd like to show you my herb garden, too. Herbs are pretty easy to grow, and so many have healing properties."

Heather glanced in the direction of the backyard. "I'd love a tour of your garden."

"Maybe next week?"

Heather looked tentative, glancing quickly at her father. "Uh, since I might be unavailable the week after that . . . maybe that's a good idea."

"*Gut,* then."

"Actually, Monday's fine. And I'll see you Sunday after dinner at the Riehls', too," Heather added. "Well, we'd better finish up our walk. Nice seeing you, Grace." Heather and her dad headed back toward the road.

Grace recalled Becky's assessment of her acquaintance with Heather. *She doesn't seem distant at all — quite the contrary.* Grace fleetingly wished she could fall into step with the Nelsons and continue the pleasant conversation. But Mandy was expecting help with the dishes. "Enjoy your walk," she called after them.

Heather and her father turned and waved again.

When Grace was back in the house, she told Mandy her plans. "I'm goin' to spend some time with the Riehls' long-term boarder Sunday afternoon." She waited for Mandy's reply, but oddly enough her sister was quiet. Grace continued, "What do ya think Dat would say 'bout us showing someone fancy the herb garden?"

Mandy shrugged. "Ask him."

"What's a-matter, sister?"

"Honestly, Grace — lately you've been runnin' off and leaving all the redding up to me."

Grace sighed. "It's becoming a chore to keep everyone happy round here."

Mandy scrunched up her nose. "*Sei net so rilpsich* — Don't be so rude!"

"Sorry, Mandy," Grace said softly. "Maybe an afternoon apart will do us both *gut.*"

■ ■ ■ ■

Once the dishes were dried and put away and the floor swept, Grace rushed out to the barn to check on Willow. She glanced at her herb garden on the way and decided the plot could use a close weeding before Heather came by on Monday.

Then, going to the part of the barn that served as the horse stable, she slipped in the back entrance to avoid running into Yonnie. Crouching low, she stroked Willow's neck, talking softly to her. "How're you doin'?" Grace ran her hand down the mare's leg, just as she'd seen her father and Yonnie do. She gave her a sugar cube and caressed her long, beautiful nose, hoping for the best. "Don't give up, ol' girl," she said before she left to return to the house, heading for Mammi Adah's sewing room.

Picking up the two pieces of the pattern, Grace sat down at the old trundle sewing machine. First she sewed the dress seams, pulling the straight pins out at well-spaced intervals and pressing them between her lips.

At last she had the long seams sewn and next, the waistband. When that was done, she glanced at the day clock on the east

209

wall, deciding she would not have time to finish the handwork before she needed to begin the evening meal. But she felt pleased with all she had accomplished, as well as a bit surprised Mammi Adah hadn't poked her head in to see how she was coming along.

Monday afternoon she hoped to make time for Mammi's fitting so that she could mark the hems for the sleeves and the dress itself. *Once all the washing is done and hung out to dry.* Grace rose and moved to the window, taking in the lovely day, and raised the window to let in the fresh air. Her eyes caught sight of a piece of paper taped to the wall; numerous names of birds and descriptions of their songs were written in pencil.

Mammi Adah had placed the list there when she and Dawdi had first moved to Beechdale Road — a list similar to Mamma's downstairs. A veritable register of pure joy for the birdwatchers in the family.

Grace hung up Mammi Adah's dress and placed the hanger carefully on the wooden peg across the room. The seams could be pressed flat with her gas-fired iron before Monday's fitting.

Thinking again of her family's love of birds, she hurried down to check on the mourning dove feeding trays Dat had set up for Mamma. She'd have to see about their other bird feeders, as well. It had been nearly a week since she'd done so, and she blamed her negligence on being scatter-brained of late. *So much to do with Mamma gone.* It was a good thing she no longer had a serious beau to busy her up. Preacher Josiah had emphasized in a recent sermon that it was better for courting-age girls not to be so concerned with marriage as a goal, but rather to think on having life hereaf-ter . . . getting into the kingdom of God.

Grace saw the wisdom in this caution. Nearly all of her girl cousins were overly enthusiastic about getting married and starting their families. Mandy, too, seemed preoccupied with courting. It was hardly surprising when they were trained from early on to become wives and mothers. There was little else for an Amishwoman to do, since education past eighth grade was forbidden and any sort of skilled job was taboo. Even so, Grace was unexpectedly glad to be free of any hope of marriage.

As she filled the trays with seed, she wondered when Dat might be assigned to have Preaching service here again at the house. Secretly, she hoped it wouldn't be for quite a while yet, since Mamma's ab-sence was so painful. Not only for her and the family, but for all the womenfolk. Her mother had done something most wives and mothers amongst the People would never consider. True, most folk — like Marian Riehl and Mamma's many sisters — had been quite considerate, choosing not to bring up what they already knew. *And what they surely dread, all of them.* Yet deep down, the silence troubled Grace. *It's almost as if they're acting like nothing's wrong,* she thought sadly.

Yonnie startled her, standing as he was a few feet away from the finches' bird feeder. "Hullo, Grace. Need some help?" he asked.

She didn't really, although the seed bag was a bit heavy. "You can carry the seed if ya want."

He quickly took it from her. "We've had some unusual birds comin' up to our feeders at home. Looked nearly like seabirds to me."

"Seabirds?" She smiled, catching his eye.

"Jah." He smiled back. "Have you ever been to the ocean?"

"No," she said, surprised.

"I have," he said, his blue eyes alight. "Just once."

Suddenly, she felt incredibly curious. "When were you there?"

"My Dat surprised Mamm last summer. She'd always wanted to go swimming." He grinned. "But that's another story."

"Oh?"

He looked sheepish. "Well, she doesn't own a swimming suit. . . ."

Grace couldn't help it; she laughed. "Ya mean she wore her dress and apron in swimming?"

"I didn't say that, no." He paused. "My father figured out something modest . . . that's all I know."

Grace felt as if she'd somehow crossed a line. It was strange talking so openly with him.

Yonnie held the seed bag while Grace dipped her cup inside. He leaned closer as she sprinkled the birdseed into the feeder. "I went looking for seashells with my sister Mary Liz and three of our younger brothers," he said. "We all went searching up and down the beach for sand dollars, and I stumbled onto a marble-sized Cape May diamond without even tryin'."

"A real diamond?"

"Not at all," he was quick to say. "But it does look something like crystal."

She'd seen crystal goblets at the Spanglers' house, in the dining room hutch.

"You can almost see through it," Yonnie

added. "It's mighty perty."

"Could you show it to me sometime?"

His eyes twinkled. "Why, sure."

Grace could scarcely believe this. Yonnie had gone to the ocean with his family and had nature's souvenirs to prove it!

They finished filling all the feeders, then walked to the potting shed where Dat kept the sweet syrup for Mamma's hummingbird feeders. Together, they filled those, too.

All the while Grace kept glancing toward Becky's house, hoping she wouldn't decide to drop by and stumble onto this too-pleasant scene. No telling what she'd presume was going on here in Grace's backyard.

Lettie was hungry and wishing she might help Susan in the kitchen. The gracious and cheerful hostess had thus far refused Lettie's offers to cook and bake. "No, no, I want to treat *you*," Susan said again as they sat down to an early supper, her face beaming. "You have no idea the joy such *gut* company brings me."

After the prayer, Lettie passed her the steaming stroganoff casserole. "Well, it's a blessing for me, too." She hadn't breathed a word to Susan yet, but now that she had Dr. Josh's name, she'd soon be on her way.

But first she must write a letter to Cousin Hallie, asking if she might be able to visit her. After all, her cousin might wonder why she hadn't heard from Lettie in more than a month, and she didn't want to show up on her doorstep, unannounced, just because she was kin. So by Tuesday or Wednesday — assuming Hallie wrote back immediately — Lettie would know if it suited for her to come for a day or so. *Just till I talk to Dr. Josh,* she thought.

For now, though, Lettie could simply relax and enjoy Susan's delicious meal. If things fell into place, she might just find her daughter — if Minnie had remembered correctly and her child was indeed a girl. Of course, it might take some doing to convince a grown woman to travel to Kidron to meet her biological father. *Samuel . . .*

She must not get into a tizzy, contemplating such things. Taking one day at a time had brought her this far. "I'll clean up the kitchen for you — how's that?" Lettie offered, dishing up more chowchow. "Since you're doin' all the hard work."

"Actually, cookin's fun." Susan smiled as she leaned forward on the table. "I don't even mind the redding up. My husband used to tease me that I worked too hard . . . liked to have things all shiny and clean.

Nearly before he was finished eatin', I'd be pulling his plate out from under his nose."

Lettie chuckled. She had done the same thing to Judah.

"Oh, how I miss Vernon." Susan continued talking, sharing about her life with her late husband. "He was the deacon here in our district for years . . . he never could understand why the Lord God chose him."

" 'Tis a sobering thing, the lot."

Susan agreed. "He took his divine appointment seriously. Really took it to heart — just as he did our marriage."

"Sounds like you were a wonderful-*gut* match, then." Lettie didn't want to press, yet each time Susan spoke of Vernon, it was impossible not to notice the light in her eyes. She had clearly loved her now-deceased husband. "Was he your first beau?"

"Honestly, there were several fellas I was fond of . . . and one I hoped to marry." Susan glanced out the window. "Vernon and I worked hard to make our love grow, even flourish. But it took a period of years."

Lettie was surprised to hear this. "Did your first beau marry someone else?"

"He certainly did — and such a long story 'tis, and rather pointless now." Susan rose

216

to get the lemon pound cake she'd baked. She sighed, undoubtedly reminiscing over the years as she placed the cake on the table. "I'll tell you this, Lettie: I'm glad I didn't wait to let Vernon know how much I cared for him. If he'd passed away, not knowin' . . ." She glanced at the empty chair at the head of the table, a faraway look in her eyes. "Might seem odd to honor him like this, but I'll let nary a soul sit in that seat right there."

Lettie recalled her relationship with Judah. Some years had been better than others, but they had never enjoyed the kind of marriage Susan and Vernon had. She felt humbled . . . even a little awed. "Denki for sharing with me."

"Happy to." Susan rose to cut a generous slice of cake and placed it on Lettie's plate. "I hope you found Minnie all right."

"Jah . . . it was wonderful talkin' with her."

"So you're in the family way, then?"

Lettie's fork dropped to her plate. "Ach, no!"

"I just thought . . . your urgency to find a particular midwife, ya know . . . maybe you'd had good experience with Minnie and wanted her again."

Good experience . . . She literally shuddered. The birth of her first baby had been difficult at best. "No, I'm not having a baby."

Susan took a bite of her cake. "All right, then."

But it wasn't all right, because Lettie felt she wasn't holding up her side of the growing friendship. A friendship that, while most likely short-lived, was becoming a balm to her soul. Susan had been forthright with *her,* but Lettie had clammed up when things got too personal. She just couldn't imagine airing her dirty laundry. *I'm as proud as I am selfish,* she realized. Ashamed, she determined to help out round here, as much as Susan would allow. Dear woman, she deserved as much.

CHAPTER SIXTEEN

As usual, Martin Puckett was right on time that Saturday after dinner. Grace stood at the end of their driveway and Beechdale Road, waiting. It was time to buy in two weeks' worth of groceries at Eli's, as she often did on a Saturday when not working at the store. *As Mamma and I always did.* Using the van to haul the many store-bought items was the best way to handle the bi-monthly chore.

"Hullo," she said when Martin greeted her.

"Looks like nice weather all weekend," he said, bobbing his head.

She still couldn't get it out of her mind that Martin had been the last person she knew who'd seen her mother. Somehow it made her feel tenderhearted toward him. "It's goin' to be mostly sunny, Dat says."

Then, just as Martin reached to slide open the passenger door of the van, Yonnie came running down the driveway, waving his straw hat and calling, "Wait up. I need a ride!"

What on earth? Grace couldn't hide her surprise as he hopped into the second-row seat right next to her. *Why not up front with Martin?*

She was taken aback by his bold, if not overly friendly manner. It was fine for him to help Dat with the lambs and her, with the birds . . . but hailing down the same van?

While Martin moseyed around to get into the driver's seat, Yonnie asked, "Will ya go walkin' with me tomorrow afternoon, Grace?"

Of all things!

She was befuddled, especially because he'd taken her walking several times last year before doing the same with a number of girls. He had spent more time with Becky than any of them, though.

"I'm busy tomorrow," she said, thinking about her plans with Heather.

"Another day, maybe?" he asked, his expression hopeful.

If she waited long enough, Martin would open his door and get her off the hook — at least for now.

"Where are the two of you headed?" Martin asked as he climbed into the driver's seat. He glanced over his shoulder at Yonnie.

"We're not actually together," Yonnie said, flashing her another quick smile. "I'm heading home, and I'm not sure where Grace's goin'."

Since Yonnie typically remained to help Dat till closer to supper, Grace was even more perplexed by his decision to head home early. Why? To ask her to go walking with him? *How many girls does he need to walk with, for goodness' sake?*

Martin peered at them in the rearview mirror. "Since Yonnie's house is on the way, we'll stop there first. That is, after we pick up Miss Becky. She needs a ride to Eli's, as well."

Oh no! Everything Grace had said to assure her friend about Yonnie would be down the drain now. She was trapped — literally — between the window and Yonnie in the second row. And if Becky laid eyes on them sitting there, with Yonnie in back instead of up front, where most men sat when there was only one young woman in the van, Becky would never believe Grace.

They pulled in the Riehls' lane and stopped at the back walkway. Becky was already coming around to the side of the vehicle, carrying a large wicker basket, and Grace wanted to shrink into her seat. And then it happened: Just as Becky was about to get in, she spotted Yonnie, her startled gaze darting from Grace to Yonnie and back again.

Grace offered a warm smile, but poor Becky was staring at the front seat, a puzzled look on her sweet face. Then, right quick, she lowered her head to look at her feet as she waited for Martin to slide open the door. Her face and neck were growing redder with each second. *She has every reason to fume,* Grace thought, wondering what Yonnie might say when Becky had to squeeze past him to get to the backseat.

"Hullo, Becky," Yonnie said cheerfully. But Becky remained silent as she got settled behind them in the third row.

Grace was mortified.

No doubt Becky was fretting, her eyes mining a hole into Grace's back.

The air was thick with tension; Grace felt her neck might snap. She honestly was sorry for Becky. What could she say to smooth things over with her friend?

I should've gone shopping yesterday! Grace thought, mentally counting the dairy cows in Andy Riehl's pasture as they rode in silence. Then she counted the pickets on the white fence as they passed the deacon's front yard. She recalled shucking corn there on the screened-in porch behind the house with Becky and her family. The pair had attempted to smoke a hand-rolled cigar Becky had "borrowed" from Dawdi Riehl, and they'd nearly choked to death. Or so they thought. With a smile, Marian Riehl had simply said, *"Love allows for plenty of forgiveness."*

The Lord says to forgive repeatedly. Yet Grace wondered if Becky ever would forgive this.

Martin stopped at the Bontrager family's gray stone house and came around to open the door, even though Yonnie needed no help getting out. "Have a nice day, Grace . . . Becky," said Yonnie, offering each a pleasing smile and a nod.

"You too," Grace answered out of sheer habit. Again Becky said nothing, although her breath was now coming in short little gasps. Grace wanted to turn around and insist that Becky move up beside her. But Martin was already closing his door up front and putting the van into gear.

Yonnie must think he can flit in and out of our lives without a single consequence.

She recalled his eager, if not jovial expression, when he'd first entered the van. Had he been watching for his chance to ride with her? She hardly thought it possible that he'd had time to wait around the barn, peering out at her.

Yonnie came around and knocked on Martin's window, his face flushed with what looked to be embarrassment. "Won't ya let me pay you for the ride?" he asked. But as Grace expected, Martin refused anything for such a short trip, and Yonnie nodded his thanks.

Grace noticed his younger sister Mary Liz, raking the side yard and wearing a dark blue kerchief wound around her head. Mary Liz had once tried to explain to Becky her brother's plan to find the "perfect girl" to court and marry. To think his own sister must've considered Yonnie's odd plan a legitimate one — nothing peculiar about it. To Grace, this had been one of the first indications the whole Bontrager family was cut from a different fabric, even though they'd transferred their church membership here soon after arriving.

Martin backed the van up the tree-lined drive all the way out to the main road. Still feeling tense about Becky, Grace kept her face forward, staring at the Bontragers' white rose trellis attached to the side of the house. She recalled going there with

Mamma and Mandy, too, taking dozens of cookies, several loaves of bread, and a sour cream spice cake to the womenfolk's initial welcoming get-together when Ephram Bontrager and his family joined church. They'd found the then-rented house to be thoroughly modern — Yonnie's father had gotten permission from the bishop to keep the electric wiring intact. But after a few months, when the English landlord allowed them to lease to own, Ephram had hired Preacher Josiah and a few other men to tear it all out. As owners, they were prohibited to use it. *'Tis a riddle,* Grace thought, *how they could use the home's electricity only as renters.*

Grace had never dreamed then she would be experiencing Yonnie's unashamed attention today . . . with Becky observing it firsthand, no less. She could only hope her friend would believe her side of the story.

But when Martin stopped to drop them off at the entrance to Eli's, Becky scrambled out of the van ahead of Grace. "I won't be needin' a ride home," Becky told Martin. She opened her purse and quickly pulled out her dollar bills, not waiting for Martin to say the amount.

Ach, is she ever miffed!

"Becky . . . wait!" Grace called after her,

but Becky was making a beeline for the store's entrance. "You don't understand," she added softly, more to herself than to her friend. *This wasn't my doing!*

When she turned, she saw Martin, still waiting near the van. His expression was concerned. "When would you like me to return for you, Grace?"

"An hour or so?" She motioned to the spot where she would wait for him to pick her up. "All right?"

"I'll meet you there." He moved back to the driver's side of the van.

"Denki," Grace said, feeling mighty glum as she headed into Eli's.

Martin Puckett had found it tricky keeping his chuckles in check when Yonnie had hopped in next to Grace as if they were a couple. But the drama had heightened when Riehls' girl came on the scene, and by the end of the drive, he'd felt downright sorry for Becky in particular.

Now that he'd deposited them at their respective destinations, he could hardly wait to get home to tell Janet. Why, this was nearly like the romance novels his wife enjoyed reading! She often sat up late in bed reading one such book after another.

Which of those girls will end up with that

young man? Although he'd seen Yonnie only once or twice before, he'd recognized him immediately, thanks to his striking blond hair — nearly an extension of his yellow straw hat.

Martin relaxed as he drove to the next passengers' home, dismissing the Amish young people for now. On the way, he turned on the radio, curious about the weather forecast. "Pleasant temperatures in the low seventies," the DJ reported. "No rain in sight."

A trial for the farmers if this keeps up. He wondered if his Mennonite neighbors up the road had observed the seventh-year rest on their vegetable garden, as instructed in the Old Testament book of Leviticus. Martin hadn't wanted to gawk over the thick hedge surrounding their property to see. But his wife, Janet, had mentioned some months ago that the neighbor's oldest son had talked of "trusting Jehovah God" during the resting of their small parcel of land. Martin didn't know anyone else — Amish or English — who observed this Sabbath rest of their land.

Martin had been contemplating the idea of observing a sabbatical rest himself, though in other areas of life. If it was good for the land, why not for people? Why was it many did not heed even the concept of resting from work on the Lord's Day . . . or at least one day a week?

He made a point of noting the time, wanting to be punctual for his return to pick up Grace Byler, who seemed to be coping fairly well with her mother gone.

Shifting gears, he couldn't imagine what might transpire in the natural foods store between Grace and her friend Becky — if they managed to speak to each other.

Grace bumped into Becky in the first aisle at Eli's, near the bulk foods of oatmeal and nuts. Her face looked like she'd eaten a jar of sour pickles.

Grace grimaced at Becky's apparent disdain. *I've got to explain to her!* But Becky ignored her and pushed her cart right past her at every juncture, keeping her eyes fixed straight ahead.

What can I say if she does stop to talk? Grace could only offer the truth, but she doubted it would be enough to convince Becky of her innocence. And since Becky was clearly in no mood to be agreeable, Grace had no recourse but to slump into silence.

Later, in the far check-out lane, Grace noticed Becky talking with several women from their church district. Becky glanced at her only once, catching her eye before looking quickly away.

Cheerless, Grace sighed. This was ever so petty. After all, if Becky sensibly considered the whole situation, she would realize Grace had not made plans to go anywhere with Yonnie — not when he was dropped off at his house and Grace had gone on to Eli's.

"Isn't it obvious?" she muttered while removing the baking items from her cart to the moving belt for the cashier. There was ample flour and salt for the next two weeks, as well as wheat germ, bran, cornmeal, molasses, and two large jars of mayonnaise, steak sauce, and a few other prepared items Dat liked to have on hand. She'd also purchased fifty pounds of unrefined sugar — in twenty-five-pound bags — in preparation for canning, coming up. Their healthy strawberry patch produced well, and she was looking forward to all the delicious jam she and Mandy were sure to make. *Mammi Adah, too.*

One final glance at Becky confirmed there would be no talking to her here. It would have to wait till later.

Outside, as she waited for Martin to return, Grace saw Priscilla Stahl coming into the store. A glance at her buggy revealed Henry sitting there, whittling while he waited for his sister.

Grace was conscious of his eyes on her from his parking spot right next to Becky's sister-in-law's buggy. Grace recognized the team by the older Morgan chestnut mare with her distinguishable white sock.

Grace hoped Martin might return quickly. She was uncomfortable, not wanting to speak to Henry and still feeling bad about Becky.

The sight of Yonnie's parents driving up in their family buggy, the seat crowded with their three school-age children, distracted her. *Yonnie's youngest siblings . . .*

It was hard not to stare as Ephram helped his wife out of the buggy, offering his hand to Irene, even though she was quite capable of stepping down onto the sidewalk herself. He leaned near to speak to her, and a long, sweet look passed between them. Grace tried to remember when — if ever — she'd witnessed such tenderness between a man and a woman. She certainly did not recall seeing this kind of unspoken affection between her own parents, even as far back as her childhood. *Truly surprising!*

Irene waited while Ephram helped the children down, patting each of their heads. *Ephram surely is fond of his family.*

Grace wondered if Yonnie might not be similar in disposition to his father. Then she caught herself — *why should I care about that?* Even so, her eyes were fixed on Ephram as he happily waved to Irene and the children, then got back into the buggy and picked up the reins to direct the horse to the parking area reserved for Amish.

Just then Martin pulled up and stopped. Grace was greatly relieved. She looked all around for Becky, in case she'd changed her mind and wanted to ride back with them, but she was nowhere to be seen.

After Martin helped her unload her groceries from the cart to the back of the van, she climbed inside and replayed in her mind the public affection between Yonnie's parents and their children. *No wonder Becky's disappointed,* Grace thought, wondering if Yonnie treated every girl as thoughtfully as he had Becky. *And me.*

CHAPTER SEVENTEEN

The van neared the Riehls', and Grace noticed Heather Nelson and her father sitting on the front porch with Marian and several of Becky's younger sisters. Had Heather told Becky that she and her father had encountered Grace on the road yesterday? *Oh . . . I wish I could've talked to Becky today!*

Another moment, and Dat's big farmhouse came into view. As Martin pulled up close to the side door, Joe and Mandy came running from the barn to help carry in the groceries. Once everything was inside, Grace dug into her purse for the payment.

"Have you heard anything more from your mother?" Martin asked as she counted out the bills.

"Just the one phone call Mamma made to you last month . . . and a recent letter."

His worried expression eased. "Ah . . . then you must know where she is."

"Well, we know where she *was*." She assumed he was making small talk — not quite as troubled as he'd seemed when Mamma first departed.

"Glad to hear she's keeping in touch." He waved as he headed back to the driveway. "Have a good Lord's Day tomorrow."

"You too." She hurried inside to find Mandy already putting things into the pantry. "I'll finish up if you need to get back to the barn," she offered.

"Denki. Another set of twin lambs was just birthed," Mandy told her, "so I should return to Dat right quick."

Grace sighed. If she stopped long enough to be honest with herself, there was no way her father would agree to let Adam or any other sibling go with her to look for Mamma now. Between the lambing and all the farm work the season brought, she doubted she'd ever find the time to seek her missing mother.

Heather had spent most of Saturday with her dad, driving around the back roads to see several of Josiah Smucker's recent houses. Most were Amish, built without the modern conveniences Josiah and others would definitely incorporate into her father's home. But several had been constructed for modern families using the ancient timber-frame technique — no nails required. It seemed clear that Amish contractors were second to none when it came to careful craftsmanship. And their strong work ethic and discounted bids were also appealing.

She and her dad had gone to look at custom cabinetry, as well, deciding on the type of wood and style for the kitchen and bathrooms. They were wowed by the skill of an Amish carpenter in Ronks and easily came to an agreement on the warm hues of maple. The minute the blueprints were finished, which would be soon, Dad planned to hand-carry them to the cabinetmaker. Josiah had urged them to have the cabinets made as soon as possible to expedite things, especially if Dad wanted to move in by midsummer.

So much had been accomplished in a few hours — they'd even taken time for a sit-down lunch at Dienner's, an Amish-Mennonite restaurant on Route 30.

Marian Riehl and her guests had referred to the delicious buffet several times. As it turned out, the place was jammed with Plain folk and tourists alike, and her dad had raved about the "seven sweets and seven sours" salad bar. Both of them had overeaten, nearly helpless to stop going back for more of the delicious food.

Now, as she and her dad sat with Marian on her peaceful porch, sipping root beer, Heather realized that, since her dad's arrival, she'd forgotten about her new online pal, Wannalive. *Dad sure knows how to fill a girl's days. . . .*

Relaxing in her porch chair, she enjoyed the sweep of fields to the east and north. In the front lawn, Becky's younger sisters giggled and ran barefoot back and forth, playing hide-and-seek. Three kittens — one pure white, one a gray tabby, and the smallest a black kitten with a white throat — frolicked about and occasionally stopped to stretch their little heads high when Becky's youngest sister, Sarah, tickled their necks. Heather could just imagine the contented purring rumbling up from each fuzzy tummy. How she missed the twin black Persians waiting for her back home!

Becky was gone from the house — according to Marian, she was out running errands. The girls came scampering toward the house again, Sarah running with the girls' obvious favorite of the kittens in her arms. Breathlessly, they sat on the porch steps to have homemade root beer and several oatmeal cookies, too.

"Mamma?" said Sarah as she stroked the kitten's shiny black coat. "Did Lettie Byler die? I never see her anymore."

Marian made a little gasp and rose from the lawn chair, and Rachel tugged on Sarah's apron, eyes wide. "Don't be sayin' that, sister."

Reaching for the empty serving plate, Marian muttered something about getting more cookies. "Come along, now, girls," she directed as she reached for the screen door.

Lettie? Who does she mean? Heather wondered. Grace's last name was Byler, too. Was Sarah speaking of someone in *that* Byler household?

"I never see her anymore," Sarah had said. Heather shivered, suddenly wishing she'd worn her jersey.

She was about to go inside to get it when Dad broke the silence. "Have you thought more about going home for your treatment, Heather?" Apparently he hadn't paid any attention to the odd reaction little Sarah's question had provoked.

Heather shifted in her chair. "Dad, no. I don't want to poison my innards."

"Honey, I'd be happy to talk to your oncologist . . . with you."

"I've already talked to him."

He scratched his head. "To put it bluntly,

236

I don't feel good about your running out on your doctor. This isn't like you at all. You've always been so responsible."

Running out?

"It's not like he's God, you know." She shook her head. "Dad, I know what I'm doing seems irrational to you, even crazy, but I really want to explore this natural option first. But don't worry — I'll get a second opinion after giving the lodge program a shot."

He gave her a measured look. "So you haven't ruled out standard medical treatment if it should become necessary?"

Heather shook her head and waited for another challenge. But he surprised her, turning to look out at the green of cornfields and grazing land and saying no more.

Her yummasetti casserole of noodles, ground beef, and peas was nestled in the oven, so Grace ran out to check on Willow. She noticed someone had recently applied yet another coating of the liniment Yonnie had mixed and left nearby. *Adam or Joe must be rubbing it on every few hours.*

Even more encouraging was the sight of Willow on her feet, eating — though still favoring the hurt leg. "Ach, just look at you. You're improving. This is so wonderful-*gut!*"

Grace slipped a sugar cube into the horse's mouth when Willow nuzzled her arm. "What would the vet say if he saw ya now?" She patted the mare's neck, then left for the sheep barn to look for her father.

"Dat just headed for the house," Adam said, leaning on his hay fork. "Why do you need him?"

"Just want to ask him something."

Adam wiped his forehead and set the fork aside. "By the way, I talked to Priscilla 'bout what you asked me. I ran into her this morning when I went to Stahls' to return an old saw after breakfast."

"Oh?" Holding her breath, she wondered if he'd just maybe changed his mind about going with her.

"Prissy said she didn't know what *gut* could possibly come of lookin' for Mamma."

Not surprising. Grace turned away, but before she could leave, Adam touched her shoulder.

"Wait, there's more." He removed his straw hat and, tucking it under his arm, roughed up his hair. "I don't know how to tell ya this, really. . . . Prissy said she's heard through the grapevine that the fellas in our church district are wary 'bout . . . well, inviting you to go ridin'." He lowered his hat back onto his head. "They say you split up with Henry for no reason."

"Such news travels too fast." But Grace no longer felt glib. For a second or two, she actually felt heartsick. "The fellas must be talkin' because Mamma left Dat. . . . And since I'm her daughter . . ."

"Could be." His eyes softened. "I thought you should know what's bein' said, is all."

"You mean what *Prissy* says?" She stared at her toes, her hands shoved in her dress pockets. "You know I wouldn't behave like Mamma, so why are you tellin' me this?"

"I care about ya, Gracie . . . don't want you to end up a Maidel, takin' care of Dat and our grandparents, 'stead of having your own family."

"It's not because of Yonnie comin' here every day?" she blurted before thinking.

"Listen, Gracie, 'tween you and me, I'd say you best be payin' attention to Yonnie, no matter what I said before. I've been observing him, and he seems like a nice enough fella."

You said the same about Henry.

She stuck out her neck. "Yonnie didn't put you up to this, did he?"

" 'Course not." Adam wrinkled his face. "If you ain't careful, Gracie, you'll be a castoff for the rest of your life."

She thought on that. "You mean like the

brethren will do to Mamma?"

Adam frowned and reached for her arm to guide her into a more private area of the sheep barn. "What are you sayin', sister? Have you heard rumblings 'bout the Bann?"

She shook her head. "It's just that it's bound to happen sooner or later."

"Well, I don't know of the brethren callin' for any membership meeting just yet."

"How long will they wait?"

"We can't know that." Adam wore a concerned look. "Is the fear of the shun the reason you want to find Mamma?"

"Ach, I dread even the thought. . . ." A great sob escaped her and she covered her face with her hands.

"Are you cryin' over Mamma now?" he asked softly. "Or for yourself?"

"I just miss her so."

Adam looked away. "Well, you're not the only one."

"I need to be alone now." With that Grace ran back to Willow, to wrap her arms around the dear mare's neck. All the while she brooded over Adam's remark: *You best be payin' attention to Yonnie.*

Chapter Eighteen

It was late that Saturday afternoon when Judah moseyed indoors and leaned against the kitchen counter to catch his breath. He'd labored since before dawn this morning and was eager to sit and relax . . . and eat. Looking at the wall clock, he calculated how much time remained before supper. It was clear by the looks of things that he'd have to wait awhile.

Rubbing his beard, he was glad to be by himself. He reached for the cupboard and removed the first large plastic glass his callused fingers touched and turned on the faucet, letting it run. He filled the tumbler to the brim and gulped down the cold water. Then yet another full glass, straight down.

He held it in his hand for a second or two, then set the glass down and went to the sitting room. He eyed Lettie's corner cupboard, with its string of teacups and saucers, and turned away. The light from the front room windows beckoned him, and he peered out, wincing at the sight of her porch swing.

The bishop's words at last Tuesday's meeting played over in his memory. *"Your wife's leaving is becoming a predicament for the People,"* Bishop had voiced sternly. That was bad enough, but Judah knew he hadn't spoken up on her behalf like he could have. *Like a loving husband would.* But then again, he had no inkling where she'd gone, aside from Grace's talk of an inn and the Ohio postmark on Lettie's terse letter. Or why she'd left. The latter was the worst of it — having no way to understand what his wife was thinking or feeling. *Is she still pained over our last talk together?* How he regretted bringing that conversation to a premature end. Unnecessarily so.

Even though Grace might think she knew, he was fairly positive Lettie's whereabouts would turn out to be a complete surprise to everyone. *When all's said and done.*

He paced the length of the front room, recalling the last Preaching service held there. Too aware of Lettie's absence, he'd worked hard to set up for that uncomfortable Lord's Day gathering. Preacher Josiah had pounded away at scriptural themes of marriage. It was as if that morning's second sermon — the longer of the two — was being preached at him. The message still rang in his ears. That, and Judah's most recent talk with the brethren. The anxious look in their somber eyes, the way they'd whispered Lettie's name as if it was somehow tainted — all of it had caused him fitful sleep these past few days.

He headed back through the kitchen and out the side door. The mourning doves' low feeding trays were full again. *Grace, bless her heart, is looking after the birds for her mother . . . looking after all of us, really.*

It was evident, too, that Yonnie had noted Grace's gentle ways. Unquestionably, he was coming each day to work because of Grace. And Judah couldn't deny, even to himself, that he was quite drawn to Ephram's son. *Neither Adam nor Joe is near the conversationalist he is,* Judah thought with a chuckle. *Ephram, neither.* He had run into Ephram over at the buggy shop enough to know the man was rather tight-lipped. He'd also noticed Ephram was still wearing the narrow-brimmed straw hat he'd worn in Indiana — too progressive for this area.

Interesting, the brethren haven't gone after him yet.

Judah assumed Yonnie had picked up his

unconventional ways from his father — and from his old Midwest church district. *And what does our Grace think of all that?* He certainly had noticed a spark between her and Yonnie yesterday, when the lad had helped her with the birdseed.

Still, it's hard to tell what girls might be thinking. Much as he cared for Grace and Mandy, he personally did not know what to do with daughters once they grew past preschool age. Girls couldn't fill silo or go fishing and hunting or muck out the manure in the barn and spread it out on Lettie's vegetable garden. They were harder to talk to, too.

Though that's not always so with Grace . . .

At the thought of her, Judah's heart warmed again. Lord willing, he believed his eldest daughter might just be his saving grace.

Grace nearly bumped into Dat in the side yard near the mourning dove feeders. "Ach, sorry," she said, catching her breath and inching back a bit. "I was lookin' for ya."

"And you've found me." He put his straw hat on his head. "When's supper?"

"Should be just about ready. I'll have it on the table soon," she said. "But while I have ya here . . . I want to ask you something."

He nodded, seemingly pleased.

"I've been thinking."

Dat smiled. "Should I be worried?"

"No, Dat." She'd never heard her father joke like this. She fidgeted with her apron and glanced past him to the deep green pastureland, stretching as far as she could see. "Would you mind . . . I mean, what would you think if I hired Martin Puckett to drive me out to Indiana, say, a few days from now?"

He grimaced. "Whatever for?"

"I have some money saved up." She hoped she didn't sound as desperate as she felt. "I don't mind usin' it . . . to find Mamma, I mean."

"Not till after lambing's done. I already told ya that."

"But time's a-wastin', ain't? Someone needs to bring her home."

Dat tugged on his black suspenders, pulling them out, then letting them nearly snap against his chest. "Ain't your worry, Gracie. Leave that to the brethren."

"So there *is* talk of the Bann?"

"You best stay put and keep house . . . look after your Mamma's parents, too."

"For the rest of your life." Adam's words floated back to her.

"It'd just be a quick trip — no matter

245

what, I'll come right back. Please, won'tcha let me?" She felt the tears welling up.

"Gracie, listen here —"

"Oh, Dat . . . don't you see?" Her lip wouldn't stop quivering. "If Mamma knew how much we want her to come home . . . wouldn't that make all the difference?"

"You're not goin' anywhere!" Dat's voice had gathered into a sudden sob, and he turned away and marched quickly to the barn.

Horrified that she'd made her father angry enough to weep, Grace hurried inside, trembling, to lay out the evening meal.

"Stay put and keep house," Dat says. What choice do I have now?

Heather plumped the pillows on her bed before plunking down to check her iPhone for emails or IMs from Wannalive. They had not exchanged actual first names yet, and she was fine with remaining anonymous. *The best way to be.*

But as she signed on to instant messaging, she couldn't stop thinking about her dad's reaction to her desire to avoid the medical approach. After all, this was her body wimping out. Wasn't her obvious weight loss only the beginning of her woes? *How many more pounds will I drop?* She couldn't remember the oncologist's grim forecast regarding weight loss. Besides, wouldn't she lose even more on a juice diet?

Finding no new communication from her online pal, she reached for her laptop, disappointed. After she booted up, she opened her journaling file. Dad's pleas for her to return to Virginia and acquiesce to the oncologist's recommendation brought her all-too-familiar frustration back to the forefront. Even so, she knew his response came out of concern and love for her.

She began to write:

> Dad's visiting here. I don't believe he's set out to upset me by debating against what I'd like to do for treatment. After all, he didn't even know I was sick until just yesterday. But he's completely old school . . . like Mom started out to be. Would she be appalled at Dad's insistence? It's hard to believe Mom wouldn't make an attempt to negotiate with him — get him to see both sides.
>
> Isn't this my life?

She paused, lightly tapping the left side of the trackpad with her thumb. "Somehow I have to win Dad over." She reached for the bottles of supplements she'd purchased at

Eli's. Might Dr. Marshall work her magic with Dad?

Laughing softly, she felt temporarily optimistic. But she couldn't depend on LaVyrle's feminine charms to persuade her stubborn father. Would he stop talking long enough to listen and see the light for himself?

Heather paused — her room had filled with a decadent chocolate aroma that had seeped through the floorboards. *Marian's baking this close to suppertime?*

Closing down her laptop, she headed for the stairs and to the kitchen. Becky seemed surprised to see her, but Marian was welcoming and smiling as always. "What are you baking?" Heather asked. "I couldn't resist coming to find out what smells so fantastic."

"We're makin' a quick batch of chocolate whoopie pies for a doin's tomorrow," Becky said, eyes bright. "Want to help?"

"Sure, but . . . I really shouldn't have any." She laughed at herself. "What are the ingredients?"

"Ach, don't ask." Marian tittered. "Fattening as all get-out."

"Well, I know I smell chocolate," she admitted, fully aware LaVyrle would advise her to steer clear of the rich treat.

"Surely one tiny taste of each kind won't hurt," Becky said. "We're making strawberry and pumpkin, too."

Such temptation was hard to resist, and Heather knew it was about time to level with them. Her days of eating decadent foods must become a thing of the past.

Starting tomorrow . . .

"Supper's on the table and getting cold!" Grace called through the screen door. She'd thought of ringing the bell, but as hungry as Dat was earlier, she figured his stomach would do the calling.

Within seconds, Adam and Joe came running toward the house as they always did — like they were starving. An outsider would never guess her brothers regularly ate like healthy horses.

She turned back to call for Mandy, who was mending upstairs, as well as to her grandparents, straightening up the hallway clutter while she went. Her grandparents didn't respond, and when she approached their kitchen, they were talking so animatedly she wasn't sure she should interrupt. Yet her supper was most tasty piping hot — the way Dat liked it.

Grace leaned against the doorjamb, momentarily resting her head on the wood, unsure when or if she should barge in.

"I'm tellin' ya, Lettie prob'ly never would've married Judah . . . if it hadn't been for our meddling," Mammi said.

"Oh, go on with you."

"No, now really. Think back all that time ago. . . ."

Stunned and too embarrassed to listen a speck more, Grace coughed slightly and moved into their kitchen. "Supper's ready," she said, her cheeks growing warm. "Dat's washin' up right now."

Dawdi rose with a grunt and reached for his cane. "All right. We're comin'." He seemed relieved to escape the conversation.

Shaken, Grace returned to the kitchen on the other side of the house. *Mamma never would've married Dat? Why?*

CHAPTER NINETEEN

Back in her mother's kitchen, Grace wondered if her grandfather had indeed arranged her parents' marriage. She'd read about such things in books, but rarely did it happen amongst the People. "What on earth?" she whispered as she turned off the oven and removed the hot dish.

She pondered hard the words she had overheard even as she passed the serving dishes at supper. If what Mammi had accused Dawdi of doing was true, then maybe *that* was the reason her parents' marriage was on such shaky ground. Could it be?

The normal suppertime chatter left Grace feeling as limp as wilted celery. Finally she asked whether Adam and Joe might be able to chop down the kudzu vine. "Or is that something that's s'posed to be reported to the authorities?"

"Keep 'em out of our neck of the woods," Dawdi Jakob piped up. "Outsiders are nothin' but trouble."

All eyes turned to look down the table at him. Even Mammi Adah's eyes were wide.

"I thought as much," Grace said, reaching for the salt and pepper. "Least I warned you. That little woodshed is goin' to up and disappear mighty quick."

"By next week?" Joe asked, his smile stretching across his face. "Can it wait that long?"

"You better just go and see for yourself," she teased him. She glanced at Dat — her father was quieter than usual, and no wonder. She'd spoken out of turn in her impatience to find Mamma. *Before the Bann falls and crushes us all.*

Now she couldn't help but wonder if what her grandparents had said about Dat and Mamma might just be true.

As the whoopie pies were cooling, Becky asked Heather, "Would ya like to have supper with us?" Her soft brown eyes were hopeful.

"Thanks, but I'd better not."

Becky tilted her head. "Are ya sure? I made tapioca pudding. Thought it might go down easy."

Go down easy? Did Becky suspect she was having trouble digesting her food? The

Amish girl was so thoughtful, she hated to refuse her.

"I think you'd like Becky's pudding," Marian put in.

How healthy is tapioca pudding? Heather wondered. She felt she ought to accept, if for no reason other than to appease Becky. And anyway, she'd been pretty good food-wise this afternoon. "All right . . . I can't pass up the pudding." She looked at Marian. "Feel free to add the meal to my weekly bill."

"No need for that." Marian shook her head. "Anytime you want to eat dinner or supper with us, just feel free."

"Mamma likes lots of folk at her table." Becky grinned. "Have you decided which is your favorite flavor of whoopie pie?" She referred to the nibbling they'd done while making the rich dessert.

Heather smiled back. "It's a tie between chocolate and pumpkin, I think." With tapioca pudding in the offing and the taste of whoopie pie still in her mouth, she felt guilty. *How can I possibly pull off LaVyrle's plan for my diet?*

Marian and Becky encouraged her to get some fresh air, nearly shooing her out for a quick walk while they put the finishing touches on a ham and scalloped potatoes dinner. She was halfway down the lane when she saw Grace Byler, walking barefoot along the roadside.

"Heather, hullo!" Grace's cheeks were rosy red as she smiled at her.

"Hello again."

"Awful nice day, ain't?"

Heather agreed. "You have the most perfect springtime weather."

"Well, we could use some more rain, for sure." Grace looked toward the Riehls' house. "Is Becky home yet?"

"Yeah. We just finished making several dozen whoopie pies."

"Sounds like I've timed my visit perfectly, then."

"No kidding. But watch out — they're addictive." For a fleeting moment she thought of asking Grace whom Becky's sisters might've been referring to earlier this afternoon — a Lettie Byler. But Grace seemed anxious to see Becky, and Heather didn't want to hold her up. "Well, I'd better walk off those whoopie calories!"

"I know what you mean." Grace headed on toward the house with a bright smile and cheerful wave. "Good-bye."

Heather nodded and continued toward the road, wondering why Grace seemed so consistently happy. *Is the Plain life really so carefree?*

Much as she enjoyed Heather's company, Grace was set on visiting Becky. Her friend's reaction to seeing Yonnie next to her in Martin's van had plagued her all afternoon, and Grace hoped the tension between herself and Becky could be talked away. *Oh, I hope so!*

Taking a deep breath, she rapped on the screen door instead of walking in as she often did. Marian called to her — "Come on in, Gracie" — before Becky even turned to acknowledge her from across the kitchen. "Come have a whoopie pie before supper," Marian said, a smudge of chocolate on her dress sleeve.

"Denki, but we've already eaten," Grace said as she opened the screen door. Truth was, snacks of any kind were the last thing she wanted as she looked at Becky's sour face. She bit her lip, wondering how she'd ever get the chance to talk to her friend alone, what with Marian's ongoing cleanup and supper preparations. Grace looked for a way to assist, going to the counter and reaching for a dirty cookie sheet. "Can I help redd up, maybe?"

"Oh, would ya mind?" Marian removed her soiled apron. "Someone needs to get to the hen house and gather eggs." And just that quick, she was heading for the back door, her bare feet padding across the floor.

Becky ran the hot water at the sink, her back stiffly turned.

"I can't stay long," Grace said. "Mandy's doin' dishes, and I need to get back soon. Here lately I've missed one too many clean-ups."

Still facing the wall behind the sink, Becky nodded.

"I know you're upset," Grace said immediately, afraid she'd lose heart. "But I hope you can understand what happened today."

"Wasn't it obvious?" came Becky's terse reply.

"I had nothin' to do with it, Becky. Honestly."

"But still . . ."

"Can't we talk about this?"

"Well, what're we doin'?" her friend snapped.

Feeling more dismal by the moment, Grace was at a loss for words. *Now what?*

"I'd prefer not to discuss Yonnie Bontrager ever again," Becky retorted. She began to scrub the mixing bowls. "If he wants to court you, then so be it."

"Ach, Becky . . . no."

"Well, why do you think he sat next to you in the van? You'd have to be blind or dense or both —"

"No need to raise your voice. We're best friends."

"Jah . . . sorry." Becky's voice softened.

"We can talk sensibly 'bout this, ain't? After all, Yonnie was just catching a ride home . . . it's not like he went off with me to Eli's to buy groceries."

"He should've sat up front with Martin Puckett in any case."

Grace reached for the tea towel. "I don't want a boy comin' between us."

It was quiet in the kitchen for the longest time, and Grace wasn't sure what Becky would say. At last her friend turned, her face sad. "It's my fault for actin' the way I did. I shouldn't have snubbed you in the van or at the store. Neither one."

Grace touched her shoulder. "Well, all's forgiven on my end."

"You sure?" Becky's eyes were brimming with tears.

"That's why I came over. I couldn't stand to have this awful wedge between us. You're my dearest friend."

Becky nodded and rinsed the mixing bowls. She wiped her eyes on the back of her arm and started to say something more but looked away. Once more she glanced at Grace . . . but still she said nothing.

What else is on her mind? Grace wondered.

Judah patted his stomach as he made his way upstairs, having eaten more than his fill. He'd sensed the strain between Grace and himself during supper. By the stricken look on her face, it seemed the small steps they'd made in their relationship were now nearly for naught. He was, after all, standing in his daughter's way of finding Lettie. Sighing, he knew he, too, should be considering such a trip, if only because of the brethren's pointed meeting with him. *I ought to be the one asking Lettie home.*

Going straightaway to his room, he closed the door and went to sit in his favorite chair, where he reached for the Bible and turned to the Psalms. Now, in the privacy of this place, Judah was alive to the stillness around him. It was the time of day when he felt closest to God. It had also been his and Lettie's time alone together, whether they spoke a word or simply lay silently in each other's arms. Were those days gone forever?

How he'd loved her when first they'd briefly courted. Lettie had made his heart sing in those early days, even though he assumed she still cared deeply for her former beau. Yet Judah had been hopeful she might come to love him with a full measure of tenderness, given time. And he believed that day had come. He'd arrived at the joyful realization soon after Lettie knew she was with child, as together they awaited the birth of Adam. Her face literally shone with affection for Judah all those months and following.

Their first days and weeks as newlyweds had been another matter, though he hadn't let on what he suspected — that Lettie had given more than her heart away to Samuel. Judah had carried that suspicion and the accompanying sadness — even disappointment — through all the years of their marriage. But never had he broached the subject with Lettie.

Closing the Bible now, he felt an unexpected desire to talk to his wife. He didn't know if doing so might bring an end to her sadness or whatever had compelled her to leave. Oh, what he wouldn't give to lift the veil of tears from his house! Judah had heard Grace and Mandy numerous times at night, sniffling and crying and talking quietly down the hall — *probably praying for Lettie.* He was not blind to the hurts and concern of his children, yet the attitude of Lettie's parents continued to irk him. Jakob had avoided him like he was contagious ever since Lettie's leaving . . . rarely coming out to the barn to help, unlike before. It no longer pained Judah; it was downright aggravating. If he wasn't one to shy away from conflict, he might've gone over and sat down with his father-in-law about it. As it was, he had little interest now in putting another ounce of strain on their lives. Or on his own.

Rising from his chair, Judah went to pray silently beside his bed, beseeching the Lord not just for Lettie but also for himself. Then he prayed for his children, that they might not get their hopes too high for their mother's return. Knowing how stubborn Lettie could be, there was no telling how long she'd choose to wander from hearth and home — or what frame of mind she might be in if she did venture back.

What was she fixing to tell me that final night? He stared at her pillow, then reached for it and buried his face.

After the evening's Bible reading, Grace and her sister prayed faithfully for their mother's safe return in the solitude of Mandy's bedroom. "We can hardly wait a day longer, dear Lord," Mandy said, and her words broke Grace's heart. She reached over and patted her sister's hand.

"Mamma's in God's care, so I trust you'll rest peacefully tonight." She wasn't as sure about herself, recalling Mammi Adah's troubling words to Dawdi. Since she couldn't begin to ask Mammi about that, she'd have to entrust it to the Lord, as well.

"Before you head off for bed," Mandy said with lowered voice, "I have something I want to tell ya, sister."

By the look of shyness and even joy on Mandy's round face, surely what she had to say was something wonderful-good. "Jah?"

"Frankly, I'd never think of tellin' a soul 'cept you," Mandy began. "You've prob'ly seen me with a certain fella lately."

Grace had observed her with more than a few young men during the past months, but she didn't want to spoil Mandy's special moment by speaking.

Mandy's eyes smiled now, the apples of her cheeks shining. "I'm hopeful that we'll need to plant plenty of celery this summer, Gracie. Maybe oodles of it."

For the creamed celery served at a wedding feast!

Goodness, she hadn't seen *this* coming! Had Mandy fallen in love nearly at first sight? Usually girls rarely told sisters or close cousins such things until they were

261

certain. "You hope to be engaged soon . . . like Adam and Priscilla?"

"It's not for sure." Mandy blinked her big brown eyes. "But I know he cares for me, and I'm so happy, Gracie."

"Oh, sister" was all she could say. Grace leaned across the bed and cupped Mandy's face in her hands. *We must get Mamma home quickly.* She wondered how her sister would feel if their mother wasn't there for her wedding. As for herself, she couldn't imagine such a day without Mamma on hand.

Mandy hugged her tight, and Grace whispered, "Wait, now, I have something for ya." She hurried off to her room.

Opening her dresser drawer, she pulled out Mamma's white hankie. She'd hand-washed it and pressed it with her iron. *Mamma would want Mandy to have this,* she thought, going back to her sister's room.

"What's in your hand?" Mandy asked, eyes wide.

"I found this in the cornfield recently." She gave it to Mandy. "It's Mamma's."

"Oh, Gracie . . ."

"Carry it on your wedding day . . . whenever that may come."

Mandy held the pretty little hankie next to her cheek just as Grace had when she'd first found it. For a moment, Mandy could not speak for her tears. "Having this . . . gives me hope," she whispered. "You just don't know."

Jah, hope. Grace knew all about that.

Twitchy and unable to sleep, Grace rose from her bed, dressed, and slipped outside to breathe in the fresh, sweet air. Dark as it was, she found comfort in the faint light of a waning moon as Adam's earlier words — hurtful as they were — rang in her head. She considered all the nights Mamma had left the house to go walking in the cornfield. *I understand better now.*

She found herself strolling along the road, something she'd never think of doing during the daytime. But this late, there was seldom a speck of traffic. Swinging her arms, she took deep breaths, holding them for five counts and then exhaling. No one had ever told her to do this, but in the past she'd discovered it helped remove the cobwebs from her brain. Helped her face her fears, too.

Adam's unexpected report had made her think twice. Not before he'd talked so outspokenly had she cared one iota about marriage. But now, knowing what the fellows were saying — or what Prissy *said* they were saying — she wondered if she should be concerned. Was it a blight on her as a woman to remain single? Adam had more than hinted that she'd come to despise being a Maidel. But wasn't it far better to live out her life taking care of the family she already had than to make a bad match out of desperation? She certainly did not appreciate Prissy or Adam, neither one, pronouncing what was going to become of her! No, in her heart she was sure she could only marry for love.

She walked farther than she had originally planned and was glad she'd taken time to dress, although her feet were bare. In the distance, she heard a horse *clip-clopp*ing up the road and the faint sound of laughter. It was a night for courting, after all.

There it was again. Goodness, if she wasn't imagining things, it almost sounded like Becky's laughter. But far as she knew, Becky was still sulking over Yonnie. *Or did Yonnie change his mind about courting Becky, maybe?*

But the farther Grace walked and the closer the horse and buggy came, the more she was convinced it was indeed Becky Riehl's voice ringing out into the night. Thinking she ought not to be seen, lest Becky and her beau think she was as peculiar as Mamma, Grace darted behind a cluster of trees.

Heart pounding, she stood there, hidden, holding her breath so she could hear more clearly. She leaned her palms against the rough bark of the tree to support herself.

The young man's voice was low at first, rising and then falling again ever so quietly. She strained to hear but was only able to make out a few phrases before his words ceased altogether. Then and there, it dawned on her that Becky was riding under the covering of night with none other than Henry Stahl.

She gasped and covered her mouth. *Well, I guess there's no grass growing under his feet! Or Becky's, for that matter . . .*

The relief Grace experienced then, as she realized it was Henry out with Becky — and not Yonnie, after all — surprised her more than she could begin to comprehend.

CHAPTER TWENTY

The Lord's Day dawned with reassuring birdsong. Grace crept to Mandy's room and opened the dark green shades to awaken her. Her sister stirred and yawned behind her, still drowsy.

Squinting into the beaming sun, she hoped to spot the various species of birds out at this hour, especially Mamma's favorite mourning doves. She remembered a lovely thing Mamma had once said — *"Birds are like little stars in motion."*

Her mother might have gotten the line from one of the poems in her treasured books. Oh, but Grace hoped not. Any link to Mamma's first beau, however slight, made her uneasy. She had mixed feelings about all of that, just as she did about the memory of last night's strange revelation. Happiness for Becky and Henry . . . and a sense of relief, too. Maybe even freedom.

She turned from the window and leaned

on the footboard, looking down at Mandy's ample form beneath the quilt. At such times she wondered if this was how it felt to be a mother. She went to sit on the edge of the bed. "I see you're awake."

"I am *now.*" Mandy smiled sleepily and sat up, pulling the quilts up close. "I slept so *gut* after our prayer. Did you?"

"Enough, I guess." Anymore a deep and restful sleep was rare and therefore a blessing.

Mandy peered out of the covers at her. "Ach, Gracie . . . you didn't sleep well."

She disregarded her sister's comment. "We need to get breakfast on the table right quick. I'll see you downstairs." She wiggled her fingers in a wave while Mandy stretched and rubbed her eyes.

Even though she looked forward to gathering with the members on the Lord's Day, in some ways she was secretly glad this was not a Preaching Sunday. She could go at a slightly slower pace — the whole family could. In her mind, she'd already planned the day, beginning with a visit to the horse stable to spend time with Willow. Bit by bit, Willow seemed to be improving. Dat and the boys had been so attentive and careful, following the vet's and Yonnie's solid advice.

Hurrying now to dress, Grace had a

hankering for apple pancakes. They might please Dat, too, for he'd always enjoyed the way Mamma grated the apples into the batter for a nice texture. Those and a homemade syrup of sugar, molasses, and vanilla — Mamma preferred that to maple flavoring — sounded just right this morning.

But will apple pancakes sorely remind Dat of her?

Truly, everything reminded them of their missing mother.

Susan Kempf had a profoundly empathetic way with others. But it was her listening ear that compelled Lettie to want to open her heart this morning . . . to tell someone why she'd left her family.

They had been lingering at the breakfast table, sunshine streaming in pleasantly as they watched a rare blue-winged warbler perch on a branch near the window. "Time for nest building," Lettie said, pointing at the petite yellow bird with blue-gray wings and a distinctive black eye line. Both she and Susan had taken only a second to spot the bright warbler after they'd heard its high-pitched chirp.

"I'm nothin' like that little wood warbler." Lettie sighed, testing the waters. "My nest is in shambles now."

Susan looked at her with soft eyes. "You've run away, haven't ya?"

Lettie bowed her head with regret, still aware of the bird's vibrant call. Why was she sticking her neck out? *Goodness, I've just met this woman.*

"I sensed something amiss when I saw you alone at Miller's."

Lettie cringed. How very awkward and forlorn she'd felt there in the crowded restaurant. "It's difficult traveling alone."

"Well, you aren't alone now, are you?" Susan smiled warmly and poured more tea into Lettie's cup.

"And I'm grateful." Her new friend spooned up two teaspoons of sugar and stirred it into Lettie's cup, just as Susan must have observed her do earlier. "I don't know when I've been so cared for." She squeezed her lips to keep from tearing up.

"I believe you'd do the same for me, Lettie."

Jah, thought Lettie, remembering the Scripture: *"Inasmuch as ye have done it unto one of the least of these . . . ye have done it unto me."* She was indeed touched by the woman's sensitivity and generosity. As she sipped her sweet, hot tea, she contemplated this safe haven the Lord had led her to.

Judah must be praying for me . . . Gracie, too.

"Your family must surely miss you," Susan said gently.

The words struck at Lettie's heart. "Oh, and I miss them, too," she said, beginning to feel comfortable enough to reveal more. "But I felt I had to do this . . . ya see, they aren't my only family." She told about her search for her child. "I was young . . . didn't know my mind, nor my heart." Between whispers and tears, she poured out her long-kept secret. "I had to find Minnie."

Susan's face reflected the anguish Lettie felt. "No wonder . . ."

Unable to speak, Lettie nodded her head slowly.

"Such a hard journey for one so wounded." Susan's lips curved downward.

"You led me to Minnie. For that, I'm ever so thankful," Lettie said, feeling suddenly spent.

"I pray you'll discover only what is best, Lettie . . . that if it's God's will, you and your child will be reunited."

"Do you mind if I lie down for a little while?"

"Not at all." Susan rose to walk with Lettie into the spare bedroom past the sitting room. "Just rest for now."

"Denki." Smiling, Lettie sat on the edge of the bed. "May the Lord bless you."

"Oh, He has, you can be sure." Susan reached for the afghan and placed it at the bottom of the bed. "I'll be in the kitchen . . . if you need anything at all."

Again, Lettie thanked the woman who, when her lips spread into a smile, looked like she might be someone's guardian angel. With a long sigh, Lettie lay down on the soft mattress and wondered if Baltic, Ohio, might just be a sampling of heaven.

Grace hurried along the road to the Riehls', aware of the *cawing* and *chit-chatter* of the crows high in the trees. Not far from the chicken house, a hen and several tiny chicks ran unsteadily across the lane. *The perfect day for a buggy ride,* she thought.

Before she could step foot in the house, Heather emerged from the back door and walked quickly to her car. "Hi, Grace! Nice to see you again."

Grace waved and smiled. "How are you?"

Heather opened the car door. "Actually, this is the first I've been outside today." She glanced at the sky. "It's warm enough to sit under a tree with a good book."

"I agree," Grace replied, surprised Heather was getting into her vehicle. *Does she assume we're driving it to Sally's?* She hesitated, hanging back.

Heather poked her head out the window and looked at her curiously. "Okay with you if we take my car to Smuckers'?"

"Actually, we prefer not to ride in cars on the Lord's Day 'cept for emergencies."

"Oh, my mistake . . ."

"I should've been more clear." Grace explained what she'd had in mind — that they might walk back to her house. "Then, we can take the horse and buggy. It's a bit slower, but —"

"No, that's fine," Heather said, getting out of the car.

Grace sensed she was still somewhat taken aback. "Sure you don't mind?"

Heather shook her head. "Not at all."

"All right, then. Let's head over to my place."

While they walked, several families in buggies rode past them on the short stretch of road. A pony cart rumbled along, too, filled to the brim with young children, an older teenage boy at the reins.

"Is there a legal age for road driving?" Heather asked. "If so, do your people adhere to it?"

"No driver's license is required, and there's no buggy training manual, either.

But boys are usually fifteen or sixteen before they drive for long stretches out on the two-lane highways."

"Such a young kid handling a buggy on a busy road . . . it seems crazy."

Grace didn't know what to say. She'd taken their pony cart back and forth to Riehls' when she was only eight. "I s'pose there's plenty that seems peculiar 'bout us," she ventured.

Heather fell silent, and Grace wondered if she'd upset her.

Once at her house, they found her father's gray buggy already hitched to the horse, and headed out onto the road. Grace tried to enjoy the landscape, but she was aware of the tension in the front seat as Heather eyed the dashboard and folded her arms. *Stiff as a two-by-four.*

Finally, though, Heather began to warm up. "What did you do this morning?" she asked.

Grace held the reins steadily as she mentioned making breakfast and reading seven chapters from Dat's old German Bible. "Then I read the same amount from the King James," she said. "What 'bout you? How'd you spend *your* morning?"

"I slept in, something I often do on Sundays. My family used to attend church once in a while . . . back before my mom died."

"No longer?" Grace asked softly.

"We just got out of the routine," Heather said. "I can't say I miss it much."

"Maybe you haven't found the right church, then."

Heather looked at her suddenly. "I guess I never thought of that." She quickly changed the subject to the health-related chat room she was enjoying visiting. "I've even exchanged a few IMs with someone I met there — his screen name is Wannalive."

"Screen name?"

Heather tried to explain instant messaging, but to Grace's thinking it sounded like a secret code. *Why not just say who you are?* "Wannalive's an interesting choice of a name, ain't so?" she remarked.

Heather laughed. "It caught *my* attention."

"I daresay." Grace urged the horse onward, glad Heather seemed more talkative now.

"But enough of that." Heather pushed her hair back behind her shoulders. She let out an audible sigh. "I don't know how to bring this up politely, but Becky's little sister Sarah asked a rather startling question yesterday."

"What about?"

Heather glanced at her. "I guess I should first ask if Lettie Byler is related to you in any way."

Grace's heart sank. "She's my mother."

A gasp escaped Heather's lips. "Well, I certainly know how to put my foot in my mouth."

"Why do you ask?"

"Well, Sarah asked if Lettie had passed away."

"Ach . . . poor, dear girl." Grace was hesitant to say more.

"She was upset. Marian took her and Rachel inside the house after that."

Grace gripped the reins taut, her shoulders tense. "I s'pose lots of young children in the church are wonderin' what's happened to Mamma." *Just as I do.* "It's become all hush-hush amongst the People."

Heather looked worried. "Is . . . your mother all right?"

Grace appreciated her concern. Everyone around Bird-in-Hand knew of Mamma's disappearance, so why keep it quiet? As they rode toward Preacher Smucker's farmhouse, she mulled over what she might say . . . and on the other hand, what might be better left unsaid.

Grace took a long breath. "To be honest with you, my mother left us . . . and I don't know why. No one does." She was quick to explain that such a thing was nearly unheard of amongst the People, "although it's happened for any number of reasons." *Ach, that was much more than I needed to say.*

"Has anyone looked for her?" asked Heather, turning to face her now.

"Mamma wasn't kidnapped, if that's what you're thinkin'."

"That did cross my mind."

Grace revealed how Mamma had hired a driver to take her to the train station. "She's since made a phone call to that person's home, just to let us know she's all right." She stopped talking to cough. "And last week, a letter came from her, postmarked Ohio."

"Surely your father must know where she's gone . . . and why."

Suddenly, the conversation had become much too personal. "Puttin' it respectfully, none of us knows. Not even Dat."

Heather seemed to consider this. "I can think of reasons why a woman might leave her husband," she offered. "But are you suggesting Amish wives and mothers don't have the same struggles as other women outside your community?"

This conversation was extending far beyond what Grace had intended. She felt nearly disloyal. "Not knowing much about English women, I'd be hard-pressed to say."

Heather looked flabbergasted. "If I may be so bold, I can't imagine living so totally under a man's control." She seemed to scrutinize her. "You appear to be rather independent, Grace — working away from home at Eli's like you do. Surely you have your own opinions and thoughts." Heather was staring at her now. "Is it . . . well, hard for you to remain Amish?"

"It's all I know . . . all I care to know."

"Did your mother have a different opinion? I mean, since she's gone?"

"That's difficult to say. But if she's not home in, say, half a year, then we might think she's left us for *gut.*" Grace saw Preacher Smucker's place coming up, and she wanted to hurry the horse to a gallop to bring this awkward discussion to an end.

"She left sometime in April?"

"The twenty-third," Grace said, recalling her birthday with sadness.

Thankfully, Heather didn't press further. In fact, she fell silent.

I wish I could be more forthright with her, Grace thought, hoping Heather, too, might share more fully about her own mother's illness and subsequent passing.

But the peaceful sweep of Josiah's rolling

green lawn and the stately rise of his three-story farmhouse lay just ahead. *Perhaps another time.*

CHAPTER
TWENTY-ONE

As they walked across the vast backyard toward May Jaberg's farmhouse on this Lord's Day morning, Susan kindly reassured Lettie. "You'll enjoy meeting May," she said, her skirt swishing against Lettie's own. "She scarcely knows a stranger."

Being it was a no-Preaching day, just like back home, Lettie was happy to visit Susan's big-hearted neighbor, with her adopted older children. "Is May comfortable talking 'bout her adoptions, do ya think?" Lettie asked, her eyes on the woman's tall, four-sided purple martin birdhouses.

"Oh, you'll see. May's quite open 'bout all of that."

I'll bring it up gently, Lettie promised herself as she matched Susan's stride and ducked her head beneath the long rows of clotheslines. Her heart sped up at the thought.

Rosy-faced and pleasantly plump, May Jaberg stood at the door, smiling broadly at the sight of them coming up the back walk. She inched out the screen door as she waved them in. "Hullo, there . . . *Kumm rei* — come in."

"Denki, May," Susan said as they stepped into May's kitchen. Then, turning toward Lettie, she added, "I'd like you to meet Lettie Byler, from Lancaster County."

May nodded her welcome, her Kapp strings tied neatly under her double chin. "Wie geht's, Lettie? Would ya care for some pie and coffee?" Quickly she put a pot of water on to boil. "Or does tea suit you better?"

Susan glanced at Lettie, a twinkle in her eye, as if to remind her of May's benevolent nature. May busied herself with cutting thick slices of banana cream pie while the water boiled. Lettie began to relax, not nearly as tense as she thought she might be. She could certainly see why such a woman might be drawn to having a good many children.

By the time peppermint tea was brewed and poured for both May and Lettie, and coffee for Susan, the three of them had already exhausted the weather talk . . . and even the subject of the hen party this coming Wednesday. "You must join us, Lettie," May invited her.

"I'll keep it in mind."

"Well, if you're still here, why not?" Susan urged.

If I am. Lettie reached for the sugar bowl.

"It'll be a nice time of fellowship and busying our hands," added May. "My two married daughters are comin' to help with the little ones, which is awful nice."

Lettie's ears perked up, and suddenly she was quite eager to take May up on her kind invitation.

Later, during a lull in their pleasant conversation, Lettie said thoughtfully, "Susan tells me you and your husband adopted several of your children." Since talking with Minnie, she'd pondered what it might mean for her own daughter to discover she was adopted.

Her mouth full, May bobbed her head, a bright smile on her face. "I must say, we were in a hurry to start our family and weren't havin' any luck at first. But once we adopted our first three, the Lord saw fit to start sendin' along a whole line of babies. So we're doubly blessed."

Lettie listened, considering what May had said. "Did any of them want to search for their natural parents?"

"Well, the oldest of the three, Ruth, wanted to, before she joined church." May wiped her mouth on a paper napkin. "But after she found her birth mother, it turned out she came to resent her, and now she has no contact with her at all. It's all very sad."

Susan caught Lettie's eye, encouraging her to ask more questions — or so it seemed.

"Did any of the other two also search?" Lettie held her breath.

"The middle of the three hasn't yet, no," May replied more softly. She paused, staring at the remnants of pie left on her plate. "But she's said ofttimes that she's never felt complete, not knowing, and talks some of wanting to find her birth mother someday."

"How old is she?" Lettie's words nearly caught in her throat.

"Vesta Mae's twenty-four."

Lettie's heart pounded. *Might Vesta Mae be my very own?*

Susan dished up another sliver of the pie and set it silently on her plate. Meanwhile, May did the same, although her second piece was more generous, and she clucked like a pudgy, contented hen.

Lettie didn't have the courage to ask May about Vesta Mae's date of birth. But the question lingered in her mind long after she'd finished tea at the woman's big kitchen table.

"Yoo-hoo!" Grace called at the Smuckers' back door.

Always fond of impromptu visits, Sally's eyes lit up when she let them in. "Oh, Gracie, so *gut* to have you visit," she said. "And, Heather . . . it's nice to see you again."

"You know each other?" Grace was surprised.

"We met the other night," Sally said, smiling. "Heather and her father, Roan, came to look over the lay of his property — on paper, that is. Josiah's buildin' them a house."

"Actually, the house is for my dad," Heather added.

"But aren't you goin' to live there till you marry?" asked Sally; then she caught herself. "Ach, I mean . . ."

Heather laughed, evidently understanding. "That's okay," she was quick to say as they followed Sally through her spotless kitchen, the dishes washed and put away.

Grace couldn't help noticing how quiet the house was. "Your little ones must be down for a nap," she said while Sally led them into the smaller sitting room, adjoining the kitchen.

"Oh, goodness, they certainly are." Sally offered the most comfortable chairs, taking the cane-back chair for herself. "So, now . . . how did the two of you meet?" she asked, folding her arms and leaning back.

"Over at Eli's." Grace looked at Heather, who seemed impatient for the small talk to be over.

"Willkumm to ya both," Sally said. "We'll have us some dessert in a little bit. I've got a homemade pie just begging to be tasted."

Grace had spotted the perfectly golden pie when they passed through the kitchen. "But I'll bet it's full of all kinds of healthy ingredients," she remarked.

Sally smiled. "And sweetened with grape juice, too."

"Sounds wonderful," Grace said. Then she mentioned that Heather was interested in hearing about Sally's healthy way of eating . . . and her natural path to healing.

"Wonderful-*gut* . . . I'd love to talk 'bout that." Again, Sally brightened, looking from Grace to Heather. "Grace may have already told you of my recovery from cancer, I s'pose?"

Heather nodded. "She shared a little . . . Grace thinks what you did for yourself might help me."

When it dawned on Sally that Heather must be suffering from a serious illness herself, she moved her chair over beside Heather's. Leaning forward, she directed her gaze solely at the English girl. "Well, let me start by saying that I believe God led me to Dr. Marshall's Wellness Lodge. I was dying, with only a few months to live, when I enrolled."

Heather's face was drawn as she listened.

"I'm free now of cancer, and I can't say enough *gut* about the program." Sally narrowed her eyes. "You . . . you're not as sick as I was, I hope . . . Heather, dear."

Heather grimaced. "As of last month, my cancer had spread to three regions of lymph nodes," she said quietly.

Sally frowned and looked concerned. Then she shook her head. "Ach, I don't know much 'bout other cancers . . . but if you make an appointment with Dr. Marshall, she will teach you all about a healthy diet."

"I've already seen her," Heather volunteered. "But I've encountered a significant obstacle."

The room was hushed, as if no one knew what to say. It was clear Heather wasn't going to reveal more.

At last Sally said, "Whatever it is, Heather,

I hope it can be solved quickly. Many of Dr. Marshall's patients have been helped greatly. There are numerous testimonials . . . all of them ever so inspiring."

Grace noticed Heather's face had turned pale, and she worried Sally might seem too pushy. "Could you maybe just share your experience, Sally?" Grace suggested gently.

Sally nodded and spent the next half hour explaining the treatment procedures at the lodge. "If you go, Heather, you'll meet some of the nicest people ever. I'm talking 'bout just the staff alone. Some were patients who were so much improved after goin' through the program, they returned to give of their time to others."

They talked further about following through with the helpful instruction offered at the lodge. Sally likened it to putting one's hand to the plow — "as in the Scripture" — and never looking back. "It's a hard row to hoe, but I want to live to see my children grow up."

Grace rose and walked to the kitchen, leaving Heather and Sally to talk more privately. She wandered about, turning her attention to the pie on the counter. Sally certainly had a talent for making delicious dishes while maintaining a healthy diet. How difficult was it to make a tender crust out of spelt flour?

Later, after they'd enjoyed the dessert, Grace thanked Sally for the tasty treat, topped off with a nondairy "ice cream" made from brown rice syrup and tapioca starch. As Sally thanked them for coming, she urged Heather, "Visit again anytime, just whenever you'd like. I'll help you all I can."

Grace and Heather left the house by way of the back door, walking through the small soap shop there. Trying to absorb all that Sally had shared, Grace stopped outside to stroke Sassy's neck and mane while Heather got in the carriage. She really hoped Willow might look as healthy as Sassy once again. *Adam was kind to lend me his horse today. How can I hold a grudge against such a brother?*

After they were back on the main road, Heather said, "Sally must be incredibly disciplined to eat that way."

"Oh, I'll say."

"Does she ever slip up and eat what she refers to as 'bad food'?"

"I really doubt it."

Heather seemed taken aback. "But how does she do it? With a husband and children, does she serve two meals every time she and the family sit down to eat?"

"Well, the whole family eats healthful, organic food now, which is an interesting howdy do."

"What do you mean?"

"You've heard of our farm diet, no doubt — mostly meat and lots of starchy foods like potatoes and noodles."

Heather said she was well aware of it. "Most people think eating heavily produces more energy, but it's just the opposite. It takes more work for the body to process and digest all that food, leaves less energy for healing."

"S'pose so."

Heather smiled. "Thanks for taking time out of your day to introduce me to Sally. I'd like to keep in touch with her."

"If it helps you get well, that's what matters."

Heather leaned back, stretching her neck. "To be totally honest, I'm really conflicted about all this." She sat up straight again.

"Oh?"

"My dad's too cautious. He's come close to demanding that I return home and start conventional treatment." Heather drew a deep breath. "He's opposed to the 'cleansing malarkey,' as he puts it. He said if I were underage, he'd drag me right back to my oncologist."

"I can see why you're torn, then."

Heather paused. "Dad's understandably concerned."

"And you're still under his covering, jah?"

"Excuse me?"

"You're in submission to your father, under his authority — just as he is under God."

Heather looked stunned. "Um . . . we don't live like that." She laughed. "If I decide to do this lodge thing — crazy as it sounds — I'll do it."

"You mean, against your father's wishes?"

"Well, does he want a compliant daughter, or a living and breathing one? My mother did things his way, and look where that got her: six feet under."

Grace wasn't at all accustomed to hearing anyone speak so disrespectfully, especially of a parent. "Perhaps you'll think this through some more?"

Heather tugged on her loose-fitting blue blouse and patted her jeans. "I'm not meek and mild like you, Grace. My mom raised me to think for myself . . . so did Dad."

Grace tinkled a nervous laugh, feeling awkward at hearing someone be so candid.

Just across the road, three little girls in pale pink dresses ran barefooted, chasing a yellow tabby cat. "Look there," Heather pointed out. "Amish children are so happy-go-lucky, like they don't have a worry in the world."

"Well, too, off-Sundays are our day for reading the Good Book and visiting relatives and friends. Things are bound to be more relaxed on days like this." Grace explained there were so many families and friends to visit, her parents had always kept track of which ones they went to see. "That way, we get to visit everyone at least twice each year."

Heather's eyes grew wide. "You have that many relatives?"

"Mamma has nine siblings. My father has eleven. And all of them are married with lots of children . . . so there are a-plenty of relatives."

"That's one thing I've often wondered about." Heather tilted her head. "Nearly all my life, in fact."

"What's that?"

"How different things might have been for me."

"With brothers and sisters?" Grace asked.

"Right." Heather stopped and drew in a long, slow breath. "You know, I rarely tell anyone this, Grace, because it's no big deal to me. But I'm adopted."

"Well, for goodness' sake." Yet even more

than this news, Grace felt surprised at Heather's sudden openness.

Heather nodded. "It's true."

"Ach, you look just like your father."

"People have said that," Heather acknowledged. "But I'm very much like my adoptive mother — or so it's turning out."

"You must feel mighty special, bein' handpicked by your parents and all." Grace didn't quite know why she said it in just that way.

"This is so out of character for me . . . telling you this. Even my former fiancé never knew this about me — can you believe it?" Heather groaned a little.

"Well, there are plenty of things I never told my beau, either." Grace confided that she had been the one to break off their engagement.

"Then we have something in common. Except that my fiancé dumped me."

They turned into the Riehls' lane, and Becky came running out the back door. "I'll keep mum, all right?" Grace said quietly.

Heather squeezed her arm. "Even better, just forget what I told you. I always had a close relationship with my mom, so I've never thought about searching like some adoptees do." Heather smiled sweetly. "Thanks again for taking me to Sally."

"You know where I am, anytime I can help."

Becky was inching toward them now, her face pink with embarrassment. "I don't mean to interrupt, but your father dropped by a little while ago, Heather. He said he'd call your phone and leave a message for ya."

"Thanks, Becky. I'll check my voice mail." Heather turned to Grace. "I hope we can talk again soon," she said. "I'm really interested in your herb garden, too. I'll drop by tomorrow, if that's all right."

"Why, sure. And you can meet my sister, Mandy, then . . . and my brothers, too, if you like."

"Evidently I've already met your grandmother, although I didn't know it at the time." Heather stretched a bit.

"Mammi Adah?"

Heather nodded. "She brought her wonderfully wicked sticky buns over the first day I arrived. I'm sure Sally Smucker and Dr. Marshall would *not* approve."

"Jah, all that decadent lard and sugar . . ." Grace noticed with some surprise Becky was already headed back to the house.

"Well, I'm sure Mammi will be happy to see you again." Grace turned toward the buggy. "She could help answer your questions about herbs."

"The healing ones, right?" said Heather.

"Where'd ya hear that?"

"Online . . . I figure if I'm dying, I need to know this stuff. Speaking of which, my laptop awaits."

Befuddled at how glib Heather was about her poor health, Grace quietly said, "A blessed Lord's Day to ya."

Heather waved and headed up the walkway and into the house.

Still perplexed, Grace spoke to Sassy. "Let's go home, girl, and see how Willow's doin'." The mare nickered softly at the sound of Willow's name.

CHAPTER
TWENTY-TWO

Why did I spill my heart out to Grace?

Frustrated at being so upfront with someone she hardly knew — *an Amish girl at that* — Heather hurried upstairs to her room at the Riehls'. She closed the door and turned on her iPhone to check for emails and listen to the voice mail from her dad.

"Hey, kiddo. Will you meet me at the house site later this afternoon? Call me."

"Is he hoping for another chance to hammer away at me?" She booted up her laptop, wanting to write in her journal for a while. Running her fingers through her hair while she waited, she got settled on the bed, sitting cross-legged. She was still surprised at how she and Grace had connected nearly from their first meeting. She appreciated how Grace had accepted first the news she was sick, then today's talk about her adoption. She hadn't given the latter a thought in a long time. It was enough to know how lucky she was to be Roan and Karen Nelson's daughter.

She picked up her phone to return her dad's call. When he answered, she said, "I got your voice mail."

"Hey, I've had a brain wave." There was an unmistakable lilt in his voice.

"About the house?"

"Can you meet me at the site?"

Now? She wanted to unwind from her visit with Sally's. "Can it wait until tomorrow, Dad?"

"Well, sure. You're probably tired. Actually, I'm surprised how you're holding up this well — *this long* — without chemo, Heather."

Here we go. . . .

"Um, Dad, if I'm not worried, you don't have to be."

"Look, kiddo, I have news for you: I'm your father, and it's my job to worry."

She sighed; she heard the trace of fear in his voice. The stubbornness, too.

"I want you to hear me out."

"Not today, Dad, please." She stopped, waiting for his retort. When there was none, she added, "Do we really have to fight about this?"

He sighed heavily. "Come home with me. That'll solve everything."

"We'll talk more about this after you meet Dr. Marshall. How's that?" It was her last attempt. She'd run out of words and energy.

"Fine. But I still want to see you first thing tomorrow. Bye, Heather."

She whispered, "Bye, Dad," and hung up.

Somewhat relieved, Heather switched over to read Wannalive's latest blog entry. She posted a comment, which he responded to immediately. It helped to think that someone somewhere was on her wavelength, even if that person was essentially a stranger.

She replayed in her mind the fascinating visit with Sally, the most disciplined person she'd ever encountered. Sally had found clever substitutes for everything from sugar to dairy. And she no longer ate red meat, saying adamantly that once her dreadful cravings ceased, she scarcely missed such foods. *"Now that I've been preparin' food this way so long, I hardly give it a second thought,"* she'd said. Heather almost wondered if she couldn't just skip the lodge and sit at the feet of the preacher's wife.

She set aside her iPhone and took up her laptop again.

I met an interesting Amishwoman today. During all of my childhood visits here with my parents, I just assumed these women were very shy. Not Sally! She was literally energized about having cured herself of cancer and was open to any question I had.

If I wasn't such a skeptic, I'd be suspicious about why I ended up here, in Amish country. Not that I think I'm a puppet on a string or anything. But how else can I explain my coming here and meeting people like Grace and Sally? It's like someone Up There really cares.

She went on, pouring out her thoughts — and questions — until she felt calmer. Finally, she shut down her computer and stretched out on the bed, wiped out. *I hope Dad's not too upset,* she thought, *for putting him off until tomorrow.*

Grace was sitting in the stall near Willow when Dat walked in and squatted down beside them.

"How's she doin' now?" he asked.

"Well, if I'm not dreaming it . . . some better."

"I thought the same."

Her heart was filled with hope.

"I've been in here every other hour — so has Adam," Dat said. "I must admit, whatever Yonnie's doin' might just be helpin'."

"You really think so?"

"Sure's hard to overlook."

"Wonderful-*gut,*" she said right out.

"If we can just get the founder under control, I suspect that's the worst of it."

"Are we givin' her enough powdered alum? That's what Andy Riehl does for his foundered horses."

"Jah, I've been doin' that, too." Dat wiped his brow. "One tablespoon of cod liver oil two times during the day should limber her up some."

"I've heard cod liver oil works for lots of older horses."

Dat nodded slowly, eyes solemn. "Just maybe we can keep her alive awhile longer."

"What about puttin' her in a mud hole with ice?" Henry Stahl had talked about this treatment some months back, insisting that it worked. A fleeting thought crossed her mind: *Has Yonnie heard of it?*

Dat's gaze was fixed on the mare. "If keepin' Willow around makes you smile, well then, we must."

It was the nicest thing he'd ever said. "I don't mean to be selfish," she whispered.

"That you ain't, Gracie."

Looking at him now, his shoulders rounded as he stooped forward, he looked like an old wounded bird. "Dat . . . I'm awful sorry 'bout asking to hire Martin to —"

"No . . . no, I understand how you feel." He glanced over his shoulder, most likely to see if they were alone. "I feel . . . the same sort of tug."

"I just see her in my mind. Already home, like she's never left."

Dat faltered as he shared how he sometimes imagined hearing Mamma making familiar bird imitations, the sweet sounds ringing across the backyard. "Or sittin' out on the porch like she does, talking to the birds that hop right up close to her." He drew a long, slow breath. "Ain't easy dismissing all of that."

All the pleasant memories.

Grace heard the note of undisguised longing in her father's voice. Was this the same man Mammi Adah had suggested Mamma might never have married? "Mamma's goin' away is the worst thing ever to happen," she said.

He was momentarily quiet, running his hand back and forth over Willow's shoulder.

Knowing she should not even think of asking, she said, "If I'm out of order, tell me, Dat. . . . Do you think it was necessary for Mamma to leave for a while?"

A long pause ensued. Then he surprised her by saying, "The night before she left, there was a problem with one of the new lambs. Adam needed my help." He sighed, rubbing his nose. "But your Mamma needed me more. . . ." He bowed his head. "I was just too busy."

She was astonished at his sincerity. "Ach . . . Dat."

"And not bein' able to make amends with her . . . that's the worst of it." Dat began inspecting the bottom of Willow's hoof. "Surely the vet checked for an abscess. But I've been keepin' an eye on it anyways."

"Well, that'd be easy to care for, jah?"

He agreed. "Just open it up, drain it, and soak it in Epsom salts." The warm solution drew out the pus and killed the bacteria inside.

"Sure would be nice if that's all this turned out to be," she said.

"Amen to that."

They remained there for some time without speaking. After a while, she mentioned spending the afternoon with Heather Nelson. "She's the Riehls' long-term boarder. I took her to visit Sally today."

Dat's eyebrows rose. "Oh?"

"She wants to see my herb garden tomorrow."

"Fine with me." Just that quick, he seemed lost in a daydream, and she wasn't sure he'd

300

heard her at all. Several more times she attempted to engage him in conversation, only to realize he must be tired. Either that or he was only able to emerge from his staid, quiet nature for a brief time. *He's sunk back into himself.*

Heather drove with her windows down after breakfast Monday, letting the warm air rush against her hair and face. The field crickets were ticking off their countdown to summer. *Ve-ry soon,* croaked the bullfrogs along Mill Stream.

She refused to set herself up for another possible dispute with her father, recalling the frequent discussions between her parents. Mom had been panicked, wishing she hadn't given in to all the pressure from both the oncologist and from Dad. Could it be . . . had she lost the will to care about living?

Sometimes Heather wondered the same about herself. Was the devastation of Devon's breakup the culprit, compounded with the heartache of losing her mother? It was ridiculous to assume she would be forever discontented without Devon or any other man. *I can be happy without a guy.*

Spotting Dad's rental car on the shoulder ahead, she steered off the road and parked.

A horse and buggy were parked there, too, and two Amishmen were talking to her father.

"Hi, kiddo . . . we're going to dowse for water," Dad called to her.

"You're kidding, right?" One of the older Amishmen held a willow branch, shaped like a Y, the forked ends held palms down. The third pointed toward the ground.

"It's willow witching," the younger farmer told her. Both wore the same kind of yellow straw hats she'd seen on Andy Riehl and his sons, and the trademark black suspenders with pale blue shirts and black trousers.

"Watch for the straight end to bounce if it detects water underground," Dad said, obviously intrigued as he followed them.

"Who are these men?" Heather whispered when they were out of earshot.

"One's Potato John — your friend Grace Byler's uncle."

She was surprised at the many connections her dad had made among the Plain folk lately. "Wow, Dad. You're becoming quite the real-time social networker."

He laughed. "Next thing, I'll need a straw hat."

"So who's the other guy?"

"Peter Stahl, Josiah Smucker's cousin. They both live up near Akron." He explained that the men were visiting relatives in the area, and Josiah thought Potato John could easily find water or even oil on the property.

"Really . . . oil? Now *that* would be nice."

Dad slipped his arm around her shoulder. "I've been thinking."

"Now that's a good start," Heather teased.

"I'll make you a promise. No more talk of chemo until after I meet your naturopath. Fair enough?"

"Deal!" She went with him to the side of the field where Potato John's willow stick was already springing back and forth.

"Here's a *gut* place to dig your well, Mr. Nelson," he announced, grinning like a schoolboy.

"Well, I daresay." Dad ran to catch up with him.

He's even starting to sound Amish. Heather shook her head. *What's up with that?*

Washday was always hectic, and Grace was mighty glad for Mandy's help this morning. She almost wished Becky might come running over and lend a hand as she sometimes did. She could see Becky and her little sisters outside in the early-morning light, hanging up their own washing together.

Grace found it almost comical that Yonnie

kept going in and out of the barn as if he wasn't certain where he ought to be. Sometimes he'd wave to her and other times he'd call, "Hullo, Grace," like he'd just done ten minutes before.

"I'd say you've got yourself a new beau," Mandy said when she came over for another handful of clothespins.

"Ach, Mandy."

"No, I'm serious. We might just need to plant a whole acre of celery this summer, what with Adam and maybe me and —"

"Yonnie's not here for *me*."

"Well, Dat's sure not over here hanging up the washing, is he?" Mandy's eyes twinkled. "What'll you say if he asks you ridin' Sunday night?"

"You'll never know, will ya?" Grace teased right back.

Mandy laughed out loud. No doubt the cheery sound carried all the way down to the sheep-grazing land. "You *do* like him!"

Her sister's carrying on so annoyed Grace, and she was worried Yonnie might overhear their nonsense. "Keep quiet."

Mandy ducked under Dat's large bed sheet, her face turning red. "Sorry, sister."

"You're anything but sorry." Grace shook her head, trying to keep from laughing.

A breeze picked up the ends of the sheets,

and a flock of birds fluttered up over the silo. Truth was, the more she thought on it, the more she worried Yonnie might be brazen enough to approach her at Singing, like Mandy suggested. Then what? Or was it best if she stayed at home and didn't go at all?

Immediately after breaking up with Henry, she'd never wanted to go to another youth gathering. Lots of the available girls — even some of the fellows — were in their teens and younger than she was. Grace was older than all of them, having been mighty picky about the boys she'd go with, then poking around too long, deciding what to do about Henry.

Yet oddly enough, she was curious to see if Prissy was right — were the fellows now leery of her? And if they weren't, what then? And, too, what of Henry and Becky — would it be awkward for *them* if she showed up? "Not that I want to court ever again," she said under her breath.

Mandy poked her head under a green dress hanging on the line. "You talkin' to yourself?"

"None of your beeswax."

Mandy let out another giggle, and when Grace glanced toward the barn, Yonnie was just heading back in, a tiny lamb cradled in his arms.

Grace felt convicted at not having kept herself in check. It wouldn't do for Mandy or anyone else to be getting any ideas. *Yonnie especially.*

"Sister?" Mandy asked. "I need to help muck out the barn with Adam and Joe. I figure you have the housework covered."

"You shouldn't be out there doin' men's work, you silly."

"It's just so much fun gettin' to know my future brother-in-law," Mandy quipped, flouncing off with a wave.

"You've got weddings on the brain!" Grace pushed a final clothespin down hard on Dat's clean for-good shirt, then returned to the house.

Adah could hear everything Grace and Mandy were saying outside. Their voices drifted right in through the kitchen window, where she was making Jakob's oatmeal — his favorite first course most mornings.

She caught herself snickering every time Grace tried to hush Mandy. *Just look what Lettie's missing out on,* she thought.

Adah reached for the cinnamon and thoroughly coated the top of the cereal. Then she made a small dimple in the middle for a dab of butter, fresh from Riehls' dairy. She placed the bowl on a tray and carried it upstairs to Jakob, who was under the weather again.

"This should make ya feel better, love," she said, going into the bedroom.

He inched his way up into a sitting position, then pulled the quilt flat against his lap. "There, now put the tray down," he muttered.

She kissed his cheek and sat down to read the Good Book aloud, but it was clear her husband was flustered.

"I'll read it myself later on," he mumbled.

"All right, then." She rose and placed the Bible on the bed. "I'll leave ya be."

"I didn't say to go away," he huffed. "Just want some quiet . . . that's all."

She wasn't sure if he even knew his own mind. "Well, do ya want me in here just a-breathin'?"

A crooked smile crossed his face. "You're a *gut* one!"

She went to stand in the doorway, hands folded, watching him eat . . . her husband sitting there, perched like a black crow in their bed. He looked so small and nearly helpless. How many more years did they have, Lord willing?

"I love you, old man," she said softly.

He turned his head to look at her, his

glassy blue eyes glistening. "I've been wonderin' when I might hear that again." He
gave her a weak smile.

"Aw, Jakob . . . what's a-matter?"

"It's Lettie. I can't get over what she's
done."

Adah reached for the cane chair near the
bureau and drew it up close to the bed.
"There, there. Our daughter's in God's
hands. Never forget."

He frowned, his right hand still holding
the spoon as it sank deeper into the hot oatmeal. "Ain't something *you'd* ever think of
doin', is it?"

"Might've thought of it . . ." Adah smiled
and he caught the joke. "Aw, you know I'd
never leave ya, Jakob Esh." And she meant
it with all of her heart, just as she had the
day they'd wed so long ago.

CHAPTER
TWENTY-THREE

Grace couldn't believe it, but there Yonnie was, stacking up the dirty dishes right behind her. She pressed her lips together to keep from smiling too broadly as she ran the dishwater. *Why is he doing this?*

Never had she known Dat or Dawdi Jakob to help in the kitchen. Men just didn't. Their realm of work was outdoors, in the barn or in the fields, though a growing number of local Amishmen spent most of their time in blacksmith or carpentry shops.

Yonnie gingerly set a pile of dishes down on the counter. "There." He eyed them. "Thought you could use some help."

"I see that."

He stood there with hands in his pockets now, grinning. "What're you lookin' at?"

"Do you sweep kitchen floors, too?" she asked, only half jesting. There seemed to be no end to the surprises where Yonnie was concerned.

He chuckled. "Sometimes."

"Indiana must be quite the strange place."

His eyebrows shot up. "Why do you say that?"

"It's just that . . . well . . . around here, men don't do dishes."

Yonnie nodded. "Actually, things aren't that different in Indiana, but my parents . . . well, they don't always observe the do's and don'ts like some Plain couples."

"Ach, really?"

Yonnie shrugged.

Grace was curious. "Like what else?"

"Well, for one thing, my Dat sometimes helped with my baby brothers." He rubbed his chin and looked away. "Better not say more."

She couldn't keep her smile in check any longer. "He changed diapers, ya mean?"

"I didn't say *that,* now, did I? But he did sometimes carry the smelliest ones to the diaper pail." Now he was chuckling. "You'd like my father, I'm sure of it."

"He must've grown up with older sisters."

Yonnie nodded, grinning.

"How many?"

"*Achde* — eight."

"*Un Bruder?*"

"Plenty of brothers, too, jah." He chuckled. "You'd feel mighty sorry for him if he had only sisters, wouldn't ya?"

She agreed. Naturally she would.

Yonnie glanced toward the barn. "Well, I ought to be goin' — your father will wonder what's become of me."

"Jah . . . Dat's waitin'." She didn't smile this time. "Denki for your help."

"Anytime," he said but stayed put. Then he pulled something out of his pocket. "Before I go, I wanted to show you this." There in his palm lay the prettiest, round glasslike stone. "It's the Cape May diamond I was tellin' you about. The one I found on the seashore."

Without thinking, she touched it. "Oh, it's so smooth . . . so beautiful."

He handed it to her. "And it's yours, Gracie."

"But . . ."

"I want you to have it."

"Yonnie . . ." She was conscious of his gaze. "You don't have to —"

"I know."

She shook her head, marveling that he wanted to part with such a lovely treasure. "I don't know what to say, honestly."

He smiled as her fingers closed over it.

"Denki . . . ever so much," she said. The sudden slosh of water behind her drew her attention back to the now-overflowing sink.

"Ach, goodness!" Grace hurried to turn off the faucet.

He said no more and pushed open the screen door, making his way down the steps.

She clasped Yonnie's sea jewel and tiptoed to the window to peer out, staying carefully out of sight, lest he turn around and see her there.

"I'm planning to bake some cookies to take to the Spanglers," Grace said as she marked the hem on Mammi Adah's almost-completed dress.

Her grandmother peered down from her perch. "Sounds nice."

"Turn slowly." Grace pulled the pins out of her mouth and stuck them in the pincushion, glad for a nice breeze coming through the open window.

Mammi rotated slightly. Then she must've raised her shoulders just enough for Grace to notice a difference in the hem length. "Marian says the family's in turmoil," Mammi said softly.

Same as us . . . Grace didn't let on what Jessica had shared with her last week. "Well, some sweets might just cheer them up, jah?" she said, weaving a pin into the hem.

Mammi Adah said nothing as Grace quickly finished the pinning. It was one thing to talk amongst themselves about the People, and quite another to waste time gossiping about their English neighbors.

When Grace arrived at their next-door neighbors to the south, Brittany Spangler came to the door. Her pretty face broke into a smile as she spied the plate heaped with cookies. "Oh, Gracie, you shouldn't have! Thanks so much!" Quickly she called to Jessica, who wandered to the door, still in her bathrobe and slippers.

"Uh, don't mind me. It's been one of those days." Jessica looked rather miserable.

"Excuse me." Brittany reached for a cookie and disappeared with a wave of thanks.

"It's great to see you, Grace. And not just because you brought some fabulous cookies," Jessica said, moving out to the front porch. "Can you stay for a few minutes?"

Grace nodded. "Sure, for a little while." She had hoped Jessica might have time to chat. With talk about the Spanglers beginning to circulate between Mammi and Marian, she was more concerned for her friend than ever.

"Has there been any more word from your mother?" Jessica asked as she set the cookies down on the small table positioned between two cushiony chairs. Grace took the chair facing toward the cornfield to the south.

Everyone seems to be asking. . . .

"I hope you don't mind," Jessica was quick to add.

"It's all right — and, no, she hasn't called or written again, if that's what you mean." Grace had mentioned Mamma's letter to Jessica when she'd stopped by with the eggs last Tuesday. "Honestly, Jessica, I've been thinking of going to look for her."

"Wow, are you serious?"

"I'm not sayin' I will. But I have considered it more than once."

Pulling her bare legs under her, Jessica draped her blue bathrobe down over them. "I can't blame you. I'd probably want to do the same thing . . . if I knew where to look."

Grace asked on impulse, "I don't s'pose you could drive me out to Indiana — if I paid for the gasoline?"

Jessica's brow pinched into a frown. "Oh, Grace, I'd love to . . . but there's just no way right now. I have to work like crazy."

"Well, such a trip's not practical for me, either, even though I'm not getting many hours at Eli's these days." She might've known Jessica's work would keep her tied down, especially with the expenses she'd

314

need to cover for her wedding next winter. "Actually, I should stay put, too. Ain't such a *gut* time, really. And Mandy's awful busy helpin' with lambing now, so I'm needed inside," Grace told her. "Sometimes Andy Riehl even comes over at night to help Dat and the boys trade off caring for the newest lambs."

"Sounds like *you're* picking up the slack for your mother, though."

"Well, it's hard to step into her shoes." Grace hadn't meant to complain.

Jessica wrapped her arms around her legs, leaning her chin on her knees. "I really don't see how you're managing . . . not knowing where she is. That would just drive me nuts."

" 'Tis hard, I'll say that."

"I assume you don't know where she went?"

Grace shook her head slowly. "I'd give most anything to know."

They sat silently for a while, staring into the distance. Grace wanted to ask how things were going between Jessica's parents but didn't have the slightest idea how to bring it up discreetly.

Just when Grace began to think she might be wearing out her welcome, Jessica said, "I've been wanting to talk to you again . . .

about my fiancé and me." Her eyes instantly brimmed with tears.

"You all right?" Grace leaned forward. "Is there something I can do for you?"

Jessica sniffled and shook her head sadly. "I'm sorry." She pressed her lips together. "If I tell you, you're going to wonder what I could possibly be thinking."

"Ach, not to worry," Grace assured her. "Feel free to say what's on your mind."

Digging into the pocket of her robe, Jessica pulled out a tissue. "It's complicated at best." She wiped her eyes. "I haven't even told poor Brittany yet."

Grace sighed. Whatever it was, Jessica needed a good friend.

"Oh, Grace . . . I've been thinking of calling off the wedding."

Seeing her friend's serious face, Grace's heart went out to her. She certainly knew how Jessica felt, and in more ways than she could say.

"I don't mean there's anything wrong between Quentin — my fiancé — and me. Actually, we're good."

Grace listened, her hands folded now.

"It's my parents causing all the upheaval — they're talking about a legal separation." Jessica stopped to blow her nose. "I can hardly think of anything else, you know?"

Nodding, Grace felt as sad as Jessica looked.

"I just wish they'd go to counseling . . . try to save their marriage. Try and do *something* reasonable."

Grace's heart sank to her feet.

"Oh, why do people break each other's hearts . . . and their children's, too?" Jessica was sobbing.

Grace felt like crying, too. *Such terrible news.*

"How can I know my fiancé will be true to me?" Jessica sputtered through her tears. "How can anyone know? You can't look into the future — ten or twenty years from now — and know what your husband will be like. It's so unfair."

Pondering that, Grace said softly, "Well, you can only know what *you'll* do. And what you purpose in your own heart to be to him . . . and for him." She was suddenly distracted by Jessica's bright toenails, which were the reddest red she'd ever seen. Not only that, but they had little white daisies painted on the big toes. Grace tried not to gawk as Jessica sat there in a ball of anguish, still sobbing as if she'd never stop.

Is anyone content anymore? Grace wondered.

"You probably don't realize it, but you'd

make a great counselor," Jessica said at last as she wiped her tearstained face.

"Oh, I don't know . . ."

"What you just told me makes me want to sit Quentin down and ask him some hard questions."

Grace shifted in her chair. "Might be better now than later."

"I only hope my parents can hold things together until after my wedding. It probably sounds selfish, but . . . I never saw this coming. Neither did Brittany."

They talked awhile longer, Jessica herself changing the subject back to the lemon cookies Grace had baked. "You're the nicest neighbor ever." She got up to give her a quick hug. "I hope your mother comes home soon," she whispered into Grace's shoulder. "I really do."

Grace struggled with the lump in her throat as they stepped apart. "I'll be prayin' for your parents . . . for peace to come."

Jessica brushed away tears with both hands, gathering herself. "My mascara probably ran all over my face."

Grace merely offered a sympathetic smile. Then, when Jessica tightened the belt of her bathrobe, she said, "Thanks again . . . for listening."

'Tis becoming what I do best.

"That's all right." Grace headed down the front porch steps. *"Da Herr sei mit du,"* she said. Seeing two hummingbirds flutter near Carole Spangler's glowing yellow forsythia bush, she whispered again, "God be with you and your family."

Relieved that Dr. Marshall could squeeze in a consultation tomorrow morning, Heather called her dad to let him know where and when. "Or since I'm heading toward Route 340 anyway, I can pick you up at the inn," she suggested.

"Great. I'll ride with you." But presently he seemed more interested in discussing the well Josiah planned to have dug. "Can you believe how fast everything's coming together?"

"Well, if you think living like a pioneer is fun, I guess . . . um, sure, Dad."

His laugh was hearty and she hoped he had forgotten the pending battle ahead. Did he really think he could persuade her that chemo was the way to go?

"Have any plans today?" he asked.

"Just a visit to Grace Byler's herb garden later."

"Herbs?" He chuckled. "Not *that* again."

"Dad . . . you promised."

He paused as if apologetic. "I was hoping

you might have time to look at some catalogs and samples with me."

"This house-building process isn't too overwhelming, is it?"

"More fun than work," he said.

"What is it today — tile choices and carpet colors?"

"Yes, and bathroom fixtures and wall paint."

She couldn't say no. "When do you want to go?"

He offered to pick her up shortly. "We can have lunch at another one of those Amish hangouts."

"They're *restaurants,* Dad."

He laughed again, and Heather cherished the sound.

The goldenrod will soon be in bloom, Lettie thought as she walked along Susan's backyard. She took in the warmth of the sun, the calming breezes. *I'll miss seeing it along the roadside back home.* How easy it was to picture Beechdale Road in summer.

At moments like this, she wished Grace was here. Or her sister Naomi . . . if she were still alive. But not Mamm. No, it was distancing enough whenever she thought of her mother's conspiratorial whispering to Minnie as the midwife had held Lettie's newborn so close in her arms. *All those years ago . . .* What had her mother so urgently advised Minnie that fateful day?

I may never know. Lettie headed for the back porch, drawn especially to the wicker chairs with plump blue-checkered pillows. There were yellow tulips in long, rectangular planters set around on the rustic wooden porch. She settled into the chair facing toward the little town of Baltic. Why was it so reminiscent of home? Was it Susan's thoughtfulness — *so like Grace?*

Her eyes scanned the farmland before her as she relaxed. There were no sheep to be seen in any of the pastures nearby. Was lambing not a profitable business here? For a fleeting moment, she almost turned to ask Judah his opinion, startling herself.

Old habits . . .

She closed her eyes and soaked in the birdcalls surrounding her. She breathed in the sweetness . . . the calm. Was it a tranquil moment before the storm ahead? Or would a peaceful resolution eventually come by talking with Dr. Josh in Nappanee? She hoped her cousin Hallie might respond promptly.

Gazing at May Jaberg's house, watching her school-age girls trimming the hedges, she let herself fall into a daydream. After some time — she didn't know how long — she heard Susan talking with someone in the house. Turning, Lettie glanced at the driveway and saw a horse and buggy parked there. Had she been so deep in thought, she'd missed hearing its arrival?

Just as the unfamiliar buggy began to pull away, Susan called to her. "Oh, Lettie, come quick!" Her voice was shrill, as if something dreadful had happened.

Lettie rose immediately and hurried into the house, where she found Susan in a heap on the wooden kitchen bench, rocking back and forth, her hands covering her face. "No . . . no . . . this just can't be."

Lettie rushed to her side, kneeling down. "Ach, Susan . . . what is it?"

"Edna, my younger sister . . . was out in the buggy with four of her little children and the new baby." Her hands trembled and Susan's face was ashen as tears slid down her cheeks. "The buggy was hit by rocks as she drove to market. Two-year-old Danny was hurt badly."

Lettie, still kneeling, gripped her hand. *Oh, poor, dear child . . .*

"I must go and help Edna with the baby and the other children." Susan returned the squeeze, then rose to head for the stairs.

"Of course." Lettie would have offered to

go, too, but she felt frozen with dread. *Help Susan's poor sister, O Father . . . and her injured little boy!* She was overcome with tears for Edna and her son.

When Susan returned from upstairs, the woman's eyes were puffy and red. "Should you be drivin' alone?" Lettie asked.

"The town's a little less than forty minutes away by buggy . . . I'll be fine." Susan pulled her shawl off the peg. "Help yourself to whatever you find. There's plenty of food in the pantry."

"Denki."

"I'll be back before dark."

"You sure you'll be all right?"

Susan must've sensed what was churning in Lettie's heart. "I travel this route several times a month." She wiped her eyes and sighed loudly. "Such a hard time for my sister. The authorities are urging Edna to press charges against the boys who did this. She'll have to go to court sometime soon."

Susan didn't mention the town where Edna and her family lived, which was just as well. *Sometimes 'tis best not to know,* Lettie thought.

"Take your time, won't ya?" she urged.

"You wanted to cook in my kitchen, jah?" They shared a sad smile. "May Jaberg will be happy to drive you if need be. She also has a telephone . . . if necessary." Susan's face was tear-streaked as she kissed Lettie's cheek. "Make yourself at home."

Lettie followed Susan down the back steps to help hitch the horse to the carriage. In the field, just beyond the fence, several farm boys in overalls with fraying hems joked and called to one another, their glee carried back and forth on the wind.

Later, when Susan was safely on her way and the back of the buggy was a small black dot, Lettie turned and climbed the steps into the house again. The quiet was nearly more than she could bear as she stood at the kitchen window, peering out at the bright day. Sunlight played off the rickety tin roof of the neighbors' woodshed, and birds of every species clambered to the sky.

She wouldn't consider a visit to May today. She was too distraught . . . too emotional. She felt nearly raw at the thought of Edna's suffering, yet Lettie knew the police would not convince Edna to file criminal charges. The Good Book instructed them to forgive "seventy times seven," and Edna and her husband would do just that, in spite of their wee son's injury. How many times had her own bishop instructed them to turn the other cheek?

Will Judah forgive me someday, too? The

uneasiness came from the depths of her heart. Lettie feared having to reveal her secret sin, protected in her consciousness for so long. *Will I have the courage to tell my husband about Samuel's and my baby . . . when the time comes? And how will Judah react when he hears?*

As if looking for answers, Lettie wandered to the room where she was staying. On the bureau she found her favorite poetry book and tenderly opened to "The Bridge" by Henry W. Longfellow. Silently, she read the entire poem, but her eyes lingered on two particular stanzas.

And forever and forever,
As long as the river flows,
As long as the heart has passions,
As long as life has woes;

The moon and its broken reflection
And its shadows shall appear,
As the symbol of love in heaven,
And its wavering image here.

" 'As long as life has woes,' " she murmured, weeping not only for little Danny, Susan's wee nephew, but for herself, too.

A sudden and gripping terror besieged her, and she found herself worried . . .

wondering if her first child was even alive. Lettie closed the poetry book, enfolding it in her arms like a baby.

What if my searching is all for naught?

CHAPTER TWENTY-FOUR

Heather dreaded tomorrow's consultation with LaVyrle. She had no idea what her father might say. *Will he voice his opinions too freely?*

The pending visit kept her from fully enjoying her time with Dad even as he kept her occupied all morning and afternoon, making snap decisions about paint and bathroom tile, sink and commode styles, and every other little detail that went into building a house. It had taken the entire day, but she overlooked it — his company was even more precious now that she might lose it. And, true to his word, Dad never once brought up her illness.

Between catalogs and store samples, they talked fondly of Mom. So much that Heather wondered if he was still coming to grips with what had gone wrong with her treatment. If so, wouldn't he consider doing things differently this time? *A second chance of sorts?* Didn't most people wish they could go back at some point and redo at least a part of their past?

On the return ride to the Riehls' place, her dad pulled over and parked near the house site. He craned his neck forward, leaning on the steering wheel as he admired his property once again. "Gorgeous, isn't it?"

She had to agree. "When will they start excavating?"

"Josiah says in a few days, once the building permit's acquired. Meanwhile, I'd like to get our present house ready to put on the market, even though it's an abysmal time to sell. Thankfully there's plenty of equity in it." He talked of having some loose ends to attend to at work, saying he hadn't told his boss that he was thinking of taking early retirement. "But with the other house to sell, there's no rush on that."

She was intrigued by his fascination with building, something he and Mom had never endeavored. Times like this, seeing him so invigorated by the challenge ahead, she wanted to take a mental picture and file it somewhere safe.

"Don't forget, we have a date tomorrow," he said out of the blue.

She nodded, not looking forward to the

discussion with him that was sure to follow the conference with LaVyrle. *Unless, of course, things go well . . .* And while he rambled on about his need to secure an electrician — something Josiah wouldn't be handling — she reconsidered the idea of touring Grace's herb garden today. *It's not as if it's going anywhere.* And as understanding as Grace had been, surely she wouldn't mind if Heather bailed.

Her mind wandered to Grace's missing mother, and she felt sincerely sad. The loss of a parent — that, she could identify with.

She picked at her shirt as they pulled up to the familiar sight of Andy and Marian's house. Their young daughters were watering the flower beds out front.

"Well, here you are . . . I'll see you tomorrow." Dad leaned over and kissed her cheek. "Thanks for hanging out with your old man."

"Oh, Dad."

"It was fun . . . at least for me."

She smiled. "See you tomorrow."

Chipper's good, Heather thought, opening the door. *Tomorrow will be a different story.*

Grace kept so busy with the washing and folding, as well as working the afternoon shift at Eli's, she forgot all about Heather's interest in seeing the herb garden until twilight. Hurrying to the front door, she looked toward the Riehls' house and saw Heather's car parked in the driveway. *Maybe she forgot, too.*

Grace had felt sure she'd gone out of her way to make the English girl feel welcome. Goodness, the poor thing was terribly ill . . . she needed all the information about natural healing she could get. But surely the visit to Sally had been helpful, and she knew Heather would soon be returning to the naturopath.

Standing there with mending in her hand, Grace suddenly remembered Mammi Adah's dress — all pressed and waiting to be worn. She made her way to the sewing room and left her mending in a neat pile on the table. "I ironed your dress," she told her grandmother, who was fussing over square arrangements for a yellow-and-green baby quilt. "It's all ready."

Mammi looked up, smiling. "You did a nice job, Gracie . . . as always."

"Let me know when you need another one sewn. I'm happy to help." Grace noticed the baby quilt Mammi Adah was working on and felt she might burst. For days now, she'd wanted to ask the gnawing question. Gathering her wits, she said, "I didn't tell you something, Mammi . . . after I called the Kidron Inn. I should've, I guess."

Mammi's smile faded to a frown.

"This might sound strange to you — well, I know it will."

"What, Grace?"

She was ever so hesitant to say. Even so, looking into her grandmother's eyes, Grace believed she could trust her with this concern. "Why would Mamma want a midwife? Could it be . . . well, could she be with child?"

Mammi's eyelashes fluttered. "What would give you that idea?"

"The innkeeper's wife said as much — about the midwife, I mean. I didn't want to mention it to anyone." She paused. "I almost didn't."

Mammi had a peculiar glint in her eyes. She was still for a moment, looking up at Grace. "Well, I 'spect that's something your father might know."

Grace shook her head. " 'Tis too awkward to bring up." She would not think of it . . . much too embarrassing. And, anyway, knowing he and Mamma had differed terribly on something before Mamma left was enough. Was it about a baby?

"I can't imagine that your Mamma's in the family way, no." Mammi's face was suddenly moist with perspiration. She picked up one of the quilt squares and fanned herself.

"You'll keep it mum, won't you?" pleaded Grace.

"Upon my word."

Worried that she'd somehow revealed something she shouldn't have, Grace carried the newly finished dress to Mammi Adah's bedroom. Her pulse pounded in her ears as she hung the garment on a wooden peg near the bureau. *Ach, I'm sorry, Mamma . . . if I spoke out of turn.*

Adah tried her best to concentrate on placing the pastel-colored squares for the baby quilt. So Lettie must be looking for the midwife who'd delivered her firstborn. That, and that alone, had to be the reason she'd left her family.

Adah's heart felt heavy . . . guilty. She was disturbed no end by her own response to Grace's innocent question. *I distorted the truth to my own granddaughter! Lied, truly . . .*

She stepped back to study the layout of squares on the table. The crib quilt would be a welcome addition to daughter-in-law Hannah's baby items. If Adah wasn't mistaken, son Ethan and Hannah's seventh child was due in another couple of months.

Stopping her work, she let out a little gasp. *Could Hannah's coming baby be part of Lettie's angst . . . and her unexpected search?*

Staring at the pattern of colors before her, Adah felt both eager for another new grandbaby and terribly convicted for her outright deceit. She would not confide in Jakob, as frail as he was. No, she must carry the weight of Lettie's pain deep within herself. Yet she knew full well that even if Lettie did come home, that would not necessarily make things better here. Particularly if word about the past got out, her return could make things even worse!

Oh, if only there was some way to make amends to her daughter. Adah placed her hand on her heart, thinking of all the years of Lettie's sorrow. *Jakob and I brought all this on her,* she thought miserably.

Judah hung back near the doorway and peered into Adah's kitchen. He wanted to talk to Jakob man-to-man, and thankfully Adah was nowhere to be seen. She must still be working on the baby quilt for yet another grandchild — or so Grace had mentioned in passing a few minutes earlier, when he'd inquired after her grandmother.

Grace had seemed downright skittish as he came through the sitting room toward the main hallway. He couldn't be sure if that was due to Yonnie's presence . . . or Lettie's absence.

He cleared his throat so as not to startle Jakob. The older man turned and waved him into the room. "Ah, Judah . . . come, pull up a chair. Rest your weary bones."

There was no getting around it: The day had been long. And he was growing tired of the routine of lambing season. He had no use for small talk, not with Adah's movements upstairs so unpredictable. No, what he had to say, he ought to just get out in the open. "I've been thinking . . ." he began, faltering. " 'Bout Lettie."

"As you should be" came the chilly reply. "She's been gone much too long."

Judah sat straight as a twig, looking across at the old man who'd brought Lettie to his attention all those years ago. "Is there anything in my wife's past that might explain her flyin' the coop like this?"

At the question, Jakob looked stunned. Then he shook himself a bit, pulling on his old suspenders. Through the open kitchen window, Judah could see the sun falling behind the horizon.

"Now, son . . . why would ya think such a thing?"

Not once since he and Lettie had become

man and wife had Jakob referred to him as son. But Judah was not inclined to sit there and be grilled with unnecessary questions. "Either ya know somethin' or you don't," he replied. "Easy as that."

Jakob scratched his wrinkled face, letting his callused fingers run down his long gray beard. "Not sure why you're so ferhoodled tonight, Judah."

"Just wonderin' if you're holdin' something back."

Jakob shook his head slowly, as if a burden had descended upon him.

"Is there something I ought to know?" Judah's ire was up but good. For days Jakob had been avoiding him . . . not even making eye contact at their shared mealtimes. He'd figured Jakob was feeling poorly, like Adah kept saying. But she, too, was acting strange, if not distant. And why would that be?

He looked again at Jakob, whose eyes seemed stripped of their usual life. Goodness, but Judah knew this man as well as he knew his own sons, and he could tell something wasn't right.

"What is it, Jakob? What can you tell me 'bout Lettie?"

Lettie had decided to wait up for Susan. She had a pot of water on the stove, ready to steep tea as soon as Susan arrived. She'd also kept busy baking chocolate chip cookies as a surprise, wanting to cheer up her friend after what would surely prove to be a difficult day.

When she heard the buggy pull into the driveway, Lettie hurried outside to help unhitch the horse. Once the chore was done, she led the animal to the stable as Susan plodded toward her home, having said little about the day.

Lettie got the horse settled in for the night with feed and extra water. Then, breathing a prayer, she made her way back to the house, the light from several gas lamps glowing in the back windows. *Like golden faces shining into the darkness . . .*

"Would ya like some sweets?" she asked when she'd entered the kitchen. She washed her hands, then dropped the tea bags into the teapot.

Susan sat at the table, her face wan. "Ach, such a hard day."

Lettie sat across from her and slid the plate of cookies toward Susan. "Maybe these will help some."

Susan gave a half nod and reached for one. "I'm all tuckered out." She began to describe her visit. The chief of police had come to her sister's house, demanding that

Edna fill out papers against the rock-throwing boys. "It was just terrible. And the authorities were baffled as all get-out . . . why she and her husband wouldn't consent." She removed her Kapp and rubbed her temples in a circular motion. "They just don't understand our way. And no explanation we gave was convincing a'tall. Edna simply refused to cast blame."

Lettie had heard before how perplexing Englischers sometimes found the People's determination to forgive as almighty God had commanded.

"One man even said the boys who did this should be taken out and shot." Susan shook her head sadly. "Such hatred."

Lettie empathized with her friend. "Where were Edna's children durin' all this?"

"Over in the *Dawdi Haus* . . . Edna and Jonas did not want them upset further."

Bad enough that they saw their little brother injured.

"We prayed before I left that God's sovereign will might be done in this calamity," Susan said in a near whisper. "Jonas has already searched out the young boys' parents, trying to befriend the boys' families. The police were so appalled. 'How can you overlook this?' one of them asked, shaking his head and growing almost angry with

337

them. I never saw the likes of it."

The tea had steeped long enough. Lettie got up and poured some into two cups. They stirred in sugar and droplets of cream, then sipped the tasty chamomile tea, eating nearly all the cookies before them. As they relaxed together, Lettie hoped to keep in touch with Susan once she left for Hallie's.

"I'd like you to know what happens with my search," Lettie said when their conversation had turned from tiny Danny, who remained in the hospital, though the doctors fully expected him to recover. "You've helped in more ways than I can say."

Susan agreed to keep in touch by letter writing. "And it looks like you might be still here for the hen party at May's on Wednesday. 'Tis *gut.*"

"Maybe so, but I trust Cousin Hallie will be quick with a reply. I should be on my way no later than Wednesday afternoon."

"Usually it takes only a day for a letter to come from Indiana," Susan said.

"That's what I'm hopin' for." The last thing Lettie wanted was to wear out her welcome here, yet in a way, she dreaded leaving. It was becoming more emotionally difficult to continue her wanderings. At night her dreams were of a vagabond, sorely lost, who did not know if she would ever be welcomed home with open arms. The daylight hours were equally filled with longing. She yearned continually for her children back home, as well as for their father . . . her Judah.

The thought of her beloved poetry books — Samuel's gift from years ago — crossed her mind. The books had been a comfort in all this. *Perhaps too comforting,* she thought ruefully.

When Susan said good-night and they outened the lights and headed to their respective rooms, Lettie found her most treasured book of poems. Holding it, she thought of tearing out the first page, where Samuel had written his greeting and signed his name on her sixteenth birthday.

But something stopped her from actually doing so. Her missing daughter — hers and Samuel's, wherever she might be — what if *she* might cherish this book? *Once I find her . . .* She considered Vesta Mae, the Jabergs' adopted daughter across the way. Lettie so badly wanted to glimpse her. "At the hen party," she whispered, putting the book on the dresser.

Reaching up, she removed her head covering and began to dress for bed. She slipped on her long cotton robe and took down her hair. Then, kneeling on the floor, she tucked the book of poems, so descriptive in its phrases, deep in the recesses of her suitcase with the others. That special book had been a crutch for more than two decades, something she no longer needed. In all truth, she believed she could walk without it . . . from here on out.

Truly my soul waiteth upon God. . . .

With a renewed sense of hope, Lettie covered the books with the clothes she'd already packed for her trip to Hallie's. She rose and, pulling back the lightweight quilt, slipped into bed.

CHAPTER
TWENTY-FIVE

Heather wended her way through a maze of Amish buggies to pick up her dad Tuesday morning. Was it just her imagination, or were the horses and carriages multiplying by the day?

She squinted her eyes, stressed at the thought of their consultation with Dr. Marshall and how things might play out. Would Dad be polite today — listen and learn? Or would he create a scene?

As she parked near the inn's entrance, he came strolling confidently toward the car, wearing a sporty navy jacket and tan dress slacks. She figured he had brought mostly jeans and khakis for the trip. "Looking sharp today, Dad," she said as he opened the door and got in.

Even before she pulled out of the parking lot and onto the highway, he began drilling her with questions about LaVyrle — where she'd gotten her credentials, what *kind* of credentials did she have, how long had she been in practice? Heather really just wanted to say, *Ask her yourself,* but bit her tongue.

The naturopath's parking lot was busier than at her first appointment last week. *Not a good sign,* she thought, worried that sitting around was sure to set her dad off even more.

Surprisingly, they waited only fifteen minutes before her name was called. She introduced her dad to the nurse who led them down the hallway. So far, he was the consummate gentleman. They followed the cheerful nurse back to LaVyrle's office, a well-decorated room with comfortable chairs across from a refurbished antique desk. Heather hadn't seen this room before, having spent the hour last time in an examination room.

The room had sea-green cloth shades that gathered at the bottom and covered the top fourth of the windows. She admired LaVyrle's taste in dark woods for her lovely old desk and the built-in bookshelves. "We should've invited Dr. Marshall to help pick out your cabinets, Dad." Despite his seeming ambivalence, she could see that he, too, was taken with the attractive office.

After being seated, Heather pointed to the wall and jokingly said, "Now's your chance to check out Dr. Marshall's qualifications. Look, Dad. I've never seen so many framed certificates."

"A dime a dozen," he retorted.

I can see it now — disaster ahead.

"Looks like she's got everything from a chiropractic degree to a license in massage therapy for sports injuries." He pointed out various certificates, then got up suddenly and went over to the wall, his nose nearly touching the glass as he peered at the words. "Unfortunately I'm not seeing anything MD-worthy."

"She's a doctor of naturopathy . . . in practice for seventeen years. Please don't judge her before you meet her, Dad."

After a few minutes, LaVyrle breezed into her office and closed the door. She wore a smart aqua suit with silver jewelry at her throat. The shade of her outfit accentuated the blue in her eyes, which fairly sparkled now as she reached to shake Dad's hand. "You must be Heather's father," she said, smiling.

"Roan Nelson." He nodded, returning the smile. "Heather's talked about you nearly nonstop since I arrived."

That's a stretch. Heather was amused by her dad's snap-to-it-iveness. *Maybe this will be a slam-dunk.*

"What can I do for you today?" LaVyrle leaned back in her office chair, making eye contact with both Heather and her father.

Dad lost no time in nutshelling the reason for their visit. "My daughter has a serious illness. She's refusing conventional wisdom. . . ."

"Which is?" asked LaVyrle.

Turning, Dad looked at Heather. "Have you filled the good doctor in?"

Yikes. She felt like a child.

"Dad . . . Dr. Marshall is fully aware of the reason why I'm here." She paused. "Why *we're* here."

This wasn't intended to be a therapy session, yet LaVyrle stepped right in and became a referee of sorts. She reiterated what she understood to be Heather's hesitations about chemo and radiation, then recited the benefits of cleansing and juicing and other important aspects of "the lodge experience."

Heather was in no frame of mind to debate her dad. "What are the drawbacks?" she asked for his benefit.

LaVyrle explained how physically challenging, even grueling, the program could be. "But I can assure you, the diet does become easier for those who stick with it."

She also offered them statistics on the success rate, without making claims. As a professional, she clearly knew better than to offer radical promises. "I believe Heather could greatly benefit by the Wellness Lodge, just as so many others have. We would love to help her."

"Any guarantees?" Dad asked, working his fingers on the arm of his chair.

LaVyrle gave him a very direct look. "I'm sorry to inform you, Mr. Nelson, there are no guarantees in this life." She glanced at Heather, a knowing look on her pretty face. "Bottom line, we don't offer easy cures here, but we do offer hope . . . through re-education, for instance. Clients learn how to work *with* their bodies to reverse the toxicities and deficiencies that have weakened the body's ability to fight off serious disease in the first place."

LaVyrle gave them a brochure listing the daily schedule and program for the lodge — including educational sessions, therapeutic massages, blood-cleansing regimens and supplements, and meals based on cleansing teas, organic juices, and other aspects of Dr. Marshall's plant-based diet, which consisted of eighty percent raw food and twenty percent cooked vegetables and grains.

To Heather, LaVyrle sounded brilliant, and she sensed anew the woman's passion.

"So let me get this straight: My daughter could endure the rigors of your program and still be sick?" Dad leaned forward, his hand in a fist beneath his shaven chin.

"I'm going to level with you, Roan. The rate of success is very low for patients who attempt this program on their own. This approach is only for those who are motivated and committed to lifestyle change. The lodge experience ensures that a person will have the needed support and guidance while going through the detox. The knowledge Heather would gain, for instance, will equip her with the skill and confidence to continue the regimen at home," LaVyrle said. "To be fair, there are patients whose illness may still require drug therapy or surgery, depending on the stage and type of illness they are suffering."

Heather eyed her father. She expected he'd heard all he needed to — that surely he would simply thank LaVyrle for her time and encourage Heather immediately to register for the earliest possible opening.

"You can also read additional testimonials from patients online, if you wish." LaVyrle folded her hands on her desk.

This is our cue the consultation is over,

thought Heather, hoping her father caught on.

"We really appreciate your time." Heather inched forward in her chair. "When does the next lodge session begin?"

Her dad ran his hand through his hair and gave her a quick look.

LaVyrle checked the computer monitor. "We have a few openings left for next Monday."

Less than a week away. "I'd like to pay the deposit today." Heather turned to her dad, hoping he'd offer the necessary money. But his eyes were sending a different message, loud and clear.

"And *I'd* like to discuss this further." He rose from his chair.

"Dad . . ."

"I think you're wasting your time here, Heather," he said, then quickly thanked LaVyrle. He reached to open the door and left Heather sitting there, bewildered.

"This is rather typical," LaVyrle said as soon as they were alone. "There are many stages of denial . . . and obviously your dad is extremely worried about you."

"He's only known for three days, so it's still a shock. And he forgets how completely debilitated Mom became from conventional medical treatment." Heather explained how hopeless they both had felt.

LaVyrle smiled thoughtfully. "I certainly understand. And I'll pencil your name in if you'd like."

"You read my mind." She realized her dad didn't have much reason to trust her decisions at this point. After all, she had withheld her diagnosis from him, although out of loving concern. But he still viewed that choice as uncharacteristically irresponsible. *No wonder he's so resistant.*

Reaching across the desk, she shook LaVyrle's hand. "Dad doesn't know it yet, but I'm planning to join the ranks of your cured patients." She mentioned having met Sally Smucker recently.

LaVyrle nodded and smiled. "Sally certainly has a supportive spouse."

Heather considered that. "Is it absolutely necessary to have a supportive, um . . . significant other?" she asked, realizing she might be going this alone without her dad's moral support.

"Well, from my experience with patients, that can be a wonderful help . . . but a good friend is equally terrific, and many clients meet such lifetime friends at the lodge."

Lifetime friends. For the first time . . . the sound of that didn't frighten her.

■ ■ ■ ■

Adah felt tense while Jakob told of Judah's visit. His sallow face was creased with deep lines; she'd forgotten how drawn he looked when he was this pale. Getting up from the kitchen table, she went to the stove to boil some water for tea. "Do ya want honey in yours?" she asked.

"Sugar's fine, love."

Gingerly she set the teakettle on the burner and set the flame to medium high. "You don't think Judah suspects anything in particular, do ya?" She glanced over her shoulder at Jakob.

"It's beyond me what he thinks he knows."

"So you didn't tell him anything, then?" She moved back to the table and rested against the back of Jakob's chair, at the head of the table.

He sat still, head bowed, breathing much too fast.

"Ach . . . *what?*" She went to sit on his right, her customary spot, and leaned forward on the table. "Jakob, you didn't." *Please, dear Lord, no . . .*

He reached for his reading glasses on the table before him. "Bring me the Good Book, Adah. It's time for the Scripture."

Her heart was heavy as she plodded to the corner table, over which the clock shelf ticked off the minutes. Obediently she carried the Bible and placed it in front of Jakob. "Please say you didn't tell Judah about Lettie's baby?" she pleaded.

Jakob reached for the heavy book and opened it to the Psalms. "You know how I love ya, Adah . . . jah?"

She nodded her head slowly, tears creeping into her vision.

"And you've always trusted me, ain't?"

Her hands trembled. "Always."

"Judah's a mighty smart man," he said pleasantly. "Wasn't that why we picked him to marry our Lettie?" His gaze held hers. "I daresay he smells a rat, which is all fine and *gut*. But Lettie's the only one who has the right to share with her husband what she did before they married, jah?"

Adah gave a deep sigh of relief. "Oh . . . thanks be to God." The secret was still safe.

After a morning at Eli's, Grace spent part of the afternoon baking lemon meringue pies — one for their supper and two she planned to take over to Riehls', hoping to run into Heather again. She wondered why Heather hadn't come to see the herb garden yet, as she'd seemed so eager to do on

Sunday afternoon.

When she arrived at the neighbors', she discovered both Becky and Heather were gone from the house. So she left the pies with Marian, who thanked her repeatedly. "I'll tell the girls that their friend dropped by."

At home, Grace stopped to look in on Willow and — surprise, surprise — found Yonnie there. "Hullo," she said at once.

"Hi, Grace." An instant smile appeared and he quickly stood up. "Willow's definitely responding to the softer bedding."

"How can you tell?"

"She's less sensitive to the touch . . . more trusting, too," he said.

"We *have* been putting the liniment on like you said to."

Yonnie touched Willow's shoulder. "Your father's not in a big hurry, but he thinks we might try to walk her slowly in a couple days. Just go a short ways."

We?

"I think you'll be pleased with how all this special care will bring Willow around eventually." He leaned toward Willow. "Ain't that right, girl?" The horse turned almost immediately and nuzzled his elbow, softly nickering like they were old friends.

"Dat doesn't think she'll ever trot again,"

Grace observed.

"Well, and she prob'ly won't ever pull a carriage, neither, but I think she'll be around for a *gut* while yet."

I think . . . I think, he says. But she was less annoyed by his assumptions today than a few days ago. Maybe it was the way Willow fixed her eyes on him. "The vet should be surprised at these small steps forward, jah?"

Yonnie agreed. "It's not so remarkable, really. A little love sure can go a long way."

Her cheeks blushed at his comment, and she hoped to goodness he hadn't noticed.

Yonnie's eyes absolutely danced now as he occupied himself with her horse. *Anyone who's this fond of an old horse must surely have a good heart.*

Grace excused herself and left for the house.

Heather's dad was on a rant. "Dr. Marshall said it herself today . . . there's no easy cure. Don't you see it?" he said.

No easy cure . . .

He'd cornered her, or at least she felt that way in the parked car. The inn where he was staying was just beyond her left shoulder, and the armrest of the car was digging into her spine, her back literally up against the door. "What I see is that you can't relinquish control even for something as vital as this," she said.

He leaned his head on the dashboard for a moment. "This? Meaning what . . . your life? Look, I care about you, kiddo." He straightened and slapped the brochure on the stick shift. "I've read every word here — 'the body can heal itself of degenerative conditions' . . . *et cetera.* Come on, Heather. You're a brilliant grad student . . . why can't you see this clearly?"

Why can't you?

She was smarter than to respond in anger. Not even LaVyrle's reasonable comments had made a dent in his inflexible veneer. "Why don't you see this as a viable alternative to chemo?" She looked at him, miserable as he seemed. "What can it hurt?"

"I'd rather not find out the answer to that," he shot back.

They were getting nowhere. "I think we should call it a day," she suggested.

"Well, I'm leaving tomorrow afternoon."

Her heart sank. She desperately needed his assistance with this — financially and otherwise. It was all she could do to keep up with the weekly rent on her room at the Riehls'. "Dad, you know I need your help to pay for the lodge program. I don't even have the fifteen hundred bucks for the deposit." Meeting Dr. Marshall today and the ensuing conversation had put the nail in what little optimism she'd had for his encouragement and support.

He shook his head and leafed through the brochure once again. "You know, Heather, if I could return to the past and do everything differently — and if it would bring your mother back — I would in a heartbeat."

"Please don't, Dad . . ."

He pulled out his wallet. "You're as stubborn as I am." He handed her his credit card. "Here's my contribution . . . at least for now."

Surprised, she accepted. "Thank you," she said, assuming he meant he'd pick up the tab for the final bill. "I wish I could say I know you won't be sorry."

"It's a crapshoot, right?"

"Maybe it doesn't have to be. Mom sometimes prayed about things." She put the card in her purse.

He nodded, turning to look at her with soft and now glistening eyes. "I'll be back to visit you at the lodge next week." He reached for her hand. "You're not going through this weirdness alone, okay?"

"Thanks, Dad." She choked back her own tears. "I mean it . . . thanks."

CHAPTER
TWENTY-SIX

Lettie awakened on Wednesday morning anticipating both a possible letter from Cousin Hallie and May's hen party. After all, May had said her married daughters were going to be present to help entertain the younger children, and Lettie dearly hoped to be introduced to them. If Vesta Mae was indeed her daughter, might the young woman resemble either Samuel or herself, clinching the truth?

With Susan off again to help her sister Edna today, Lettie needed to keep her mind and hands busy. Rolling out pie dough with a group of other Plain women just might be her cup of tea, especially when she was discouraged at not having heard back from Cousin Hallie yet.

Moving about Susan's kitchen, Lettie hummed while packing the food to take for the noon meal — her contribution. She'd already discussed the items with Susan:

three dozen pickled red-beet eggs, a generous bowl of potato salad, and the remaining chocolate chip cookies she'd baked Monday to cheer up Susan.

Glancing out the kitchen window now, Lettie saw several black buggies already pulling into May's narrow, tree-lined lane. As she watched the flurry of activity, a sudden urgency gripped her. The loneliness she felt was enormous. She must hasten to go, must see for herself if May's adopted daughter was truly the reason she'd found herself here in Baltic.

Will I see her face-to-face at last?

Lettie had no idea they would be making pastries and cookies, as well as enough fruit mush to feed seven neighboring families. The enormous batch, to be frozen for next winter's meals, consisted of crushed pineapple, sliced bananas, and maraschino cherries in a syrup of orange juice, sugar, and water. She'd often made the concoction with Grace and Mandy, but there were thirty women on hand this morning — a very efficient assembly line. May comically offered a running tally of helpers as she welcomed Lettie at the back door.

Worktables had been set up in the kitchen and sitting room. Three young women were already mixing batter for four hundred cookies — peanut butter oatmeal and snickerdoodles. In one corner of the kitchen, there were food hampers filled with sandwiches and other luncheon items brought along for the noon meal. And two women were working together in the summer kitchen, setting a long table with paper plates and plastic utensils. *Like a picnic,* thought Lettie, enjoying herself.

All the while she kept an eye out for May's daughters, Vesta Mae particularly, although one bubbly woman said they were upstairs telling stories to a group of toddlers. "The children are draping themselves with old scraps of quilting fabric," she was told.

Since Vesta Mae's married, does she have little ones? That thought led to another, and in short order Lettie imagined what it might be like to not only meet her daughter, but her first grandbaby! *How can I manage to sneak up there and have a look?* She kept glancing toward the stairs, hoping the girl might simply appear.

May, however, was nearly omnipresent as the ultimate hostess, flitting from one location to the other as she coordinated the various groups. She chattered as they worked and visited leisurely. May took the time to talk with one young woman, who looked downright blue. "Oh, Anna," she said, "I know it isn't easy, but try even harder, dear . . . marriage is a sacred thing. You just have to work it out."

Try even harder, thought Lettie as she pulled out a chair and introduced herself to a woman around her age named Maryann. They began to cut oodles of fresh pineapple, gently putting the small squares in a large bowl. And because Maryann seemed nearly as shy as Judah always was, Lettie found herself recalling her wedding day. Her husband had never smiled as much in all the years she'd known him. She remembered being a little startled at his happy state and wishing she might have felt the same. *For his sake.* Truly, she had been ever so grateful to wed a hardworking man who was so well thought of, especially by her father. *By Mamm, too.*

The conversations between herself and her mother had dropped off drastically following their return from Ohio, Lettie with empty arms, yearning for her wee babe. Yet Judah had never been the wiser. It was as though he just assumed her leaving town had made her realize she cared more for him than for Samuel.

Now, as she pondered that chilly November wedding day, she wondered if Judah had ever considered that she had been less than happy from the start of their union. If so, it must have been so distressing for him to suspect he was her second choice . . . though her father's *first* choice in a mate for her, according to Naomi.

Reliving her marriage vows, Lettie recalled how bashful she'd been, standing before the bishop and all the People . . . before almighty God, too. Judah was as soft-spoken as she had expected. Yet, at the same time, she had sensed in his gaze his unwavering commitment to her — he'd believed she was the bride for him.

Does he know that I grew to love him, too?

After filling several bowls with pineapple chunks, Lettie had a kink in her neck. She rose to go into the front room and stretch a bit and discovered two women nursing their babies. Turning toward the stairs, she heard a small child crying and continued up, her heart wrenching at the desperate sound.

She followed the sobbing to a large bedroom, where a pretty young woman sat, rocking a tiny boy, cooing into his ear. "There, there . . . you'll be all right," the girl said, rubbing the boy's back. "Shh, dear one."

Is this Vesta Mae with her child? Lettie tried

not to gawk, but she was so drawn to the lovely dark-haired girl with big brown eyes — nearly black. "Maybe I can help?" Lettie said, going into the room, moving quickly past the bed and around several small children sitting on the floor, playing with blocks. Some still had remnants of play-clothes wrapped around their shoulders.

In that moment, when her eyes met the young woman's and held for the longest time, she realized anew how she longed to know the truth. "Are you Vesta Mae?" she asked softly.

"Jah . . . my Mamma's the one hosting the hen party." She rose gracefully from the rocker, walking now and swaying with the towheaded boy, who looked about two, nestled in her arms. His wailing had ceased, but she continued to kiss his chubby red cheeks. "This is my son, Levi." She stroked his hair. "Smile for the nice lady."

"I'm Lettie Byler." She glanced toward the window, giving a nod of her head toward Susan's house. "Stayin' over with your neighbor for a little while."

"Ah, Mamma mentioned you'd come by." Vesta Mae brightened. "Said you were askin' about adoption."

Lettie scarcely heard her now — she was so fascinated by the shape of Vesta Mae's mouth . . . the deep, rich hue of her hair. *Samuel's father had dark hair.*

"There's a doctor we know who places babies fairly quickly. . . ." Vesta Mae's voice trailed off as Lettie blocked out her words, still taken by the arch of her eyebrows . . . the line of her chin.

Even now, all these years after the fact, she knew Samuel's face by heart. Lettie's gaze darted now to little Levi and she searched his face, as well . . . hoping for some clue. He was as blond as Lettie had been as a youngster . . . as blond as Adam and Grace still were.

Lettie's eyes traced the boy's chin line, his nose, and the set of his eyes. Then, searching . . . searching, she did the same with the young woman, Vesta Mae.

But, standing there, she knew without question this was not her daughter and grandson. As much as she'd wished to, she had not stumbled miraculously into her missing daughter's life.

"You have a precious son . . . mighty nice meeting ya," Lettie mumbled awkwardly, moving past the cluster of children on the floor, toward the hallway. She felt spent. "Sorry to bother you," she said over her shoulder, hoping May's daughter hadn't felt slighted.

Don't give in to sadness, she told herself. *Keep your head up.*

Gripping the railing, she inched back down the stairs, thinking of the psalm she'd read just that morning: *"Why art thou cast down, O my soul? . . . Hope in God."* Heartened, she made her way back to Maryann's table and the fruit mush. Lettie was not a quitter; she would finish the task. But all she could think of now was Dr. Josh, the man who'd helped place her baby.

Please, Lord, let me hear from my cousin soon!

Returning to the bustling kitchen, Lettie glanced at the banana-slicing table, then back where she'd sat. Someone had taken her earlier spot, so she walked to the sink to get a drink of water. She looked at her wristwatch. *Nearly time to eat.* She felt as if the other women were gawking at her. She was, after all, a stranger to them. How could they possibly know why she'd come?

She poured a glass of water and drank nearly all of it before stopping to breathe. Then, setting the glass to the right side of the sink, behind a scouring pad set in a small white cup, she turned around and looked for an empty chair where she might sit and resume her work. *Someplace to gather my wits.*

It was then she noticed Nancy Fisher and her sister Sylvia across the room near the double oven, pulling out several hot cookie sheets.

Quickly, Lettie turned away, hoping not to be seen. As she did, she bumped against a soup ladle on the counter, and it fell clattering to the floor. The abrupt noise made such a ruckus, the Fisher girls looked up . . . right at her.

Nancy's eyes were wider than walnuts, and Sylvia audibly gasped, "Ach, Lettie Byler . . . what on earth. Is that *you?*"

Lettie clenched her hands, struggling to keep her emotions at bay. She knew full well this news would quickly wend its way to Judah's ears.

Ach, no . . . now what?

CHAPTER
TWENTY-SEVEN

Heather sat on her bed at the Riehls', eager to tell Wannalive her plans for the Wellness Lodge. He would be in favor of her decision, having gone through something similar months ago in another state.

> Hey! I made my deposit for the lodge program. Next Monday's the first of ten days. I'm ready for the deep-tissue massage, but I'm less sure about the one-on-one counseling and, of course, all the detoxing my body can withstand. Any advice for handling it?
>
> Thanks for your encouragement. I really appreciate the input I got from your blog . . . and from your messages. I'll let you know how it goes.

After sending the message from her phone, Heather opened a window and peered out, hungry for some sunshine and fresh air. Sitting near Mill Creek with her laptop would certainly qualify as the *somewhere tranquil* LaVyrle had emphasized in her brochure. Stress, after all, had the power to create a host of health problems . . . as did unresolved grief issues. Physical detoxing was only part of the getting-well equation. Since emotional trauma had a way of getting trapped deep in the muscles — and other places — it was as essential to detox the emotions as it was her body. *I need to maintain a mellow mindset.*

Heather heard the chime signaling she had a new email. She picked up her phone to check who'd written and found a reply from Wannalive. He must have been online when she'd sent hers.

Courageous move!
Be forewarned that something mimicking euphoria might sneak up on you during the first few days at the lodge. It hit me on the third day of the cleanse regimen — an amazing feeling, like floating through space.
On the fifth day, though, I sank like a rock. It was the day of the liver flush, and I was depleted of electrolytes and dehydrated, according to the doc. But you'll do fine if you go into the whole thing with a

good mental attitude — and drink lots of water. Prayer helps, too.

I believe God leads people who are open to divine intervention. You may have come to the same conclusion. Just think of your upcoming lodge stay as a powerful nudge in the right direction. How's that?

I wish you well!
Wannalive (aka Jim)
P.S. Keep in touch!

"Jim? So we're on a first-name basis?" She laughed, feeling a surge of elation. She stared at her iPhone. *Do I dare reveal my name?* He was probably right there, still online. And he would guess that she was, too. *Will I appear too forward if I reply now?*

She really wanted to comment on his idea of divine direction — what the Amish around here called Providence or the sovereignty of God. Becky had talked about just that, one of the first times they'd gone riding together.

"Get over yourself, Heather," she muttered. Why not respond to his nice email? After all, they were adults.

She began to key in her response.

Hey, Jim,
Your comment about divine guidance

has me thinking more about "our great God," as someone recently posted in your blog comments. The Supreme Being with a strategy for the universe He created and for every person on the planet.

I have to level with you, Jim: I never considered much of this until my diagnosis — I kind of gave up on the whole notion of God after my mom's death. Then getting slammed with the prospect of dying jolted me into a whole different sphere of thinking. Is there more to life than what we see around us? IS there a great Hereafter, just waiting for us to show up?

That's where I am now — thinking about my present life and the possibility of the next one coming sooner than I'd planned. And how/where my belief system fits into that reality . . . IF it's real at all.

I guess you are far more connected to spiritual things than I ever was or cared to be. But even if I get lucky and cure myself, it might be time to give the God-thing a closer look. . . .

Thanks for being there,
Heather

She refused to second-guess having signed her name. A guy who was interested in talking about God seemed pretty harmless.

That, and incredibly fascinating.

Reaching for her laptop satchel, she slung it over her shoulder and headed downstairs through Marian's kitchen. "I'm out to catch some rays," she said, feeling exhilarated. "Oh, and by the way, has anyone called for me this morning?" She laughed at her own joke.

Marian and Becky snickered, too, their hands deep in bread dough. "Well, Gracie Byler was here lookin' for ya yesterday. Does that count?" Marian asked. She sported a healthy smudge of flour on her cheek.

Grace probably thought she was forgetful or fickle for not showing up to see the herb garden. "Sure, thanks. I'll definitely catch up with her soon."

Feeling surprisingly carefree, she waved to Marian and Becky and headed out the door. She glanced across the pasture toward the Bylers' house and spotted a group of sheep bunched up along the fence. She remembered how Grace had thoughtfully given up her Sunday afternoon to introduce her to Sally Smucker.

Heather searched for the perfect place to sit, eyeing several locations in the grass, near the running stream. At last she found a pleasing spot beneath a cluster of willows and settled in for an hour or so of writing.

It was time she caught up her daily journal.

The day had turned overwhelmingly sunny — a perfect one to do some gardening. Grace had been at it for some time, and now she stopped to raise her head to the sky, squinting up and adjusting her blue-and-white bandana. Yonnie had announced he'd be unable to work this morning, and Grace felt free to roam about the backyard — had even spent a full hour weeding her herb garden. The chives especially needed attention. She still hoped Heather might come to see it, especially now with everything looking so tidy.

Rising to catch her breath, she'd nearly completed the last long rows. A pot of suey stew had been cooking on low heat in the oven, enabling her to work outdoors for as long as she wished. Closer to time for the noon meal, she would fry up some melted ham and cheese sandwiches.

For now, though, she was itching for a walk. In the distance she heard a dog barking as she wandered toward the road, turning north toward Becky's house. She paid little mind till she saw Yonnie running on the opposite side of the road, jogging this way, his German shepherd straining on the leash.

"Grace — hullo!" he called, halting the dog.

Nearly like a runaway horse, she thought of his large pet.

"Nice day," she said.

His familiar smile was infectious as he wrapped the leash around his wrist several times. Quickly, the dog sat at his feet. "A wonderful-*gut* day, jah?" Yonnie's hair shone nearly gold in the sunlight.

She breathed in the fresh fragrance around them. "Smell that?"

"Won't be long till summer."

Had he somehow planned this encounter? But how could he have possibly known she needed to stretch her legs after hours of weeding?

"Out walkin' alone?" he asked.

She glanced down at his compliant pet. "I only have barn cats to keep me company, and they don't much like a leash." She didn't know what had gotten into her, joking like that.

"Well, walk with *me,* then." His lips parted, waiting for her answer . . . his blue eyes wide with hope.

"All right." She fell into step with him.

They walked for a ways without speaking. Knowing Yonnie's inclination for wanting to talk, she was surprised he was this quiet, yet the silence wasn't at all uncomfortable. She enjoyed watching Dat's young lambs darting about just beyond the sheep fence.

After a time, he looked at her, a questioning expression on his face. "You know, Grace, I've never said anything, but I can see how sad you are 'bout your mother." His tone was thoughtful. "It wonders me."

Not willing to disclose anything, she merely nodded. Did he assume her initial unfriendliness was due to her distress over Mamma?

"I've been thinking a lot about your family. What I mean is . . . this must be a difficult time for *all* of you."

She'd never experienced such caring from a fellow — except for Adam, of course, though they were siblings. She recalled Yonnie's gentle way with animals. Maybe this was just part of his nature.

"My prayers are with you," he added. "I wanted you to know."

She had to look away. "Kind of you," she whispered.

Yonnie glanced over his shoulder. "Something else, too," he said, looking now at her. "I bumped into your father at the blacksmith shop recently. I believe it was Providence." He paused, offering his winning smile.

"Why would ya think that?" Grace wasn't sure why the shop was so special — here lately Yonnie'd seen plenty of Dat. *All of us, really.*

He stopped walking and removed his hat, pushing it under his arm. "I hope you won't think I'm too plainspoken, but I talked with him about something important. And I want you to hear it from me."

She listened, quite befuddled. How intriguing for him to want to be so open. She thought of Henry — it was hard not to compare him to her former beau, if fleetingly.

"I asked your father for his blessing," Yonnie said.

"Sorry . . . you did what?"

"Where I come from, askin' the father's go-ahead before courtship is essential. Some bishops strongly urge it."

Her mind whirled. "Oh, Yonnie, I think you're mistaken."

He frowned, his eyes intense. "You mean you're spoken for?"

She thought about what she'd said to Becky.

"*Are* you engaged, Grace . . . as your father supposed?"

"I was . . . but no longer."

His swift smile gave him away. "Then I'd

sure like to court ya — that is, if you're so inclined."

Before Henry came along, she had been interested. Then, while Yonnie was getting acquainted with other girls, she had dismissed him, thinking he was fickle . . . or worse. And Becky's heartache had complicated even the most subtle feelings Grace had managed to squash. But now, with Becky seeing Henry, what would her friend say to this? Didn't that give Grace some kind of permission?

"I'd be willing to wait for the appropriate time," he pressed.

So it wouldn't look fishy . . . after Henry, she presumed.

"Well, there's a wonderful girl for you right next door." She pointed toward Becky's house. "What about her?"

"What do ya mean?"

"I know for truth she really liked you. I don't know what you're thinkin', passing her up."

"Becky's a sweet girl, I'll say that." He paused, his eyes fixed on Grace. "But she's not *you.*"

She was speechless — Yonnie's eyes were soft. He cared for her; that was clear.

She sighed, pushing a pebble aside with her bare foot. "I couldn't think of hurting my dear friend. . . ."

"I'm talkin' about *us* now — you and me, Grace. I want to court you . . . when enough time has passed, if that'd make you feel better." He wanted an answer, and Grace knew he deserved one.

"With Mamma missing, things are so unsettled."

Yonnie frowned. "Missing?"

Grace noted his strange look of curiosity and suddenly realized that he must not be privy to the whole story. Well, at least the things she and her family knew. Most likely he'd kept himself clear of the sordid talk of local gossips.

His frown deepened. "I thought she was . . . visiting friends."

"Not that we know of." She shook her head. " 'Tween you and me, we haven't been able to find her."

He put his hat back on, eyes serious. "Grace . . . what if I told you I know where she is?"

She studied his face, disbelieving. "How can that be?"

"I'm tellin' ya, I know right where your mother is."

If this was a joke or he was making light of it, she didn't find it one bit funny.

"Listen," he said. "The grapevine takes

only a few minutes to travel from Baltic, Ohio, to Bird-in-Hand."

Baltic's close to Kidron, she thought, stunned. *He must know what he's talking about!*

"Two of your friends from Eli's saw her just today — less than two hours ago."

Grace's breath escaped her. "Saw Mamma? Where?"

"Nancy and Sylvia were at a doin's with other women, Mary Liz told me. Your mother was making fruit mush."

"How'd your sister hear?"

He explained that Nancy Fisher had access to a telephone in an Amish-Mennonite woman's house. "They're visiting their father's cousins, the Jabergs. Anyway, Nancy called Sally Smucker's cell phone . . . the one she has for her little soap shop."

Grace had passed through the shop just last Sunday. "Did your sister mention the name of my mother's friend . . . where she's staying?" Grace asked, still unbelieving — she'd never heard Mamma speak of anyone in Ohio. Was she a new addition to Mamma's circle letters, perhaps?

"Her name's Susan Kempf. She lives right behind the farmhouse where the Fisher girls are visitin'."

"Oh, this is so wonderful-*gut!*" She wanted

to let him know how grateful she was, but right quick she squelched the thought of a spontaneous hug. "How can I thank you?" Truly, Yonnie deserved more than a token of appreciation for this information . . . and for everything else he had done, too.

"Your happiness — just seein' it on your face — that's enough thanks for me, Gracie."

She'd never cared much for the nickname, but hearing Yonnie say it made her feel warm all over.

Brushing back her tears, she glanced toward the house and suddenly remembered her big pot of cubed meat and vegetables. "Ach, my dinner!" She wrung her hands apologetically. "I'm so sorry, but my suey stew's goin' to overcook."

He grinned and tapped his hat brim. "Well, then, by all means hurry!"

The courtship question circled in Grace's mind all during the noon meal — the table seemed quite empty without Yonnie.

Ach, I never gave him an answer!

CHAPTER
TWENTY-EIGHT

Heather leaned back to look at the sky and shielded her eyes. She marveled at the beauty surrounding her, here in this quiet haven she'd claimed for herself. Was the day unusually pleasant due to Jim's comments about God? Or was it his abandoning the screen name for the more personal Jim? *How do I know that's his real name, anyway?*

She couldn't let herself fall for someone she'd met online, could she?

Refocusing her attention on her laptop journal, she was suddenly aware of the friendly voices drifting down the road. Long before she ever saw the couple, she could easily make out their conversation . . . embarrassingly so.

One voice was unmistakably Grace Byler's. The other apparently belonged to a young man named Yonnie, who seemed pretty worked up about Grace's mother. Heather looked up from her laptop, unable to keep from listening. She wondered if Grace realized that this Yonnie guy was totally into her.

Heather wanted at least a glimpse of them. But she wouldn't stare, even if she had the chance when they walked past the willow trees. It was bad enough she had heard such a personal discussion!

To think she was listening in on a real-life Amish romance. It was just as she might imagine. *Well, not actually.* As of yet, she hadn't noticed any suspicious pauses, and she very much doubted kissing was even in the cards. But there was definite longing in Yonnie's voice.

Now Heather was second-guessing her decision to put off the herb garden tour. Why had she failed to make good on the invitation when she'd found Grace Byler so engaging?

Don't I owe it to her to keep my word?

She pushed the laptop into its case and hopped up from her grassy perch. Slipping the strap over her shoulder, she glanced toward the road again. Not spotting Grace and her guy just yet, she ambled toward the creek. *Has Grace's mom really been visiting friends all this time?* If so, why hadn't she told her family?

Talk about an Amish riddle! And Yonnie's

sister had heard it from the proverbial grapevine? How was Grace expected to cope with such a revelation?

Shortly, she saw Grace running this way . . . *away* from the blond Amish boy who earlier had proposed courtship. Heather saw both of them now — Grace in a dull gray dress and long black apron, her hair the color of raw honey. She had a blue kerchief in her hand as she ran.

Quickly, Heather called, "Grace!" not certain why she was so compelled. "Over here!"

Grace stopped her mad scramble and waved. She wiped her brow, out of breath. "Ach, I didn't see ya. How've you been?"

"Just great . . . spending time with my dad." *Making plans to extend my life.* Heather walked toward her. "Looks like you're in a rush."

"I need to get back to cookin' dinner." Grace was out of breath, and now she glanced back toward Yonnie and his dog. "Would ya like to see my garden sometime today?"

Heather assumed she was making small talk, especially because she was noticeably preoccupied with Yonnie. "Sure . . . I'll come over later." *What can it hurt?*

"All right, then. See ya." Grace lifted her

skirt, her apron flapping as her bare feet flew across the road. She darted over to the grassy area along the shoulder, then toward the sheep fence, and slid under. She ran through the pasture. Now Yonnie was jogging this way, his dog at his side, his eyes still fixed on Grace.

Heather would soon be face-to-face with the young man who loved Grace far more than Devon had ever loved her — she was willing to bet money. As he ran this way, Yonnie's eyes met hers and he looked away. His face turned instantly red. *Does he guess I heard them talking?*

"Good morning," she said as he grew closer.

"Hullo," he replied. He was visibly uncomfortable being addressed by an outsider — and a feminine one at that.

Watching him jog away, Heather replayed the conversation she'd overheard. *If only I had the chance to retrieve* my *own mom,* she thought wistfully and wondered if Grace would want to go and visit her mother in Ohio.

Heather's mind began spinning with ideas. *The lodge program doesn't start until Monday. Would Grace be allowed to drive out there with me?*

There was only one way to find out. It was

the very least Heather could do for someone who had been so incredibly generous.

Lettie stood in Susan's front yard, pacing as she waited for the mail truck, which she could see at the end of the road. The morning's catastrophe had left her exhausted. She had excused herself following the noon meal and rushed back here, hoping for some peace of mind. But that was next to impossible. She could just imagine the reports flying to Bird-in-Hand. All too soon her husband and family would know where she was staying. Perhaps Judah might come calling himself . . . or send Adam out here to fetch her. She contemplated the pain of such a confrontation — forced to reveal the ugly truth. And Lettie shivered at the thought of her sin laid bare.

She held her breath, watching for the mail. Surely today Cousin Hallie's letter would come!

Judah stood in the barn, watching Grace walk with the Englischer from Virginia. He felt he was intruding on his daughter's privacy somehow, despite the fact he could not hear a single word she and the tall young woman were saying over there in the herb garden. As he observed them through the smudged window, he was amused now and then by Grace's bending low to pick off a leaf of spearmint or lemon-scented thyme. She offered each sample to the girl, who either tasted or pinched it, sniffing the fragrance. *This one knows little about gardens,* he decided as he watched the Riehls' boarder trailing Grace through her beloved herbs. The fancy young woman squatted and ran the palm of her hand lightly over the low mounded chamomile, with its white daisylike flower. She looked as if she was in awe of the leafy vegetation rising out of their rich black soil.

But it was the way the two girls lingered, as if conspiring together, that gave him pause. Wasn't this the young woman Andy Riehl had described in hushed tones? The one whose father had hired Preacher Josiah to build a house? Andy had said the young woman spent hours alone in her rented room. He'd even found her once late at night, curled up in the haymow with a small black computer, weeping like her heart might break.

Judah moved toward the barn entrance, more curious now as Grace strolled back toward the road with the girl, the two of them just talking up a storm.

■ ■ ■ ■

"How did ya know I want to go to Ohio?" Grace asked as she and Heather walked back toward the Riehls'. Her heart had sped up at the Englischer's words.

"I need to level with you." Heather admitted to overhearing Grace and Yonnie's conversation. "My guess is you probably wouldn't think of traveling alone to see your mom, right?"

Grace agreed it was out of the question. "My father made that clear days ago."

Heather was staring at the road ahead. "You've got to be having a difficult time of it," she said quietly. "With your mom being gone."

Grace's heart warmed to Heather's remark. "I guess we both know what that's like."

Heather gave a slow nod. "Well, would you like to go?" she asked. "I'd be glad to drive you."

Grace looked curiously at her. "Do you honestly want to?"

"It'll help me take my mind off my own issues," Heather said. The afternoon humidity hung around them like a veil, heavy and still.

"This is such a surprise!" Grace wanted to hug her. "You're an answer to my prayers. Truly you are."

Heather hung back, her eyes blinking rapidly. "Well, uh, how soon can you leave?"

Grace considered that, knowing nothing stood in her way except her father. "If I can get Dat's permission, I s'pose we can go right away."

They walked farther, the sunlight turning the kudzu vines into a shining green cloak that nearly concealed the woodshed to their right. *Spreading nearly faster than the Amish grapevine.* But today Grace had no complaints whatsoever about that.

"Okay, I'll wait to hear back from you."

"Denki . . . I'll see what Dat says, then come over and let you know either way." Grace walked with her to Marian's kitchen door. For some odd reason, it was hard to part ways. And she hoped she might get even better acquainted with Heather on the long ride to Ohio.

Hopefully, Dat will let me go.

Judah steadied the ewe during her intense labor. He recalled Yonnie's way with the birthing ewes, how he talked softly to them after the labor was past . . . when the young lamb wobbled to its scrawny legs. That boy seemed to know more about God's creation than Judah had ever given a second thought to. But recently he'd shown too much interest in Lettie's absence, even asking him guardedly if Lettie had ever tried to tell him why she wanted to go. *"Before she left."*

Since Yonnie's first day helping, Judah had been telling the lad things he hadn't found the ability in his heart to tell even Adam. Things a man might only share privately with a preacher, really — someone with a powerful sense of understanding. Not with a mere boy who, while he was still wet behind the ears, seemed wiser than Judah himself in the area of relationships.

Mandy had informed him that Yonnie and Grace were seen on the road before the noon meal today, walking and talking together.

Maybe he's got Gracie figured out at last.

Heather assumed her father had checked out of the inn hours ago, since she hadn't heard anything more from him. She'd forfeited her usual stint at the coffee shop that afternoon, afraid it would present too much of a temptation, and was now nibbling on a few almonds from her vantage point on the front porch, where she sat. She was surprised to see her dad's car pull into the driveway.

"You're still here?" She hurried down the steps to meet him.

He kissed her cheek. "Come walk with me," he said, eyes smiling. "I need some exercise before my long drive."

"I bet you want to go over to the house site, right?" *Where else!*

He nodded. "Okay if I leave my car parked here?"

"Sure, as long as there's still room for the team to come and go."

He looked momentarily puzzled. "Oh, you mean the horse and buggy."

"Hey, you catch on fast!"

They headed north on Beechdale Road; a warm, gentle breeze came up as they walked. Delicate clouds played on the horizon, near the green hills to the far north.

It didn't take long for them to arrive at the place where they had parked yesterday and debated Dad's side of things. "You sure know how to pick a pretty spot, Dad," she admitted. "But I still don't quite understand why you chose this area to build."

His eyes caught hers, searching her face. "I'm ready for a change."

She weighed that, confused. "But . . . Dad, at the height of your career? I mean, you're leaving everything behind. Everything you've built to get where you are."

"It might appear that way." He pushed his hands into the pockets of his khakis.

"Isn't it a gamble?"

He led her to the edge of the property.

She studied him, this man who rarely acted on impulse. "I don't get it, Dad. Why?"

He faced his four acres and squinted. "There are things your mother and I never told you." His voice was suddenly ragged.

"What things?"

He shielded his eyes with one hand. "After Mom died, I started thinking we needed a change of scenery, you and I. Everything in the house reminded me of her . . . everywhere I looked."

Which is why I love it.

"We came here to Lancaster County so often as a family 'to soak up the peace,' as your mother liked to say. But she and I came for another reason, too." His eyes bore a new softness when he turned to look at her.

"What reason?"

"We wanted to build a house here someday. Your mom and I thought it might be fun for you to experience something . . . of your family roots." He paused, jingling the coins in his pants pocket. "Actually, kiddo,

I'm talking about your *Amish* roots."

"My . . . *what?*" she sputtered.

In that moment, Dad's eyes registered the gravity of the years. Everything around them slowed to a stop — even the breeze seemed to die down. "Your birth mother was a young Amish girl, Heather."

"You can't be serious." She locked eyes with him. "Did you say Amish?"

"That's a *gut* thing, jah?" He offered a smile.

"You have to be joking."

"Well, when we first heard about you from friends of ours in Ohio, your mom said it was the sweetest thing."

Sweet?

"And when we flew out to see you, we fell instantly in love with the most beautiful baby girl we'd ever seen."

She tried to wrap her mind around his words.

"We had to make you ours." He explained that although they were approved for an in-state adoption with a local Richmond agency, the two of them had started to feel discouraged . . . nearly given up hope. "We'd waited so long. Your mom had begun to pray every day."

Heather had heard most of the rest of this story before, but never about the prayers.

"Really, Mom prayed?"

"Let's just say she made frequent appeals to God."

"Wow, I didn't know."

Dad looked proud suddenly, like the rooster that owned Andy Riehl's barnyard.

"Why didn't you tell me before? Why didn't Mom?"

"It didn't seem important until now." He slipped his arm around her as they walked. "From the moment we brought you home, you felt so much a part of our lives. Frankly, it was difficult to think of you as coming from anyone else apart from your mother and me. We truly adored you. Still do."

She leaned against his arm. "Oh, Dad . . ."

"I'm telling you now only because it clarifies why I want to settle here. Ohio would have been truer to your roots, but since Lancaster County's closer, this is where we liked to visit — the place where our family really connected with one another."

She swallowed hard. "You know, it doesn't make any difference to me who my birth parents were. It was so great growing up as your little girl . . . yours and Mom's."

"And a thoroughly modern girl, no less."

With Amish blood coursing through my veins . . .

They'd reached the middle of the plot.

Sunshine spread across the cornfields and grazing land beyond. "I want you to have this land and the house we're building someday."

"Not for a long, long time, though, right?"

He sighed, reaching for her hand. "You're going to beat this disease, right, honey?"

"Sure, Dad." Heather smiled up at him, tears falling down her cheeks. "That's the plan."

By the time they walked back to the Riehls', Heather's dad was starting to make noises about getting on the road. She kissed and hugged him in response to his wholehearted promise to return early next week. Watching his car creep down the lane, Heather was still surprised at her parents' long-held secret. All the same, knowing it changed absolutely nothing about her feelings for either of them.

She noticed Becky and her mother tossing feed to the chickens across the barnyard . . . and Becky's barefooted sisters squealing with glee as they played at the well pump. She was seeing them in an astonishing new light. Heather glanced down at her attire, mentally comparing her sleeveless blouse and faded jeans to the Amish cape dresses. *The way I might've been raised . . .*

She wandered around to the front of the Riehls' roomy old house and sat on the porch steps. Looking to the south, she watched the littlest lambs *ba-a-a* and bleat as they followed their mothers on the other side of the fence. And not far from where she sat, four young finches chirped happily in a birdbath.

"Unbelievable," Heather whispered, leaning her chin on her hands. She reveled in the spread of the immense front yard before her and the flat, fertile fields on either side, gazing in all directions.

No wonder I'm so at home here. . . .

CHAPTER
TWENTY-NINE

Grace hurried inside and pulled down Mamma's biggest kettle. Spaghetti sounded so good for supper! While she worked, it crossed her mind that she should cook ahead a couple days' worth of meals for the family. *If Dat allows me to leave tomorrow.*

Goodness, she could scarcely believe Heather had offered to drive her all that way. She filled the kettle with water, thinking how much easier it might be to simply write her father a note of explanation. *Just sneak away after dark like Mamma did.*

She carried the kettle to the stove and turned on the gas, knowing she couldn't bear to hurt her father that way, nor the rest of her family. She went to the pantry and found the packages of noodles she'd purchased at Eli's and resolved to talk to Dat immediately. She must be respectful and ask for his consent, praying his answer might reflect the Lord's own will in this.

■ ■ ■ ■

Judah heard Grace's footsteps on the driveway. He'd come to check on Willow after
eating too much again at supper. Grace had
surprised him when she'd leaned over to
whisper in his ear as she put dessert on the
table, asking if she might talk to him. Now
what was on her mind?

He patted Willow's neck and back, feeling
the strength of the mare's muscles. The last
thing he wanted was another rift with his
eldest daughter. He almost wished it was
Jakob asking to speak with him tonight. Far
as he was concerned, the conversation
they'd had was less than satisfying. Nothing
had been accomplished — Jakob had thrown
the wrench back at him.

When will I ever see Lettie again? Judah
wondered.

Grace arrived carrying a lit lantern, even
though twilight was at least another hour
away. He braced himself as she appeared
and stood there before him.

"Ach, Dat . . . I have such *gut* news! I
would've told you — and everyone — at
supper. But the timing didn't seem quite
right."

What the world was she babbling about?

"So I waited to tell you privately . . . first."

He took the lantern from her and set it down, away from Willow's bedding straw. "What's on your mind?"

"It's Mamma." Her voice wavered. "I know where she is."

His breath caught in his throat. "How's that?"

"Yonnie told me today."

Judah was stunned. He hadn't expected this.

"Yonnie heard it from a reliable source. And I'd like to go and visit her, Dat."

"Where?"

"She's staying with a friend in Baltic, Ohio."

He rubbed his face, heart pounding. "You know this for certain?"

"The Fisher girls saw her this very morning at a work frolic."

"In Baltic?" He'd been waiting . . . hoping for such news all along. And yet, hearing it now, Judah felt bewildered, like he didn't know what to do first.

"Can I go, Dat? Heather Nelson, the young woman staying with Andy and Marian, asked if she could drive me. And since I know where Mamma is staying — I've got the woman's name written down — we won't be gone but two days." Grace continued, reminding him that she'd met his earlier conditions. Sure, lambing season wasn't quite over, but she wasn't asking to take Adam or anyone else away from helping with the sheep. It was as if she'd rehearsed every word, at least in her mind.

The first thing that popped into his head was to put his foot down — simply refuse her again. But it was hard to overlook the fact this just might be a second chance for him. And wasn't it a good idea to let Grace decide some things for herself, now she was twenty-one? All grown-up . . . nearly past courting age, too. Judah wanted her to know she could come to him and talk things through — like the adult she'd become. *She's always been such a steady and faithful daughter. . . .*

"When would you want to go?" He looked at her standing there in the shadows, oh, so hopeful.

"As soon as possible, I'm thinkin'."

"Well, then, so be it."

Her eyes filled with tears, and she touched his arm. "Dat . . . do ya mean it?"

"Go and visit your Mamma," he eked out the words. "Maybe she'll want to come home at last."

"Oh, I hope so." She glanced at the lantern, then at Willow. "Denki ever so much.

You don't know how happy I am."

"By the look on your face, I'd have to say that I do."

Grace smiled and turned to leave, her skirt swishing past the glowing lantern.

Judah watched her go with a twinge of sadness. Yet as protective as he'd always been of his girls, something felt different now. Standing taller, he sauntered out to look in on the newest lambs, feeling mighty proud of himself . . . in a humble sort of way.

Adah had seen Grace hurry to the barn with the lantern and wondered what she was up to. Surely there was something, for she'd noticed Grace glancing over at her father every few minutes all during supper. Living with folk in such close proximity, she had no trouble noticing this kind of hesitancy, if not apprehension, coming from her grand-daughter.

What can it mean?

It had been some time since Adah had attended any work-related get-togethers. Most of the womenfolk were busy tending gardens and doing spring housecleaning. Some of the younger wives were helping their husbands rake hay, too. Anyway, she hadn't heard much of the usual tittle-tattle.

"Jakob, love." She looked over at him, sitting in his favorite chair, there in the front room. "You don't s'pose the Riehls' boarder and our Gracie are becoming fast friends, do ya?"

"How would I know?"

"I saw them walking together today, just a-talkin' to beat the band."

He turned his head slightly. "Is that so."

"I sure hope that Englischer doesn't put a spell on our Gracie." She frowned.

"Now, Adah, what on earth?"

She pulled a hankie from beneath her sleeve and began to fan herself. "It's just a peculiar feelin' I have."

"Borrowing trouble, I daresay."

She looked up and there stood Grace, the biggest smile on her face.

"Am I ever glad to see you're both in the same room," Grace said, looking first at her, then at Jakob.

"What's on your mind, child?" Jakob sat up, more alert than before.

"I know something that's sure to make you smile." Grace came into the dim room and sat with them. "Word has it Mamma was seen this morning in a little town south of Sugarcreek, Ohio." She explained that a friend of hers had heard it from Nancy and Sylvia Fisher. "They saw Mamma with their own eyes."

"Well, for pity's sake!" Jakob said.

Adah fanned herself even more briskly with the hankie. "*Gut* news, indeed."

Grace began to share all sorts of details, but then, in the midst of that, she startled them by saying she'd gotten her father's permission to travel there. "I'm leaving tomorrow . . . with Heather Nelson." Grace motioned toward the north window. "But we'll be gone and back before ya know it."

"Goin' to fetch your Mamma?" Adah asked.

"If she'll agree to come . . ." Grace looked momentarily sad.

Jakob had fallen silent. And there was nothing more Adah could share, either, that would benefit Grace. Nothing at all. Even though it was wonderful to know where Lettie was, she was in turmoil. Why would Grace want to go with a near stranger? And what had gotten into Judah to say that she could?

"It won't be long till we're all together again," Grace was saying. "Least I hope so."

"We'll pray that way." Adah looked at Jakob, wishing for all the world he'd say something.

"You don't seem as happy as I thought you'd be." Grace turned in the chair, folding her arms. "Neither of you."

Jakob spoke at last. "No one knows why your Mamma up and left like that, Gracie." He drew a slow breath. "Seems she just might need to decide when to come home . . . on her own."

"You really think so?" Grace asked.

Jakob tugged on his beard and nodded.

"We'd hate to see you disappointed," Adah said.

"Well, why not look on the bright side? Maybe knowin' how much we all miss her will encourage Mamma." Grace rose suddenly, looking as though she might cry. "I best be getting back to Mandy and the boys. Dat will be starting evening prayers pretty soon."

"Jah, 'tis that time." Jakob reached for the Good Book.

"Pray for us, won't ya?" Grace said before slipping into the hallway.

"Ever so hard, dear one," Adah whispered.

Sleep would be difficult to come by tonight, Adah knew, thinking now of her favorite psalm. While Jakob thumbed through the Bible to find his place, she recited the verse silently and embraced the truth of the words: *Yet the Lord will command his lovingkindness in the daytime, and in the night his song shall be with me, and my prayer unto the God of my life.*

EPILOGUE

Before dawn the next day, I packed a few things in a small suitcase I borrowed from Mammi Adah. Not wanting to awaken Mandy or Dat, I merely looked in on my sleeping sister and then crept down the stairs, eager to get an early start on the trip, as Heather'd suggested when we discussed it last evening.

In the kitchen I chose two firm bananas from the bunch and sliced some sweet pumpkin bread made fresh yesterday — a poor substitute for a hot breakfast, but I wasn't certain if or when we might stop for the noon meal.

Outside, I waited silently for Heather's car to appear. Across the meadow to the north, the Riehls' rooster was crowing. The morning stillness carried the familiar sound like a loudspeaker. And as the rooster heralded the coming dawn, I wondered if it was somehow a good omen — a declaration

401

of happy things to come — even despite the damper my grandparents had thrown on my leaving.

Heather soon arrived, the blue of her car blending in with the darkness. *"I'll come up the drive without headlights,"* she'd said, wanting to be considerate and not cause a rumpus so early.

We exchanged "hullos," and I got myself settled in quickly. Then, as we backed up to the road, I found myself staring at the tall outline of Dat's big house — the place I'd always called home. A lump crowded my throat as I realized we were heading in the same direction Mamma had gone, leaving behind the familiar landscape I loved.

To think I'd agreed to travel so far with Heather in her fancy car with what Heather called a GPS. Whatever that was! And I mean fancy, with her small, portable telephone guiding our way. She sat in the driver's seat, surprisingly relaxed, tapping her long fingers on the steering wheel in time to a peppy song. Perhaps it was the music that made her cheerful — the "tunes" on the radio nestled into the dashboard, nearly in front of my nose. The worldliest music I've ever heard. She seemed so happy-go-lucky, I wondered if she looked on this trip as a final adventure before her stay at the Wellness Lodge.

In no time, the highway seemed to open up, with little traffic due to the early hour. I spotted the exit signs for the city of Carlisle, already missing the lush, thick carpet of green meadowland where our white lambs frisked about with their mothers. Where Becky's father's herd of cattle grazed — all the cherished sights fading with the miles.

Goodness, but it seemed like just yesterday I'd planted all the new herbs, replacing those lost to winterkill. Mamma still was at home with us during that garden-planting time. I doubt she would've believed I'd be leaving now for Holmes County with an English girl I'd just met. Despite that, it was a blessing how things had fallen into place.

As we continued onward, the sun gradually peeped over the hills behind us. I could see the golden gleam in the mirror jutting out from my side of the car. No turning around now, even though I could still smell the earthy fragrance of our gardens back home. I'd left both plots well weeded and watered. I had also checked each of the birdfeeders. The black-capped chickadees had certainly moved in again, making themselves at home in our yard. I'd paused to watch three of them fussing over the sunflower seeds Yonnie and I put out. It was sweet the way they held a seed in their black beaks and shook their little heads, their white cheeks twittering with their whistle-like song: *fee-bee-ee.*

Does Mamma see different kinds of birds where she's staying? Has she started a new list of sightings? Oh, surely she hadn't begun putting down roots anywhere else. When I allowed myself to ponder such things, I felt ever so sad. But I didn't want to distract Heather with my sniffling. No, she needed to keep her wits about her and watch the road as the signs and cities flew past us on our long journey.

Long, indeed. Heather told me it might take till midafternoon to arrive, what with stopping for gasoline and a sandwich or something to drink. Honestly, I didn't dare get my hopes up about bringing Mamma home. I'd be misleading myself. Even so, I wondered how I'd feel if she refused my invitation. Yet at the same time, it was hard not to consider what life might be like if she *did* agree to return. How long before Dat and all of us might begin to understand what had compelled her to leave in the first place? *How long before the pain and sadness fade away?*

Sighing, I leaned against the headrest and

closed my eyes, trying to imagine Mamma's face at first seeing me. *Will she be pleased?*

If all went well, our family would be complete once again. Oh, such a joyful reunion that would be!

Surely you're ready now, Mamma. Surely you're longing for home. . . .

ACKNOWLEDGMENTS

Offering the words *thank you* is the mere tip of the proverbial iceberg for the gratitude I wish to extend here. While Heather Nelson's story is entirely fictional, her decision to choose naturopathic treatment is based on years of my interest and research into the topic, including interviews with and invaluable gleanings from many helpful sources, including the following: Joel Fuhrman, MD; David Frahm, certified naturopathic doctor and co-founder of Health*Quarters* Ministries; Gabriel Cousens, holistic MD; and Judith Chandler, NP. However, I do not endorse any particular healing methods — conventional, holistic, or otherwise.

My constant thanks to David Horton for shepherding this new trilogy with much joy; and to Rochelle Glöege, my line editor, who finesses my writing with such grace. My content editor, Julie Klassen, and I had great fun poking around the quaint town of

Baltic, Ohio, and eating at the well-known Miller's Dutch Kitch'n during my recent book tour. Thanks so much, Julie!

Great appreciation to Hank and Ruth Hershberger, who graciously answered my questions about Ohio Amish tradition. As for Pennsylvania Amish, my Lancaster County consultants have gone the third and fourth miles on a regular basis, for which I'm ever grateful. Hugs to Carolene Robinson, who drops everything to answer my medical questions no matter the time of day. I appreciate you!

To my faithful reviewers, Ann Parrish and Barbara Birch — thanks so much. Also, I cannot imagine writing a single novel without each of my devoted partners in prayer.

As always, thanks to my husband and first reader, Dave, for all the sacrificial hours and sweet encouragement!

Finally, all praise and honor to our heavenly Father for anything that is considered good or redemptive in these pages. *Soli Deo Gloria!*

For reading group discussion questions and additional book club resources, please visit *www.bethanyhouse.com/anopenbook*

ABOUT THE AUTHOR

Beverly Lewis, born in the heart of Pennsylvania Dutch country, is *The New York Times* bestselling author of more than eighty books. Her stories have been published in nine languages worldwide. A keen interest in her mother's Plain heritage has inspired Beverly to write many Amish-related novels, beginning with *The Shunning,* which has sold more than one million copies. *The Brethren* was honored with a 2007 Christy Award.

Beverly lives with her husband, David, in Colorado.